THE TIME OF LIGHT

GUNNAR KOPPERUD

THE TIME OF LIGHT

Translated from the Norwegian by Tiina Nunnally

BLOOMSBURY

c.1

First published in Norwegian
by J.M. Stenersens Forlag A/S under the title *Lysets Tid*
First published in Great Britain 2000

Copyright © 1998 by Gunnar Kopperud
Translation copyright © 2000 Tiina Nunnally

Quotations from II Samuel 23: 5–7 on p 101, and
Amos 3:1–2 on p 109 are taken from *The Holy Scriptures*,
The Jewish Publication Society of American, 1917

The publishers gratefully acknowledge a grant from NORLA
towards the translation of this book

Published by Bloomsbury Publishing, New York and London.
Distributed to the trade by St. Martin's Press

A CIP catalogue record for this book
is available from the Library of Congress

ISBN 1-5823-4088 9

First U.S. Edition 2000
10 9 8 7 6 5 4 3 2 1

Typeset by Hewer Text Ltd, Scotland
Printed in Great Britain by Clays Limited, St Ives Plc

DAY ONE

'I woke this morning to the song of war and the smell of tears. The war must have been going on for a long time: my pillow was wet, very, very wet.'

The priest studied the man who was speaking. He had to be around seventy, a little younger than himself, and slimmer, more compact; with sharp features, round glasses, and a thick silvery mane combed straight back. He spoke Armenian almost without accent; it was only now and then that a different melody would slip into his intonation, like a memory of another language, another place.

'When I got up I could hear the war outside my house, when I turned on the radio I could hear the war inside my house, when I brought in the newspaper I could read about it, when the gardener and housekeeper arrived I could see it in their faces.'

The man hadn't sent for him; it was others who had asked, cautiously, uneasily, whether the priest had time to stop by.

'I sent them home. They were frightened, frightened and proud, the way people are when a war starts.'

The man added, almost as an afterthought: 'Too bad. I was thinking the gardener and I could gather the goutweed leaves together; winter is coming.'

He gave the priest a searching glance.

'To use for a compress for gout. *Aegopodium podagraria*, also called "German cabbage." I grew up in a library.'

The priest nodded. The man leaned back in his chair and

turned his head, as if to look at something, something far away. The priest leaned forward.

'Is there anything I can help you with?'

'This.'

The man pointed to his own eyes.

'I've been crying all day, I can't work, can't talk to anyone, all I can do is cry, shut myself up in the house and cry.'

He said this without embarrassment.

There was silence in the room. Through an open window they could hear the sound of tanks and boots, thousands of boots, interrupted only by an occasional shouted command. The battle for Nagorno-Karabakh had begun.

'This war has been under preparation for a long time, it comes as no surprise. But to prepare for a war is one thing, suddenly to go to war is something else entirely. Could it be something about the actual outbreak of war that's making you cry?'

The priest waited. The man didn't reply, didn't turn his head.

'Nagorno-Karabakh is an ancient Armenian territory. Our leaders claim that all peaceful means were attempted and now they see no alternative but to go to war. Could it be something about this attitude that you're reacting to?'

The priest waited tensely. The man replied in a low, almost indifferent voice, so low that the priest had to lean closer to hear him.

'We're in the Caucasus, and war is an integral part of Caucasian culture.'

The priest took note of the word 'integral'; it told him something about the man.

'I've counted them up; at this very moment we have thirty-seven armed conflicts and fifty disputed territories here in this region; next year there will undoubtedly be more. I've lived all my adult life here, and if I was going to cry over every war that broke out I wouldn't have time for anything else. May I offer you a cup of tea?'

The priest stood up and went over to the window while the

2

man put the kettle on and brought in some cups. He had crossed the marketplace on his way from the church to the man's house, making his way through the soldiers and onlookers and armored cars and artillery. Soldiers and civilians alike had moved aside for the robed priest and allowed him through, but just barely, just barely; a different era seemed to be on the threshold. From the window he could hear shouts from the marketplace, first a solitary agitated voice, shrill, then the reply from thousands, deep and dangerous. The priest was new in town, he hadn't yet managed to take its pulse, hadn't been able to find it, not until now.

The man came and stood behind him. The roars from the marketplace rose toward the sky like black birds; the priest and the man stood in silence and watched them flap their wings, slow and menacing.

'All this fervor. What purpose does it serve?'

The man was almost whispering.

'They're young, they live in a fervent time.'

The priest turned around and saw something pass over the man's face, something that might resemble a smile. He accepted the cup of tea and sat down at the dining table, a heavy, solid table of imported beechwood with inlaid crystal mosaic. The cups were hand-painted porcelain with gilded rims. The man sat down on the other side of the table, the priest looked at him and asked in a low voice:

'Who are you?'

The man sat in thought for a long time before he replied.

'Markus Wagner, German. I came here fifty-three years ago, in the fall of 1941, in uniform.'

Something came to an abrupt halt in the room and held its breath, as if something forbidden had been said, something everyone knew but never mentioned.

The priest pulled himself together.

'Go on.'

June 22, 1941: Germany attacks the Soviet Union with 3 million soldiers, almost half of its armed forces, along a front that stretches from the Baltic Sea in the north to the Black Sea in the south. Romania, Hungary, Slovakia and Italy eventually join the campaign, which is the largest military invasion in human history. The attack is based partly on ideology: Communism must be eradicated. Partly pragmatic: New territories for settlement and raw materials will be secured for the German people. Opposing the Germans is the world's largest army. The Red Army is estimated to be 7 million strong, but at the same time the Communist system is considered so rotten that 'all it would take is to kick in the door to make the whole thing collapse.' Thus the prevailing opinion is that the war against the Soviet Union will be over before winter sets in. The head of the German general staff, Franz Halder, writes in his journal: 'The campaign against Russia will be won in 14 days.'

The horizon curved gently around the cavalry clad in black coats. The man in front raised his hand, turned slightly, and signaled. The group started off, dust from hundreds of hooves swirled up. A faint breeze tugged lightly at the long coats, one of the men pulled the brim of his hat down over his eyes.

On both sides of the cavalry and behind, the rest of the plain started moving. Slowly it surged forward, a rolling plain of dark figures; the dry sound of boots, the muffled sound of tanks. The cavalry approached the edge of the plain; young, expectant faces, some smiling, others somber, on horseback, on foot, on tanks and artillery. The clamor grew with them, rising from a menacing rumble to a splitting roar from the airplanes. And singing; the cavalrymen were singing, confident of victory.

The first shots were fired somewhere in the distance. The cavalrymen looked up in surprise, looked at each other; the first shots in a war always seem unreal. No one sought cover, instead they urged their horses into a gallop, toward the shooting. It was early in the morning, the infantrymen who followed saw the cavalry etched like black silhouettes against the sunrise.

They stood in their stirrups, struck their horses on the flanks, rode toward the shooting; a splendid picture, full of light and power.

The rider on the right flank was the first to disintegrate. Suddenly both he and his horse exploded in a gush of blood that glistened against the backlight. Two horses reared up, pranced sideways around the slow, red rain; the rest of the group continued on. The riders on the two rearing horses tried to regain control, had almost managed it, when they suddenly stiffened in the saddle, lurched several times, and fell forward. Their horses ran in terror out of the picture.

The other riders sought refuge in a hollow at the edge of the plain, where the slopes began. The horses pranced, sideways, backward. The safety catches clicked, two artillery guns were rolled forward.

One of the cavalrymen rode in front of the group, turned around and signaled to the young boys wearing black coats, raising his hand for quiet. The group gathered round. The leader began, his voice resonating, not in the hollowed terrain but in their terror, the quivering terror lodged in the pits of their stomachs, in every last one of them.

His voice was drowned out by the roar of a tank. The cavalrymen had a respite from his words, long enough for them to sense what lay next to their terror: anticipation.

The tank stopped, idled, the voice carried.

'That's all. May God have mercy on anyone who doesn't give his utmost.'

Dense forest, a low range of hills; the army stood eight rows deep along the whole perimeter of the woods; motorized cavalry on each flank, artillery behind, the horse cavalry in the middle, men shouting in front of each company, men shouting in sharp voices. The faces were still young, but serious now, uncertain. Some adjusted their gear belts, others checked their rifles, glancing at each other. A signal was given, the army started moving, dark figures running toward the dark forest, first one wave, then another, and another and another. The sound of thousands of boots on the forest floor, the ringing of metal, gasping breath.

The cavalrymen stopped at the top of a hill, straightened their caps, and looked down at the lights on the opposite side. The town seemed to be asleep, only a few lights on here and there, otherwise nothing; not a sound, nothing moving. The army massed behind the cavalry, silent, waiting. The rider in front turned around and looked back, raised his hand once again, and shouted.

The army started moving like an avalanche, slowly released. The avalanche rolled down the gentle slope and surged toward the town, bigger and bigger, faster and faster. The flash from artillery strikes in the town glinted on sweaty faces. Two young boys looked at each other and smiled, reached the first buildings, huddled behind the wall of a house. They were filled with anticipation now, excitement. They watched the group of riders assemble and then ride into the town, pushing their way in; they stood up and followed. From one section of the assault came excited laughter, from another the sound of singing.

A wind from the east suddenly streamed over them, wind from a universe that had collapsed because of the choices made by men. None of them noticed a thing, the wind was a Buddhist legend, and the boys had just finished high school; they hadn't made it that far in religion class.

Inside the town a little girl's face turned toward the sound; two dark, frightened eyes stared toward the singing and the laughter, uncomprehending, sitting up in bed, her arms around her knees.

The war had arrived the way wars almost always do, of its own accord, and no one was fully able to explain how. One day there was warm sunshine and a lush play of colors and peace; the next day there was warm sunshine and a lush play of colors and war. People talked to each other in the streets, wondering:

Could a country at war be so beautiful? Could a war be so radiant?

The people who said least were those who had fought in the previous war; they merely looked at each other, and in their eyes lay trenches and barbed wire and no-man's-land and bodies and defeat. Most of them were middle-aged and didn't figure on being called up, but they had sons of draft age, and they gave their sons the look that fathers have always given their sons when war breaks out: a look torn between sorrow over a history that no one can stop, and pride at being called upon by history.

The people who said a little more were those who had lived through the previous war; they straightened their backs, as if rising up from the rationing and the sound of hammers when the casualty lists were posted in the marketplace, the telegram from the defense department, the medal hung on the son's photograph, the defeat, and finally the humiliation and the sound of crutches everywhere. Those who had lived through the previous war looked toward the new war with a kind of hope.

The people who said the most were the new ones, those who didn't know what war was; they had merely assimilated the humiliation. They greeted the war with a mixture of pride and excitement; convinced they were right, they carried the banners and beat the drums and paraded through the streets the way people always do before going to war.

Later a time would come when historians would discuss the cause and judges would discuss the blame, but at that moment neither of these words existed. The country went to war because it had to, and if there was anyone who could have stopped the war, they spoke so softly that their voices were drowned out by the roar from the mass rallies. The country went to war because it wanted to, in warm sunshine and a lush play of colors, and people lifted their faces toward the beautiful weather and thought: What a magnificent day to go to war.

★　　★　　★

'As citizens of a country, we have certain obligations, Markus. Certain obligations and certain rights. They go hand in hand.'

His father was sitting behind the counter in the library. Markus stood leaning his elbows on the counter with the draft notice in his hands; it occurred to him that what personal conversations he and his father had were largely conducted across this counter. Later he would speculate that his father seemed more secure in the role of librarian than in the role of father, more secure in the public place than in the private. Here he could offer his son guidance without subjecting himself to close contact with him. But back then, that's not what Markus was thinking, back then he was simply uneasy.

'Erich Maria said no.'

'That's not an option. We have a legally elected government supported by a majority of the people. If the government thinks it's necessary to go to war to ensure the country's security, then it's our duty to participate.'

'Our duty?'

'My duty is to send you off, your duty is to go.'

'And what if I don't want to go?'

'Desire and duty have nothing to do with each other, Markus. Remember what our philosopher said: If you do something because you want to, you act well, but amorally. It is only when you do something out of duty, out of respect for your duty, that you act morally.'

Markus stood turning the letter over in his hands as he pondered this. He had read enough philosophy to recognize his father's reasoning, but he hadn't imagined that philosophy would one day catch up with him in this manner.

'Is it moral to go to war against other countries?'

'At the moment you haven't been called up for a war, but for military service.'

'That's sticking your head in the sand, Father. We both know what they're building up for.'

'It's the only possibility for us to survive as a nation, Markus.

The Treaty of Versailles took from us practically all the opportunities we had for acquiring wealth; we either have to expand or run aground. Ask your teachers, ask the priest, ask the public officials, they'll all tell you the same thing.'

How strange, thought Markus, to go to war with your head full of arguments in favor of it, and your stomach full of protests against it.

Quiet days and the sound of seagulls above a bare rock face; salty skin and sunshine. She lay next to him, he turned his head and looked at her, she noticed, met his glance. Salty skin and sunshine and the water 19° C; she blew water out of her nose and pushed her dark wet hair out of her face as she resurfaced after a dive. He had never seen a girl dive before, he thought they all jumped, with their legs tucked up under them. She had dived right in and shouted to him, teasing, when she broke the surface again. He had dived after her, swum over to her as he laughed, splashing her; she splashed him back. They swam next to each other, playing, and suddenly she brushed against him and he against her; they both noticed it and looked at each other, shy, that was the first time. They pulled hastily away, as if in apology, but not fast enough to deny what had happened.

Quiet days and the sound of seagulls above a bare rock face; salty skin and sunshine and someone who took his hand, cautiously, without looking at him. Something burst inside him and overflowed; a light, a joy, at knowing that he belonged to someone, someone he would long for, someone who would miss him, worry about him.

July 6, 1941: The Russians retreat, the Germans advance on all fronts. During the first four months of the campaign they take 3.6 million Russian prisoners of war. In some places the Russians are so unprepared that the streetlights are burning and buses continue to run as the Germans attack.

The cavalry halted and looked at the lights in the distance. One of the men shook his head.

'God Almighty.'

By now they had ridden hundreds of kilometers, deeper into the countryside than anyone before them for over a hundred years, and they still felt like seducers. Unsuspecting, the land submitted to them with almost no resistance and allowed the cavalry to enter, naively, as if the thought had never arisen that that's what they wanted. The cavalry had subdued village after village, subdued and abandoned them, as the men had moved from conquest to conquest, their backs getting straighter, their smiles prouder.

But they had never been welcomed with streetlights before, had never seen a town turn on its lights for them in the middle of a plain and whisper: Come on, take me.

'God Almighty.'

It was the same cavalryman; he had a narrow face with dark, shifting eyes and a seducer's contempt for his victim. He shook back a lock of black hair from his forehead and glanced at the others, without excitement, without curiosity, guided only by a plan, a plan that had to be carried out.

The cavalrymen rode toward the lights and watched them moving; they rode closer and watched them approach like great illuminated surfaces with shadows behind.

'God Almighty. Buses.'

The seducer again, half astonishment, half disappointment; it shouldn't be this easy, there's no honor in it. The cavalry stopped, dismounted at a bus stop, stood under a streetlight and watched the bus approach.

The seducer stretched out his hand, the bus turned in and stopped, opened the door. The cavalrymen got on, one after the other, the seducer first. A woman was sitting behind the wheel, young, blonde, with big, incredulous eyes. In the bus behind her sat ten or so people, dumbstruck.

'Where to?'

She tried to resist by asking the question, tried to hold onto reality the way it was before, right up until now, tried to hold tight to what had always been.

The seducer pretended not to understand, took a firm grip on the back of her neck with one hand and pressed a pistol against her temple with the other, motioning with his head.

'Drive.'

She didn't understand the word, but she knew what he meant, what he wanted; she had known this might happen one day, known it as an uneasiness, a possibility, a biological inevitability. One day someone might arrive who would exploit her innocence and take her firmly by the back of her neck and force her wherever he wanted to go, without asking. The seducer waved his pistol now and then, to show her which way to turn, tightening his grip on her neck if she tried to protest.

She grew frightened, he pointed to a street she had never driven down before, it led to a section of town that was forbidden to her, she had heard of it, had heard others whisper about it, but had never ventured there herself.

'No, no, please no.'

She was pleading now, whimpering.

The seducer pressed the pistol harder against her temple and yanked her head against him, using the hand around her neck, until she was locked between his hands; then he slowly turned her toward the entrance to the forbidden street.

Markus was scared. He lay huddled around a submachine gun behind a low stone wall and he was scared. At intervals of several meters along the wall lay other soldiers, completely still. Some had shut their eyes, some were staring at the ground; everyone was waiting.

Shout, whispered Markus, shout, shout, shout, let's get it over with. On the other side of the wall lay a village; in that village a group of partisans had dug in. Markus had volunteered for the mop-up operation.

He had heard a voice right next to him and watched the others turn toward him in surprise when the lieutenant asked for volunteers; it wasn't until a few seconds later that he realized he was the one who had responded.

During the advance on the village he tried to figure out why he had volunteered, but couldn't find an answer. The only thing he had managed to put into words so far was the feeling of finally taking his fear all the way out, holding it like a spear in front of him.

The war had taught him what fear is and what dread is. Dread of the unknown, fear of the known; dread sits in your soul, fear sits in your body.

The recruit school was dread: sudden cold shivers of dread, of the war that lay before him, about which he knew nothing. The campaign was fear: intense, nauseating fear of suddenly having half his head blown off or his groin or stomach ripped open.

He had learned something more about fear and dread, but there his words deserted him; the closest he could come was that dread was somehow connected with a person's individual experience and could thus be chronic, while fear was connected to something more universal and for that reason erupted only under very specific conditions.

Markus checked the safety on the submachine gun for the twelfth time and thought: Those very specific conditions are right now, those very specific conditions are this stone wall, this stone wall right here is very special, and suddenly he had the stone wall under his right foot and his left foot was on its way over the top, and he realized that the lieutenant had shouted the order. On both sides of him he could sense the other soldiers on their way over the wall, and fear forced its way like nausea into every cranny of his body. His body conjured up the instincts of prehistoric man: his muscle armor tightened to receive blows, he hunched over to become the smallest possible target, hunched over and ran; keep moving, never stop moving, and the first building drew close, coming toward him with dark, dangerous windows. Markus glanced at the other two in the patrol, one on his left and one on his right, they nodded and Markus stormed toward the door with his gun ready. His first submachine gun, it had been given to him when he volunteered, his first close combat, the rifle he had been issued wasn't suited to close combat.

He set his boot against the door and kicked, and with that kick he encountered the war for the first time. Until that moment the war had been far away, something on the other side of the plain or up on a ridge they had fired on and received a reply from; until that moment the war had been shells that fell without warning and transformed his company into a running, shouting swarm. Markus kicked in the door of the first building, flung himself in sideways, and opened fire, and above the deafening, lethal hammering of the submachine gun he could hear a voice screaming shrilly, his own voice, and he suddenly noticed that his fear had left him; he kicked and screamed it out, and something else replaced it, something that filled him, bursting and gushing from the muzzle of the submachine gun and its strong recoil. Glorious.

Something moved inside the room and struck the door frame next to his face, splintering it once, and then again before Markus hurled himself out of the doorway and stood with his back pressed up against the wall outside. He nodded to the other two; together they covered the door and windows, knowing that another patrol was covering the other three sides of the building, and Markus took his time getting out the hand grenade. He could hear movement inside the building and pulled out the pin, now he could hear voices. He lobbed the grenade in a gentle arc, heard it thud against the floor, and everything grew quiet inside, the voices fell silent in the two endless seconds between the instant they understood what had been tossed onto the floor and the instant the grenade exploded, and hot compressed air flung the rest of the voices out through the windows and doorway.

The three soldiers looked at each other, expectantly, until Markus and the one who had covered the windows both stood staring at the one who had covered the door, and he nodded, looked down and went inside the building. He had a long face with high cheekbones, rather delicate lips, and a puzzled look in his eyes, as if there was always something he didn't quite understand. When he came out of the building, he first turned away and threw up, then he faced Markus and the other soldier with his puzzled eyes full of tears.

They moved on to the next building; running, hunching down, taking cover, running. On both sides they could hear commando shouts and shots, they could sense others advancing as they did, fitfully, the way an organism registers all movement; but at the same time their world was now a closed, isolated system, defined by the narrow alley with the three buildings assigned to them.

The next building came toward them and suddenly a machine gun fired from one of the windows, the shots struck the stone wall behind them with sharp, dry slaps. Markus and the two others threw themselves behind the cover of the wall and yelled, yelled for their lives, as they watched the shots from the machine gun blast the wall to bits. Two men with a bazooka came slithering over, studied the building through a square green periscope and took aim. Markus shut his eyes and listened for the whistling sound of the shells shooting out, almost like rockets in a fireworks show, so innocent. But the booms from the other side of the wall were not innocent. After the second boom the machine gun paused, and it was like a pain suddenly easing, only to strike again, and the two men with the bazooka shoved another shell in the tube, another boom followed, and then the machine-gun was silent. The two men with the bazooka smiled, and the other three jumped back over the wall and ran toward the building. Markus and the boy with the puzzled look covered the third man as he went inside. They heard two short submachine gun bursts, not fully understanding; they looked at the figure that came out of the house, not fully understanding, but they pressed on toward the next building, and Markus thought: How long does a war actually last?

It was his turn again, and the two others covered him as he ran toward the door and kicked it in, he was quicker now, more confident. The building was bigger than the first one, he stood in a small hallway with two doors and hesitated for a moment before hammering a burst at one of them and kicking the other one in. Behind the falling door he caught a glimpse of movement, two arms reaching out and a face between them, a face with an expression and a voice. Markus raised his submachine gun to waist level and took aim, bending his knees slightly and steadying his body behind the weapon; in a fraction of a second his movements were transformed into a graceful ballet, a lovely dance with his gun, a ritual. He looked at the man behind the outstretched arms; he was grizzled, unshaven, unkempt, his clothes were rough and worn, but his gaze was sharp. Clear, alert eyes stared at the bullets coming toward him at the speed of three thousand meters per second; flashing, rotating steel projectiles that aimed straight for his stomach and threw him against the wall, blasting everything out of him. The man raised his glance toward Markus, and Markus aimed the steel projectiles at his eyes, erasing them from their sockets. At the same time something gushed out of Markus, a force, a discharge, a surrender; something he had only felt once before, just once.

Quiet days and the sound of laughter in a schoolyard. They went to the same high school, but were in different classes; the world had not yet dared allow boys and girls to be in the same class, and besides, he was two years ahead of her. The separation was transplanted to the schoolyard; boys and girls stood in separate groups, each in its own section. Once she turned around and looked at him just as he turned around and looked at her; he smiled at her cautiously, a quick smile, she smiled back just as quickly and looked down.

Three days later he looked at her again. She had positioned herself near her girlfriends so that she could just manage to watch him out of the corner of her eye, and made them move so that he would have to turn around if he wanted to look at her. She saw him turn his head and look at her once; she lifted her chin. He turned back to his friends and kept on talking, then he turned around and looked at her again; she gave him a brief glance. Now they both knew.

The next time they met was in the municipal library where his father was a librarian. Markus had practically grown up in the library, exploring the shelves meter by meter, from the first books of fairy tales to the dusty leather volumes. He used to sit there with his homework in the afternoon; there was a sense of peace that he liked.

Rachel had never been in the habit of going to the library, had never been encouraged to do so; her father was convinced that everything she needed to know was in the books in the synagogue, but it's never too late to start, she thought with a smile.

She walked lightly up the steps to the library, pulled open the heavy doors to the reading room, and looked inside, then let go and ran back down the steps. Markus was sitting in the very back of the reading room. She took a deep breath and climbed the stairs again, opened the door, went inside, steered straight for where Markus was sitting, her chin jutting out slightly, almost there, almost. He looked up.

'Hi.'

'Hi.'

She ran her hand along the spines of the books on the shelf behind him, he was so close to her now, so close, if she reached out her hand she could touch him, she feigned nonchalance.

'Are you looking for something?'

He had taken off his glasses to look at her, the big round horn-rimmed glasses, his big eyes staring at her inquisitively.

'An elf. People say that elves live behind the books in a library.'

Markus smiled.

'He just left for lunch.'

'What are you sitting there reading?'

'Hugo Gressmann, Oriental eschatology.'

Rachel fell silent, she didn't know what eschatology was but didn't dare say so. Markus was silent too, he regretted using the word, it had created a gulf, and if he explained it the gulf would be even wider.

They were silent together for a long time, she standing and he sitting; they gave each other a brief glance, gave the wall a brief glance. Rachel turned away and Markus turned away, and from the books on all four walls came angry shouts; one of life's golden moments would have been wasted if each of them hadn't suddenly turned toward the other and started to say something but stopped to allow the other to speak, and they both burst out laughing, and the books breathed a sigh of relief and watched them as they left, walking side by side toward the door after Rachel had taken another deep breath and asked if he was going to take a break soon, and Markus's face had brightened and he had folded his horn-rimmed glasses and stood up. The books looked at each other and smiled as the two young people disappeared out the door.

Later Rachel looked up the word eschatology and read about the belief that the world can be cleansed by first being destroyed and then rising up again; she stared straight ahead, trying to picture Markus thinking about eschatology. Why did he do it? There was no reason for it. Then she looked up Hugo Gressmann and a sunbeam lit up her heart. The theology professor had written the book of eschatology teachings for her own people, and Rachel sensed that Markus was now saying something to her, something more important than what they

17

had said to each other out on the terrace in front of the library when they talked for the first time and both of them tried to follow unwritten rules, managing to do so with their words but not in the way they said them. And when it was no longer possible to postpone it and they had to say goodbye, each went home, knowing that something had happened, and they both had a black, numb feeling deep inside their bodies, because they came from different cultures and lived in a period when more hatred existed between those two cultures than it had for hundreds of years.

The submachine gun emptied out and was silent. Suddenly Markus heard the man groan, gasp; he fumbled for a new cartridge clip with his left hand and shoved it in as he kept an eye on the bundle over by the wall, but he didn't have time to protect himself before the blow came from behind, his face slammed against the door frame and the submachine gun was shoved into his stomach.

A strong, lean hand grabbed hold of his gun and tore it away from him; he spun around and stared straight into the eyes of a young woman with long brown hair and brown eyes. She pointed the submachine gun at him and pulled the trigger, and he looked for the steel projectile but heard only a click and her scream when she flung herself out the door as she pulled back the bolt to load the first round into the chamber. He heard two rapid bursts of gunfire and got to his knees just in time to see her running past his two comrades. The sight of a woman had made them hesitate the split second she needed to kill them, run to the wall, leap over it, and scream again, but a different kind of scream this time, prolonged, plaintive, as if someone had punctured her grief, and her body came back over the wall, slowly, with her arms spread out and the submachine gun hanging limply from one hand; a young woman with long brown hair and brown eyes impaled on a bayonet protruding from the spot where her ribs met. A dark splotch grew from the bayonet, and blood trickled down the rifle toward the fingers of the soldier who was holding it; he stared at the blood with disgust in his eyes and did what he had been drilled to do thousands of times during training with hay dummies: He gave the bayonet a swift twist and pulled it loose with a sideways motion, the blade flat between the ribs, and the woman fell straight down onto the wall with a hollow thud and lay there motionless.

Markus ran toward the wall and looked at the soldier with the bayonet as he picked up his submachine gun; the soldier first wiped the blood from his hands on the pants of his uniform, then he cleaned the blood from the bayonet by thrusting it into the ground. Markus ran over to his two comrades and turned them over; empty eyes stared up at him, so he ran back to the wall and leaped over. The soldier with the bayonet sat huddled with his back against the wall and his rifle in his lap. Markus sat down next to him. Neither of them spoke until the soldier with the bayonet turned and whispered:

'What's your name?'

'Markus. And yours?'

'Manfred.'

All around them the war went on. Soon an officer would appear and bellow at them to get moving, but at that moment they could sit still for a bit, next to each other, with their backs against a stone wall and that sense of solidarity that only violence can give.

That evening, after he had returned to his company, Manfred heated water in his helmet and tried to wash his hands. He whittled a point on a thin twig that he used to clean his fingernails, he walked up to the road and scraped together sand and gravel that he used to scrub himself; for over an hour he sat with his helmet in front of him, washing and washing his hands.

The others in his patrol and platoon left him alone. Some of them had also taken part in the mop-up operation in the village; the others had seen the change in the faces of those who came back after completing their mission. Deep inside, at a level of consciousness beyond words, everyone understood what Manfred was doing.

They had set up camp at the base of a ridge and been told that they would be staying there several days to wait for supplies. The soldiers used the time to rest and inspect their gear. Some wrote letters which they doubted anyone would ever receive, some washed clothes in the river they were camped beside, some went in search of a swimming hole. It was a brilliant late-summer day with clear skies and a dark green in the shrubs and trees. Manfred walked away from the camp area until he could hear no other sounds except the river and insects; then he sat down with his back against a rock and took out a little harmonica. He tapped it on the palm of his hand a few times without knowing why, just something he had seen in a movie, then he started in on a calm, low melody, a love song from the previous war. Life was always easier when he could play; music had been given to him at birth, and he had learned to use it to express himself. At any moment he could compose a tune that gave a precise picture of whatever mood he was in. Once he had heard a legendary American band leader say on the radio that all good music tells a story. The band leader had started telling the story behind a piece he had written and Manfred had run to get his sister and made her sit next to the radio and write down the story while he stood in the other room with his fingers in his ears. Later they went to a music store and asked to hear the piece – this was before that kind of music was banned – and Manfred had listened to the music and the story it told and looked at his sister and said:

'It's about a young girl who's sitting on the steps outside her house and every day a young boy walks past and smiles at her, but one day her mother says that she can't sit on the steps anymore, and so she sits alone on a bench inside the house. Mood Indigo.'

Manfred's sister gave him a resigned look.

'Am I right?' Manfred was excited.

His sister walked toward the exit as she thanked the shop-keeper. Manfred followed close behind.

'Thea, am I right?'

Thea turned around as soon they were out on the street and the shop door had closed behind them.

'You make me sick.'

He was twelve and she was nine; nine and just as determined as she always had been and always would be. She stomped away from him with her nose in the air, holding in her hand the piece of paper on which she had written the story from the radio. Manfred ran after her and took the paper from her hand and read the story word for word as he had heard it in the music, and Thea kept two paces ahead of him and said: 'I bet you're a terrible kisser.'

Later she turned fifteen and he was eighteen, and she had the loveliest body in the whole school; boys walked right into lampposts or the gutter whenever they caught sight of her, and she knew it and was grateful but never let it go to her head. Now they both had something, although they didn't have much more than that. They had a mother who was depressed and a father who sat in the pub all night long; after he lost his job he spent all day in the pub too. Their mother grew more and more depressed, and their father grew more and more hazy. Manfred and Thea learned to take care of themselves; they developed strong ties to each other and accepted that life had dealt them a mother who closed herself off and a father who was sinking into dissolution. Someone had to get the losing card so that the others could win, as Thea used to say, but they both took their revenge. Manfred developed something called selective dyslexia; he could read and talk and write just as correctly as everyone else except for one thing. He couldn't handle names. As soon as he came to a name, the letters would jumble together, often with disastrous results. Thea sometimes suspected him of developing name-blindness on purpose, but she never said a word; it set up a barrier between her brother and the rest of the world, and intuitively she knew that this was exactly what he needed. She took her own revenge in a less direct way; she joined a Catholic convent as a novice, first just in her free time, but later, after she finished school, full-time and forever. In this manner she robbed the world of what it liked best about her. Only once did she take direct revenge; that was when three boys in her class put a vulgar note in her locker. Thea knew instantly who had done it. She went right over to them, hauled them along to an empty storeroom, locked the door, and stripped – thoroughly enough and languorously enough that several weeks later the three boys were sent to the nurse because they were weak and pale, and they came back with gauze boxing gloves that they were supposed to wrap around their hands at night before they went to bed.

Manfred continued to play calm, low ballads that lulled everything around him and called down the evening darkness. When Markus came looking for him, the other soldiers nodded toward the river, and Markus walked toward the sound, first of the river and then the harmonica.

Manfred looked up at Markus, lowered his harmonica, moved over a bit and patted the ground beside him. Markus sat down, not really knowing what he wanted to say, not really knowing why he had come. They sat for a while in silence, the way they had sat near the stone wall, and yet it felt different; by now the events in the village had settled inside them.

'Was it your first?' Markus's voice was low, a little hesitant. Manfred nodded.

'What about you?' Manfred had turned to look at him.

'Inside the building. An old man.'

They didn't say anything else for a long time. A melody took shape inside Manfred; a slow, painful melody that rose and fell, rose and fell. Markus sat beside him, sensing a question take shape, a question that loomed larger and more urgent than any other. He tried to put it into words but couldn't. The question writhed and wriggled and stared at him impatiently.

Almost imperceptibly they leaned toward each other until their shoulders and upper arms touched, and neither of them tried to pull away; it was the closeness they needed to dare to open up. Markus talked about Erich Maria who had simply said no when he was called up; he hadn't shouted it, he hadn't shrieked it, he had simply said it – to himself. And it was almost by accident that Markus understood and asked Erich Maria: 'Do you know what's going to happen?'

Manfred picked up his harmonica and told the rest of the story; he told about the interrogations and the screams and the blows and the judge's gavel and the black hood over his head at four in the morning.

Markus listened to the melody; in it he could hear Erich Maria, hear his pulse, hear his breath against the cell wall, hear him say 'no' one more time. The melody rose slightly, shifted, grew heavier, and Markus saw Erich Maria's father, he was standing next to the grave with the light extinguished and asking: 'What did you accomplish with this?'

Manfred stopped playing and they sat for a while longer as the camp settled in for the night; then they stood up and brushed themselves off, and Manfred said: 'Good night, Kusmar,' and Markus stood staring after him, smiling. The image of the old man against the wall inside the house had separated him forever from the images of young boys back home who thought and felt the way he did, but he had gained something else in return.

Fall 1941: Special units follow the advancing German forces with a directive to liquidate the political leaders in Russian society and see to it that new ones never re-emerge. The directive was issued as early as March 1941, an important factor in the evaluation of the ideological impetus behind the attack. The special units introduce a reign of terror in the occupied territories and kill people indiscriminately.

The cavalry stopped and gazed at the village, fifty or so small, dark, timbered houses scattered across a bare plain with a white-painted church in the middle, like a glimmer of light. The horses stirred restlessly, shifting sideways; there was snow in the air, a chill, the fall colors were starting to fade.

The army gathered behind the cavalry, silent, tense, as if aware that they were standing on the verge of something new. The tank crews listened to the engines and adjusted the ignition, the artillery crews polished the barrels, the infantry-men were quieter than usual, squatting down to check their gear, over and over again, without looking up. Way up ahead the cavalrymen were arguing about something, fragments of angry voices rose and fell above the drone of the engines and the click of bolts being pulled back and shoved forward. Two of the cavalrymen split off and rode back; the other riders turned around to watch them go. They had all grown thinner, more defined, older in the eyes.

The cavalrymen pulled their scarves up over their mouths and noses, looked at the village and the white church against the clear blue autumn sky and the silent, silent countryside. Then they spurred their horses forward, riding at a calm trot onto the plain. Sounds now came from the village. The army followed close behind the cavalry, like a menacing, creeping shadow.

The sounds from the village grew louder as it came closer. The timbered walls creaked, trying to pull away. The army advanced on all sides, boots and weapons and tanks blotted out the sun, and a milky white smoke shrouded the countryside.

The cavalry rode into the village in slow motion; they stood gracefully in their stirrups with pistols held above their heads.

The horses galloped down the main street in a languid, elegant run, their muscles rippling. On the sidewalk a woman pulled two children into a narrow alley; one of the children fell and started bleeding. Slow motion. The woman picked up the child and carried him. Slow motion. Blood dripped down her shoulder.

In front of the church an old man tried to seek safety; he got up from the wooden bench where he was sitting, turned to face the cavalrymen with an astonished look in his eyes, took a few steps, and gazed down at the red patch that was spreading across his stomach, looked back up at them. His body shuddered, a hole gaped in his chest, a hole as big as both of his palms, filled with blood and scraps of clothing. The man tried to cover the hole with his hands but didn't have time to protect himself before the first horse kicked him to the ground. He fell hard on his face, breaking his nose and teeth; horse hooves smashed the back of his head in slow motion and trampled him into the ground, a tiny convulsion in the old body with every horse.

The cavalry halted in front of the church, turned around, and looked at the army that was approaching from all sides, approaching like black smoke from burning, timbered houses; shrill screams from women and children and old men, who came stumbling and tottering and running toward them, fleeing from the army, fleeing toward the army.

The cavalrymen fanned out and blocked the way of those in flight; the advancing army formed an arc, closing the circle with the horsemen. The villagers stopped, surrounded, and drew together. One woman fell to her knees and began weeping and pleading, others followed; soon the whole village was on its knees with hands clasped and stretched out toward the soldiers. A cameraman ran forward, lay down on his stomach in front of them, and started filming; the sound man followed with his microphone pole, carefully wending his way among the pleading people until he stood in the middle of the crowd. The cameraman zoomed in close on the face of an old woman, tilted the lens slightly toward the sky, and followed the snowflakes as they floated down onto the lined cheeks, melting and mixing with her tears. The sound man stood on tiptoe, holding his microphone, to record the chorus of hundreds of voices, not individual voices; the chorus of voices from old people and children which rose up toward the cold sky.

One of the cavalrymen rode to the side, making a gap in the circle. The pleading people looked toward the gap, straight at the open church. A brief shout of command. The soldiers fixed bayonets to their rifles and walked toward the pleading people; the crowd crept backward, whimpering, many of them still on their knees. The first supplicants reached the church door and disappeared inside, others followed; the soldiers jabbed their bayonets at those who dawdled until everyone was inside and the door was bolted.

Another brief command shouted. The soldiers spread out, ripped roof beams and doors from the closest houses, came back, used hammers and nails and pounded the boards over the windows until they were sealed. From inside the church came the sound of hymns; one of the soldiers stopped to listen with his hammer raised. An officer yelled at him harshly.

The soldiers retreated as the flame throwers arrived, specially trained soldiers wearing gas masks, with steel canisters on their backs. They took up positions around the church, aimed the nozzles of the flame throwers at it, and opened fire. Like biblical archangels they opened fire. Fire shot out with violent force, toward the hymns and the church walls, tearing at the white-painted planks until it caught hold and colored them yellow, red, blue, black.

Inside the church the shouts rose, the congregation pounded on the door, the walls, the boards that were nailed over the windows. Some people coughed, some shrieked in mortal terror. The flames caught better hold, spread up the walls, onto the roof. Black smoke began seeping out from the boarded-up windows; now the congregation was screaming in pain – prolonged, naked screams. Something was thrown against the boards on one window, two of them came loose, fell away, an enormous baptismal font appeared, a battering ram. Two old men, their clothes on fire, forced their heads and shoulders through the opening and searched for something to hold onto, something they could use to hoist themselves out. The flame throwers aimed at them and opened fire again. The men put their hands to their burning heads, screaming, and vanished. The flames continued to spread until the whole church was engulfed and sections of the roof fell in and the flames mounted like a roar toward the sky; a roar of sparks and flames and shrieks. Both the cavalrymen and the soldiers had to retreat farther back from the intense heat. The flame throwers fastened the nozzles back on the steel canisters, and someone lowered the sky and stepped down with black clouds underfoot and placed hands over the church and silenced the shouts and the flames and the screams.

DAY TWO

'Is forgiveness possible?'

The priest looked up in surprise, as if he didn't understand the question. Markus had invited him, it was the second day of their talk together, and both knew that they were going to be friends. The soldiers had left the city now, taking along the shouts and songs, going off to war; now the marketplace was deserted, and the first reports from the front had not yet arrived, the streets were abnormally quiet, it was as if the whole town was holding its breath while it waited.

'Forgiveness for what?'

Markus raised his eyes.

'The war.'

'Which war? This one? Or the one you were in?'

Markus shifted uneasily.

'The one I was in.'

'You're asking a priest whether forgiveness is possible?'

Markus looked embarrassed.

'Forgive me, Father.'

'You don't have to call me Father. That title belongs to your own church.'

'I'm sorry.'

'But perhaps God's forgiveness is not what you're looking for.'

Markus's eyes were filled with tears.

Far away they could hear thunder, a slow, muted rumbling. Markus looked at the priest to see whether he understood that

29

it was cannons and met himself in his gaze; the priest had heard cannons before too. They paused, listening; the cannon thunder rolled in waves at intervals of several minutes. They looked at each other; now the waiting was over, now the shouts from the marketplace had reached the front, now it was only a matter of waiting for the tide to turn and come back the same way, as casualties or prisoners or soldiers in flight, and if it was soldiers in flight who came, then other soldiers would follow, in other uniforms.

Markus went on.

'Is it possible for a person to receive forgiveness without God's help?'

' "If someone falls, he falls alone; but no one is saved on his own." '

'Alexei Khomyakov.'

The priest was surprised.

'You're a well-read man.'

'On this particular topic, yes.'

'Have you thought about seeking forgiveness in the church?'

'In the orthodox church, possibly. You have a different sense of fellowship from us. But you too have conceptions of sin and atonement. Nonetheless, I'm a Catholic by birth, a German Catholic. In my church there's a dispute about whether someone can save himself or whether he's dependent on God's mercy, but there's no dispute about one thing: You *can* atone for sins. The only question is how. And I have atoned, God knows I have. But have I atoned enough to gain forgiveness?'

'The Roman Catholic church requires that the extent of atonement correspond to the seriousness of the sin.'

The priest was making a statement, not asking. Markus nodded.

'In what way have you sinned?'

Markus hesitated a moment before he replied.

'It's a widespread view that in war it's permitted to kill military personnel but not civilians. The First World War was a war of military personnel; it cost ten million lives, but primarily soldiers. There were few who talked about atonement back then. I was born five years after the war, I grew up as the country attempted to lick its wounds. It was reconstruction that people talked about, not atonement.

'The war I was in was different. It cost thirty million lives, and half of them were civilians. Half civilians. For every soldier who fell, one child, one woman, or one old person was killed.'

The priest interrupted him.

'Except here in this country. Here two were killed: two civilians for every soldier who fell. The Russians, as you Europeans call us, lost twenty million people in that war, and thirteen million were civilians. Yes, I can see that atonement is important for you, Herr Wagner.'

'Not just for me, Father.'

'You don't have to call me Father.'

'I'm sorry.'

A plane thundered low over the house, then another, and still another. Markus and the priest grabbed hold of the edge of the table and hunched forward. When Markus continued in the silence that followed, his voice was far, far away, as if the planes had taken it with them.

'I went off to war with a friend. We had grown up together and had close ties, we had been through childhood and adolescence together, I think that creates especially strong bonds. Later on I've wondered what happened to us: whether we were different and grew more alike, or whether we were alike and grew different. His name was Dieter, his name is Dieter. He was more sure than I was, less in doubt, had no doubts at all; he got mad at me when I hesitated.'

———————————

Quiet days and the sound of thousands of wings. Dieter looked up at the sky and the birds gathering high overhead. He had

31

always liked the fall, always liked it when the birds departed, leaving the silence in peace, always liked it when the sun stayed low and the nights turned colder; as if the low beams lit up the world at a slant and altered the shadows, as if the chill nights soothed a fever in nature, an ache.

It was his mother's sister who came to get him at school. Dieter heard the sound of thousands of wings beating at the very moment he saw her enter the classroom behind the headmaster, above the sound of thirty students getting to their feet to stand beside their double desks. She peered around the room for him as the headmaster whispered something to his teacher, who stood at attention; he saw the hand the teacher raised to beckon cautiously. His aunt had smiled at him, but uncertainly, as if she wasn't convinced she'd be able to smile, or whether it was proper for her to do so.

'Dieter Rauschenbach, it is my sad duty to report to you that something has befallen your father.'

The headmaster had waited until they were out in the corridor and the classroom door was shut.

Befallen? Dieter had stared at him. Befallen? What kind of word was that? Had something fallen on his father, had something knocked him to the ground?

'Wait until we reach your mother, she can tell you about it.'

His aunt was practically running as she dragged him along, practically running as she crossed herself and moved her lips and fingered a rosary.

People were standing outside their door when they reached home, a small group of silent people and an ambulance; two men in white coats came down the stairs carrying a stretcher, and he could see there was something lying under the wool blanket.

His mother followed the stretcher down the stairs, and she screamed when she saw him and pushed her way past the stretcher and pulled him close.

Quiet days and the sound of thousands of wings, and Dieter

looked up at the sky. His mother had told him about the shot in the study in such a way that he could hear it, hear it forever after. She had told him about everything all around it, everything that was cut short by the shot; about the groceries she was putting away in the cupboard when it went off, about the music from the radio on the windowsill, blithe morning melodies, about the sunlight and the green leaves that had just appeared; everything that his father had put out and turned off and shut down when he pulled the trigger. He escaped the bankruptcy and the social disgrace and the dole, but he had to put everything else behind him as well, put the light behind him and enter the darkness.

Dieter was just a boy back then, and he adapted to his father's death as something inevitable. His mother and aunt never used the word 'suicide'; they spoke of his death as an unavoidable result of something external, something that had to happen, never as the result of something internal, a choice, something that could have been avoided.

In the midst of his sorrow and loss Dieter sensed another emotion, one he couldn't define, and it wasn't until he joined the Party that he managed to give the emotion direction and see it clearly. It was when he learned about the others, those who were responsible for his father's death, that he suddenly released his hatred and shouted: 'How could you do that to Father?' Not: 'How could Father do this to me?'

Quiet days and the sound of thousands of wings and Dieter who stood with his draft notice in his hands and looked up at the sky and felt proud; at last he would have the opportunity to retaliate.

Dieter studied the pine forest. The trees stood at regular intervals, as if they had been planted, on a flat mossy-green terrain. Their trunks were slender and straight, their crowns high overhead fractured the sunlight, filtering it in narrow rays slanting toward the ground.

33

Hesitantly they moved forward among the trees. There was something about the forest they didn't like, something about the silence, something about the light. For the first time they didn't have the cannons and tanks behind them because they had been sent around the forest to a rendezvous point.

They had orders to advance in absolute silence; they used prearranged signals when they wanted to communicate with each other. The last row walked backward.

Gradually the forest closed around them and changed them. They knew they were advancing but not in which direction; they knew time was passing, but not how quickly; everything around them was exactly the same, they no longer had land-marks by which they could orient themselves.

An hour passed, maybe two, possibly three; their wrist watches told them nothing, they were meaningless instruments for measuring something that existed elsewhere, outside the forest.

Dieter was part of the left flank, in the middle. He let his eyes shift back and forth, 180 degrees at five-second intervals; never fix your gaze: back and forth, back and forth, until you see something new, something that wasn't there before, a move-ment, a shape. He felt unreal, as if it was another Dieter walking along, a stranger. The real Dieter was somewhere out there, outside the forest along with time and space.

His feeling of unreality continued even though the back of the man's head in front of him disappeared; one minute it was there, the next minute it was gone. Just a dark, gaping hole. Dieter registered this, observing it from the distance that only unreality can give. He asked himself whether the man in front of him had seen the bullet coming, seen it coming toward him, rotating, red-hot; it must have flashed as it crossed the beams of light. Somewhere in his consciousness the man in front must have registered images of the bullet and sent out an order that didn't reach his body until the bullet had shattered his forehead and cut off his consciousness.

Dieter saw the man in front of him raise his arms toward his head in a kind of reflex before he fell, not forward like in the movies, but backward, like in war. The shot threw him backward with violent force and tipped his helmet over his eyes when it was struck in the back, from the inside.

Quiet now, Dieter, quiet. He moved the few paces ahead to the man in front of him, bent down, and rolled him over. He looked around; the company had stopped, the soldiers were hunkered down, each behind his own tree trunk, looking at him. Dieter put up his hands and crossed his wrists: the sign that he needed stretcher bearers. An officer shook his head. Dieter stared at him for a long time, then he bent down again and put his hand on the dead man's neck, found the cotton cord with the metal tag and tore it off. The metal tag was divided into two parts by a perforated line, ready for breaking. On either side of the line were stamped two numbers, an identity number and a blood type number, one for those who were killed and the other for those who were only wounded. Dieter broke the tag in half and shoved one part between the teeth of the dead man; the other he stuck in his left breast pocket. Then he nodded to the officer.

The feeling of unreality had deserted him. Something else had taken its place now, something steadier, stronger. He could taste it, bitter, in his mouth. For the first time in his life his body knew that someone was aiming at it, preparing to destroy it, to press a trigger and blast it apart; his body reacted by mustering its forces, tensing up. Dieter read the signals in his body with astonishment; he hadn't imagined that it would be like this to die, so simple, so inescapable. He had been taught to believe that life was something he could fight for, that death was something he could conquer, and yet his body suddenly knew that it was now completely at the mercy of someone else, completely defenseless; and in spite of all awareness and insight and reason, there was nothing Dieter could do about it.

Dieter waited, the company waited, the slender pine trees stood in silence and looked down on them and waited.

35

Something had happened, it felt as if someone had stopped time and made all of them hold their breath, someone had said that the first man to breathe would start time again and then someone would die, because time is what we die from; if we stop time, we stop both life and death.

It was a soldier two rows ahead of him who broke the spell; a thud and a brief scream as he was slammed against the tree trunk he was squatting next to, and black blood between his fingers which examined in surprise the hole in his chest. An officer pointed in the direction the shot had come from and gave Dieter's platoon orders to advance; a sergeant gathered the platoon together and instructed them with hand signals, without a sound. He gave them their bearings, showed them what the orders were if they encountered snipers, fixed a rendezvous for returning to the main force, and waved them off.

Dieter felt a sense of relief as he started moving. He was still at the mercy of someone else, a sight and a trigger, but he was no longer standing still and waiting; now he was on his way toward the threat.

The tree trunks gave way and allowed him to pass, they seemed to be guiding him, bending back and nodding in the direction they wanted him to go. He turned around, the trees stood watching him, smiling encouragement and pointing. He glanced to one side, the platoon was fanning out, the man on one side of him was thirty meters away, there; the man on the other side, there. They waved to each other, kept going. They could no longer see the main force, the forest floor was no longer flat, it was rolling, with small hills and gullies, ideal terrain for both the hunter and the hunted, and Dieter realized that right now he was both, both predator and prey. He saw himself as if in a film, alone in the woods, his gun ready to fire, quiet, light slanting down through the crowns of the trees, bird song, dangerous. He saw himself turn back toward the main force with the trophy, heard two officers praise him, make note of his name; he saw the others scrutinize him with a different look in their eyes, but he couldn't manage to see what lay between those two scenes.

He emerged from a hollow and was on his way up the slope when he discovered that the men on either side of him were gone; it didn't surprise him, it was to be expected. He knew that soon he would find tracks, hear a sound, that was also to be expected. That's why he wasn't surprised when he saw the glint of an empty cartridge case on the ground. It seemed almost like a touch of parody.

He lay down in the heather and moss and slowly crawled upward, stopped, listened, kept on crawling, stopped, listened, kept on crawling, stopped, listened.

A sound. Dieter looked up at the sky, looked at the silver spider's thread he had crept along, down toward his destination, his landmark. Now the consequences lay before him, a sound in a landscape and something imminent, something abrupt.

He listened, took his bearings, managed to distinguish one or more low voices. He moved, listened; his movement didn't affect the sound. He crawled onward, one meter, two meters, stopped, the sound continued; he crawled onward, three meters, four meters, stopped; the sound continued, clearer. He released the safety on his weapon, millimeter by millimeter, and crawled onward, up a little, over a little, and suddenly there was nothing between him and the sound. He could look down at it, hear it distinctly; he was lying at the edge of a gully, staring down at a voice that was talking, a figure in civilian clothes, turned away from him.

Dieter got to his knees and took aim at the figure. It didn't turn around, didn't seem to notice anything, kept on talking. Something swelled inside him, an ignition, a feeling of power; he could kill now, and the man or men the figure was talking to would come after him, and he could kill them too. It kept on swelling inside him; he wanted more than to kill, and the only thing that surprised him was the sequence. He stood up and leaped at the figure before he realized that it was a woman and that she was kneeling in prayer; he landed on her back and pressed her flat against the ground. She tried to scream, but her voice was strangled in the moss. He put his hand around her throat and squeezed; she struggled, her body struggled under his, and something rose up in him, like a gust of wind. He squeezed her throat harder, she whimpered, the sound filled him with elation; she was defenseless now, the way he had been back there.

He shoved his hand under her and loosened a belt buckle, she tried to yell something, tried to twist away, he tightened his grip around her throat. She was young, slender; he put his hand under her sweater, searching.

He lay on top of her and paused; not for a moment did he have any doubts. He enjoyed the anticipation and the power, the feeling of total control, total, total control; the feeling his father had lacked when he took his own life, the feeling his mother had lacked when she fell apart, the feeling an entire nation had lacked in the years since the previous war, but most of all the feeling he himself had lacked during the whole campaign until now. He took her with a smile and a thrust and a force, and when it was over he still had no doubts. He moved his hand to her forehead and yanked her head back; her neck snapped with a dry crack, he let go of her head and lay there on top of her before he stood up, buttoned his fly, picked up the gun and her boots – trophy and proof – and moved on. King Dieter, he thought and smiled, King Dieter. He knew he could have been shot at any moment as he lay there, and he could be shot at any moment right now, but he hadn't been shot and he wouldn't be, because he was invincible and he had just taken his first woman without looking at her face. It was of no interest.

Quiet days and a sun-bright Sunday and the crackling of a loudspeaker outside a school. Dieter stood guard at the door, in newly pressed uniform and shiny boots, a clear sky above him

38

and a sense of confidence inside him. Crowds of people arrived, wearing their Sunday best; they sat down on the benches set up in the schoolyard and looked expectantly at the speaker's platform and the flags and the banners. The speaker stood talking to the organizing committee, a little off to the side and yet positioned so that everyone could see him; he seemed relaxed, self-assured. Dieter was looking forward to hearing him; he had heard him many times before and knew word for word what he would say, but he wanted to hear it again.

Dieter studied the people who streamed in through the doorway and felt proud, proud to be part of it all, giving them something they needed. Many years later he would read in a history book that it was the unemployed who had voted the Party into power; he read this over again, in disbelief, then he closed his eyes and called up the picture of that Sunday morning at the school door. Those who streamed into the schoolyard were not unemployed, they were ordinary people who needed something to hold onto, people who felt that they had been robbed of control; things happened, without anyone being able to explain why. The old society was collapsing, and they knew nothing about the new one; the economy was in chaos, and they had no idea how to restore order to it. The Party gave them an explanation and a way out, and they let themselves be filled the way people let themselves be filled with a national anthem; the Party gave them a cultural idea of the others, they sighed with relief. Finally they had an explanation. They had not lost control, it was the others who had taken it from them. The old society was collapsing because the others wanted it that way; the economy was in chaos because the others wanted to harm them. Now it was time to take up the battle. Dieter had listened and smiled, nodded and shouted, looked forward to taking part.

July 3, 1941: Joseph Stalin declares that the Soviet Union will be defended using the scorched-earth tactic. Gradually a secret civilian army of partisans is organized, first under local leadership, later under the direct control of the Communist Party. The partisans operate with voluntary or compulsory support from the local populace, contrary to international rules of warfare, which require the use of uniforms for all participants in battle. The partisans function more like an active army than saboteurs or militiamen; they take part in regular attacks on the Germans and inflict great casualties. The tactic contributes to an increase in German brutality. The leader of the German high command, Wilhelm Keitel, later gives his forces the order to 'counter the eastern bandits' resistance with brutal measures in order to prevent our divisions from ending up defenseless before them in short order. The troops therefore have the right and the duty to use any means, even toward women and children.'

An officer rode in front of the group of cavalrymen, a red scarf around his neck, dust and dried blood on his face, a gash in his long coat. He rode back and forth in front of the group several times before he began.

'There are rules for peace and there are rules for war. One of them is that prisoners of war should be treated with respect.'

The officer signaled, and a caisson with a tarp over it was pushed forward. The officer folded back the tarp, the cavalrymen stood up in their stirrups, craned forward to see, then turned away. The horses sniffed uneasily, their nostrils flaring.

On the caisson lay three cavalrymen wearing long coats. Their eyes had been dug out, their ears and noses slashed, their fingers and toes cut off. The sweet smell of blood hung heavy over the caisson. The heads of all three had been severed from their bodies, a wooden plug shoved into the bloody necks. Their mouths were stuffed with something, their cheeks bulged.

The officer put the tarp back in place and looked at the cavalrymen.

'Another rule is that anyone who participates in battle must wear a uniform.'

He signaled again and three civilian prisoners were brought

forward, bound together, their hands tied. Two men and a woman, wearing rough, drab clothing, their feet bare. All three were young, but adults, with high cheekbones and eyes full of defiance. The men looked at the officer, the woman stared at the group of cavalrymen.

'These three were caught in the village over there; they blew up two tanks and killed eight of our men. We found the three on the caisson with them.'

The officer dismounted and walked over to the prisoners, the guards released the safeties on their rifles. The prisoners stiffened at the clicks, glanced uneasily at the guards, at the officer. He stopped in front of them, pulled out a knife, held it up in the sharp sunlight.

The officer grabbed one of the male prisoners by the hair, bent his head back, and slit his throat with a swift incision. The prisoner stared straight ahead in disbelief, touched his throat, held out his hands and stared at the blood.

The other male prisoner tried to cover his neck with his hands as the officer came toward him. The officer shoved his knife into the man's stomach, the prisoner screamed, doubled over, tried to grab the knife; the officer quickly yanked it out and cut his exposed throat, a strong, swift slash.

The woman looked from one to the other of her partisan comrades; both were clutching their throats with blood gushing between their fingers as their bodies slowly collapsed and sank to the ground.

The officer moved behind the woman and placed his arm around her neck in a chokehold. With his free hand he un-buttoned her blouse, cut off the belt to her pants, sliced through her underwear. The woman was voluptuous, beautiful; she tried to cover herself with one thigh, tried to hunch her shoulders forward over her breasts. The officer struck her hard on the back, she straightened up. Two of the cavalrymen shifted uneasily, from the ranks behind came voices. The officer let his hand glide over the woman's naked body as he whispered in her ear.

41

Then he pushed her forward into the group of cavalrymen and onward into the ranks behind, the ranks of men who hadn't seen a woman in months. One hand grabbed hold of the remnants of underwear clinging to one hip and pulled, another hand pulled off the open blouse.

October 1941: The German campaign develops problems and comes to a partial halt; autumn rain, day after day, saturates the roads, and the tanks become mired. In November the autumn rain is followed by frost and snow; the German soldiers are not equipped with winter gear, so certain were the army commanders that the campaign would be over before winter. The temperature drops to minus 30° C, in some places the snow is six meters deep. On December 5, 1941, the Russians launch a counterattack and strike the Germans in unprotected terrain and extreme cold. By December 1, Marshall Feodor von Bock had written that 'the troops are completely exhausted.' During the following weeks the Germans are forced back 250 kilometers from their forward positions.

Winter came early that year. It began with a biting cold and gray light. The cavalrymen pulled their scarves up over their mouths and noses; steam rose from the horses. After a while the ground grew harder, ice covered the puddles in the road, crunched under the hooves.

Back through the ranks something was spreading, an uncertainty, a tension; they knew what winter was like, but they didn't know what winter was like *here*, they were strangers in this landscape. The ridges grew darker, the valleys narrower, the horses whinnied uneasily.

The first snow came late one afternoon, while they were resting, and it was different from the snow they were used to. It swirled around in tiny flakes, barely visible, as if it were snowing and not snowing at the same time, as if the snow couldn't make up its mind.

The plain gave way, did not continue; mountains rose up

42

and stopped it, first with sandstone cliffs, low and with vertical grooves, as if the one who created them had drawn his fingers over them. After the sandstone cliffs came the ridges, five hundred meters and steep, but still covered with trees, thick, thick trees.

The cavalry dismounted at the edge of the plain to reconnoiter. Some lay down to rest, some studied maps, some stared at the steep ridges; they knew that the word 'ridge' didn't cover what they saw, but it was the only word they had; it covered the reality they came from, but not this.

Beyond the ridges towered the mountains: three, four, five thousand meters straight up; dark, unapproachable, snow-covered, more vast than the sky. Again an uneasiness rippled through the cavalry.

'Are we going over that?'

The man who asked had a boyish face with delicate features; he was prepared to wage war against men, not against this.

'Are we really going over that?'

And yet he was only looking at the precipitous ridges, wondering only how they would get the horses and artillery and crates of shells and tanks and provisions and everything else up there, because now they were so far from home that they had to transport everything they needed; the supply lines had grown too long. The cavalryman studied the precipitous ridges, moved his eyes along dry riverbeds: There it might be possible to try, and there, and maybe there, and yet he was still only looking at the ridges.

Not once did he raise his eyes to look at the mountains, the mountains where no pass was lower than three thousand meters.

A scouting party was sent out, a patrol went off to the nearest village to find a guide. It was snowing harder; the silence that always accompanies snow wrapped itself around the cavalry. Some of the men continued talking to each other, but in more subdued tones and with longer pauses. The scouts returned, said they thought they had found a road; the patrol returned from the village with a guide in tow. He pointed out the same road.

The cavalrymen began mounting their horses without a glance at each other, without a word; it was as if the mountains up there already held them in their grip. Now the ground had turned white, along with the trees and the sandstone cliffs; only on the clothes of the riders did the snow fail to stick. It melted and allowed the dark figures to continue upward through the whiteness; small black dots on their way toward a mighty cathedral. They approached it the way people approach a cathedral: slowly, hesitantly, with reverence. When they rested, some of the horsemen leaned against the nearest trees and closed their eyes as they moved their lips.

The rest periods and ascents merged into one another. The men were leading their horses now, pulling them along, turning to look down the slope of the ridge at the artillery and tanks, turning to look upward, continuing. Steam rose from the horses, steam rose from the cavalrymen, their breath hung in the air before them.

The ridges came to an end, the trees came to an end, the dry riverbed grew narrower and narrower, split in two. The men reached the door of the cathedral, opened it, and rode through the nave, a white valley with vertical walls rising up one thousand meters and blue sunlight high overhead, through a window in the dome.

The cavalrymen could hear the others behind them, could hear sounds meeting the silence, and for the first time they were unsure of the outcome. They had grown up with sound breaking silence; now they stood before a silence which they knew could break sound. The rider in front raised his hand, a black leather glove beaded with melted snow, and signaled to the rear until everyone had seen it and understood. The engines were turned off, movement halted, conversations ceased. The silence released something else, another silence. The horses heard it first; they glanced up at one of the side naves, a narrow valley filled with boulders and deep shadows. The cavalrymen followed the gaze of the horses and heard the other silence, heard it grow from the shadows in the side valley. A song, an antiphony, between clear sopranos and deep basses, calm, without haste, between two choirs that had the whole day, a whole lifetime. A lead singer came in and started off, the sopranos replied, the basses came in below them, rose up to meet them. The choirs billowed toward each other, making their way along the mountain walls in the cathedral, rising up to the windows and the light.

The cavalry commander gave the signal to continue without saying a word, it wasn't necessary. The riders set off without a sound. The Gregorian hymn from the cloister hovered like a mirage over the landscape, and the men bent low so as not to intrude upon it or disturb it.

They rode on through the valley, through the cathedral, toward the altar and the light. They noticed that there was someone or something next to the altar looking at them, studying them; someone or something that knew they were coming and was waiting for them. The light changed, grew stronger; they looked around in confusion. It was as if the light suddenly flooded in from all sides, poured in, stronger and stronger until everything was backlit and they could see only the silhouettes of each other. The silhouettes moved, changed, took shape; it looked as if some of the cavalrymen were now holding lances, and some had swords; it looked as if they were riding out of the darkness and into the light, out of something disquieting and into something calm.

They rode past the altar and on toward the pass. They could sense that someone or something near the altar was staring after them, following them with its eyes, a presence. And they felt that they were riding out of time and into something greater, something cyclical. Whatever it was next to the altar that was staring after them had seen others head the same way before and knew that more would follow.

On the other side of the mountains winter awaited. The cavalrymen rode into it a little hesitantly, their eyes uncertain, as if it were something they didn't fully understand. They rode into the whiteness and looked around in amazement, without speaking a word. The snow was already deep, but it was something else that made them uneasy: They knew what a meter of snow meant, but it was the other, the unknown, that they didn't yet know.

They stared at each other in disbelief as the snow gradually increased and all trace of reality was erased; only the unreal whiteness remained, the unreal whiteness that continued to fall, night and day, without ceasing. Their progress grew slower and slower; now it was the snow they were battling, not men, and at last they had to give up and stop, overpowered. They were not allowed to turn back and couldn't have done so anyway because there was just as much snow behind them; they were given the order to make camp and wait.

'Wait until spring?'

One of the cavalrymen tried to warm his hands by blowing on them. Another replied without turning around.

'How do we know it will ever be spring here?'

It was when they made camp that they understood what the other was, the unknown. During the night the weather cleared and the next morning they saw that they were alone on an endless plain; the horizon lay utterly flat and utterly unbroken in all directions.

Over the next few days the temperature dropped. By now they thought they were prepared; they stared at each other with the same disbelief, huddled together under the tarps, trying to keep each other warm. It felt as if the cold would soon rip out their guts. They dozed a few minutes at a time, never really slept; their wounds refused to heal. They huddled together and thought: How long will this last?

They were under attack and could barely manage to defend themselves. The machine guns didn't work and the tanks failed to start. They didn't get enough to eat; the provisions never reached them. They huddled together and thought: This will never end.

Some of the cavalrymen kept diaries, one of them drew pictures, drew a man with a worn wooden crutch under his left arm standing motionless, studying the snow-covered plain. The man had only one leg, his head was wrapped in a filthy gauze bandage, his long uniform coat had a rip in the right shoulder. Beneath the gauze bandage the lenses of his glasses glinted, two imprisoned eyes trying to peer out.

The man took a step toward the white eternity, moved his crutch and hobbled after it; then he stopped and gazed into the distance. One step closer to eternity, and yet just as far away.

In a letter to his wife, the German tank-corps general Heinz Guderian writes: 'Only someone who sees the endless Russian steppes, covered with snow in this, our despondent winter, and feels the icy wind blowing across it, burying everything in its path in snow; who drives hour after hour through this no-man's-land, only to find at last an all too paltry shelter along with inadequately clad, half-starved men; and who also can see the contrast: the well-nourished, warmly dressed, fresh Siberian soldiers, fully equipped for a winter war; only the person who is familiar with all of this can truly judge the events that came next.'

Almost a million German soldiers fall during the Russian counter-offensive.

May 17, 1942: The Germans begin their counteroffensive. The Russians eventually have to retreat, the Germans now advance on Stalingrad, Leningrad, and the Caucasus. After three months the

German forces reach the Volga River, one of the most important traffic arteries in the Soviet Union, and attack Stalingrad, the city that controls the river. The Germans take Stalingrad street by street, building by building, in close combat with the Russian soldiers who stubbornly defend every meter. The German armored forces have trouble maneuvering in the streets among the ruined buildings, and the battles gradually develop into hour-long duels between snipers. By autumn the Germans have control of nine-tenths of the city but can't manage to drive the Russian soldiers from the west bank of the Volga.

'They're attacking our flanks.'

The cavalry commander looked up at the men who were talking. One of them was gaunt and unshaven with a terrified, almost wild look in his eyes; the other had a bulky body and looked ill.

'How many are there?'

'A lot.'

'Will the flanks hold?'

The man shook his head.

The cavalry commander stood up and went over to a map on the wall. The river was drawn in red, the city in blue; on one side of the river he had cross-hatched the position of his own forces, on the other side the enemy's forces. He drew two arrows across the river, at the top and bottom of the cross-hatched areas.

'We're not allowed to return without orders.'

The two men followed him with their eyes. They already had a long ride behind them.

'The orders are to stand your ground. I'm sending in reinforcements.'

The cavalrymen saluted and left.

The commander went back to the map on the wall. They had reached the city a month earlier; now the cavalry controlled nearly all of it, but they hadn't managed to drive the defenders from the opposite side of the river.

The commander carefully unhooked the map from the wall, rolled it up, and left the room. He nodded to an adjutant and went down the corridor, then took the stairs two at a time until he was up on the roof terrace. He took a pair of binoculars out of a leather case and rested his elbows on a cornice.

Dusk had started to fall; still enough light for him to view the contours of the land but dark enough for him to see the war. Right before him lay the city, a barren desert landscape of blasted façades and heaps of rubble. Beyond the ruins lay the river, one of the vital nerves in the mighty empire; control of this river would be a stranglehold. On the other side of the river the adversaries had dug in. He could see them as brief, sharp flashes from cannons and gleaming streaks from tracer bullets. Inside the city, machine-guns hammered between the buildings.

He turned the binoculars upstream, along the river, and could see that the upper flank was under attack; the cannon flashes and lights of tracers were fierce over there, like a frenzied, staccato pulse. He turned the binoculars down toward the lower flank; exactly the same. Something filled his throat, something that prevented him from swallowing. He waved to his adjutant, gave him two brief orders, and pointed. The adjutant listened and nodded and looked; then he saluted and left.

The commander stayed where he was. He took out a canteen and drank, grimaced, drank some more. It grew darker, colder, the moon came up and was reflected in the river. The river raced like a silver ribbon into the distance; he could see the silhouette of the city against it. Now the battles subsided among the ruins, the snipers withdrew to their positions and made do with keeping watch.

At the upper and lower flanks the flashes and tracers continued, denser and fiercer. The cavalry commander positioned the canteen and binoculars on the cornice so that from where he stood they concealed the battleground; in this way he

49

could see whether the fronts moved. Then he went back downstairs to work. He sat down with a pile of reports, took out his glasses, and had just screwed off the top of his fountain pen when the adjutant came in.

'The reinforcements couldn't make it through.'

The commander nodded. He read reports for an hour, then he went up to the roof and took the measure of the canteen and binoculars. The battles had shifted. He felt a tightening in his stomach, a cramping. An hour later the cannon flashes and tracers had shifted even more; now they were behind the building, he had to turn around to see them. He stayed up on the roof until the battles died out, stayed there until the adjutant came to get him.

'A radio message.'

'I know.'

A Russian voice with a thick accent crackled over the receiver. The commander knew who he was; they knew about each other.

'Comrade Commander?'

'Here.'

'You are surrounded.'

'I know.'

'You have twelve hours to surrender.'

The commander broke off the connection.

Surrounded. He let the word sink in, raised it back up. Surrounded. Captured, locked up, imprisoned. He sensed that the word alone made something beat faster inside him, the same thing that makes a trapped animal hurl itself wildly and blindly at its attackers, completely without fear, driven by a primal instinct which tells it that to surrender means certain death.

He called in his men and briefed them, decided on a time and direction and stood there watching them ride back to their companies, watched them disappear into the cold dark of night with their long coats flapping. He knew that he had only hours to make a retreat, he had to break holes in the ranks of attackers before they managed to dig themselves in. He rolled up the maps and packed his things, sent a brief radio message to headquarters and was on his way out to the command post when the adjutant called to him.

'Another radio message. From headquarters. They won't allow us to retreat. We have to stay here.'

The cavalry commander turned to look at the adjutant; the adjutant met his gaze. For several long seconds they looked into each other's eyes without saying a word, and during those seconds they both saw it all: what had happened and what was to come, and they accepted it the way men in war accept an order.

November 19, 1942: The Russians launch a counteroffensive along the Volga, focusing their thrust against poorly equipped Romanians, Italians and Hungarians in the flanks, and after four days they manage to surround the German 6th Army of 270,000 men. The commander in chief, Brigadier General Friedrich von Paulus, requests permission to attempt a retreat, but is turned down: 'No one will be allowed to drive us out.'

DAY THREE

'How could the church?'

Markus left the question hanging. The priest didn't speak. They were sitting at the big dining table with a simple salad and a basket of sour rye bread. From a radio in the next room voices shouted, excited and shrill; from the stairwell came the sound of hurried footsteps; from the rooms above came the sound of moaning and now and then a prolonged scream. A nurse with her arms full of bloody towels crossed the room and disappeared into the stairwell, another followed with a washbasin full of blood. Neither of the men at the table looked up.

The wounded were the first to come back from the front. Markus had awakened to pounding on the door; it was the captain of the medical corps who had requisitioned his house for the receiving station, politely but firmly. They had their eye on his house quite early in the planning of the war; it had many rooms, newly renovated water pipes, a new electrical system, diesel generator, and electric water pump. Markus was not only a prosperous man, he had also learned something about living in a socialist republic.

Markus had opened his house to the medical corps with no sign of emotion whatsoever; he had walked from room to room and studied the rows of cots they set up, the operating table rigged up in the library with water hoses leading to the bathroom, and the drain they made by knocking holes in the wall facing the garden.

'How could the church?'

'What do you mean?'

The priest had arrived right after the first ambulance brought the wounded, ready with incense and holy water. He had worked all night, sitting with the wounded and comforting them, holding their hands until they died, blessing them with holy water on their foreheads and lips. Markus had held the cushion bearing the incense and water and the black silk ribbon. When morning came and the priest needed to rest, Markus had shown him to a cot that wasn't in use. Markus himself slept on a mattress in the hallway to the bathroom; the priest was awakened several hours later to tend to more of the dying; afterward he went back to his cot. This was where he now lived.

'How could the church what?'

'Precisely. That's exactly part of the problem. I was once a Catholic, probably still am, but I saw the church drop out. That's a good expression, isn't it: drop out? But when I try to determine in what way the church dropped out, the words escape me. I don't know what to ask.

'I was ten years old in 1933 when the so-called concordat was entered into between the German state and the papacy. For me, the church was Sunday school and mass and the boys' choir, a stern, somber church that made demands, always demands.

'Later I've read what the concordat was all about: the Catholic church agreed that the German state would be allowed to determine the political, social, and organizational activities of the church. In return, the state guaranteed that the church would be allowed to work freely and promised to protect the church schools and properties.

'Subsequently the Catholic church assumed a benevolently neutral position toward Nazi policies. That's another good expression, isn't it? Benevolently neutral. I've tried to imagine what it means; what did it mean, for example, to be benevolently neutral toward the policy of extermination?

'I managed to find a reputable European religious lexicon from after the war. It says that anti-Semitism with a religious emphasis continues to flourish in abundance in certain Catholic countries, and that the Polish Catholic church, for instance, is considered to be "incurably anti-Semitic." Is it true that the Catholic church is still benevolently neutral?'

The priest looked up sharply, as if to stop him. Markus didn't notice, or ignored it.

This is a question that I ask myself now, thought Markus as he helped himself to more salad. Back then I didn't ask such questions. I was an adolescent; I fantasized and took communion and admitted it when I went to confession. The priest would grow furious and call me a swine, yank me out of the confessional by my ear and give me a slap. That's the way the church was back then, it was part of our everyday life, we grew up with it, we encountered it in nursery school, in grammar school, on the sports teams. And another thing: The priests didn't move away. They stayed with the congregation until they died, they followed us from childhood to adulthood, they knew practically everything about us. Whenever I did something wrong, it was always the priest I feared most.

Markus continued.

'In high school I started asking myself how the teachings of Christianity could fit in with the Nazi theories about the state, leadership, and the races, but I still went to mass; it was as if those kinds of questions had nothing to do with my church, or my priest.

'Later I read that the word "church" means two things: the church as an organized power structure with popes and cardinals and bishops and priests; and the church as the body of Christ, the ultimate fellowship among the faithful. We enter into this fellowship when we drink of his blood and eat of his flesh.

'So, Father, do you understand now why I don't know what question to ask? Is it the church as power structure or the Christian fellowship that I feel has dropped out? And if it's the Christian fellowship, then what should I ask? Should I ask whether it was Christ himself who dropped out?'

'You don't have to call me Father.'

'I'm sorry.'

An ambulance stopped outside. Markus and the priest went over to the window. The wounded were lying three high inside the ambulance, all of them with intravenous bags hanging above their stretchers. Markus continued talking in a low voice as they watched.

'During the campaign we had units with us that had special assignments. We were told that they were supposed to stabilize the areas we seized and that they had quite extensive authority; in practice, they were supposed to eradicate all undesirable elements, of which there were many. The first time I witnessed their tactics, I was shocked. They gathered an entire village of women, children, and old men inside a small wooden church and nailed shut the doors and windows before they set it on fire. I could hear the screams of the people day and night for weeks afterward. I went to the army chaplain and asked him how the church could defend such actions, participate in such actions. That was before all of us got involved in it, before the partisan war had brought out the greatest brutality in all of us. A partisan war has that effect; I know even the Americans experienced the same thing in Vietnam. When the enemy doesn't wear a uniform, he could be anybody, anywhere, and his pinpricks will slowly drive you mad. Almost never open warfare, just snipers, snipers, snipers. The Russians deliberately focused on partisan warfare; they have to share the blame for the way the campaign turned out.'

'What did the army chaplain say?'

'That it's not the job of the church to defend anything at all. "God has a plan for everything, but it is not given to us to understand it. He will allow us to understand in due time."'

'But?'

'Is there a "but" here?'

'It seems that way.'

'Two days after we attacked the Soviet Union, the council of

German Catholic bishops approved a declaration supporting the attack. Did God allow the bishops to understand something?'

Markus stopped talking. The priest's face had turned gray and he was holding his hand to his chest, breathing heavily.

'What's the matter?'

The priest shook his head, walked slowly back to the table, and sat down.

'Nothing, just nature running its course.'

'Shall I get you a glass of water?'

'If you wouldn't mind.'

When Markus came back with the water, the color had returned to the priest's face. He accepted the glass gratefully.

'That was kind of you. Would you like to continue?'

'Does this happen often?'

'Now and then.'

'Have you seen a doctor?'

'I don't think a doctor could tell me anything I don't already know. We're both old enough to understand.'

Markus nodded.

'Would you like to continue?' The priest set down the glass.

'I made friends with a musician during the campaign, a church musician. It sounds strange when I say it that way; we're not used to thinking about soldiers having any other identity. He was an organist, a student; sometimes I wonder whether he was drafted simply to set the war to music.'

One of the nurses had come into the room as he spoke. Markus glanced at her. She was young, with thick brown hair and brown eyes. She met his gaze, he could see the words 'set the war to music' reflected in her eyes, creating a bridge across the room.

Quiet days and the sound of church bells in the warm morning sun in a clear and pure Sunday sky. Manfred counted the number of peals as he looked down on the heads assembled in the nave:

men's gray heads, most of them with bald spots, women with hats and locks of hair combed over the brims or knotted at the nape of their neck. They slipped into the rows of pews as they rubbed together the fingertips of their right hands, a Catholic reflex, to wipe off the water they had used to cross themselves. Scientific studies have shown that Catholics have twenty-two per cent less sensitivity in the fingertips of their right hands than Protestants, said Thea, so don't ever ask a Catholic to use his finger.

Manfred shook his head and shut out his sister's voice as he smiled, counted the peals of the bells and smiled, four thousand more peals and then it was his turn. He let his feet slide over the pedals and placed his hands lightly on the lower keyboard, pulled out one of the stops of the organ pipes and looked at the priest as he entered from the sacristy.

Manfred fixed his eyes on the sheet music merely to have some place to rest them. He heard the priest begin the first prayer and knew that it was almost time; he straightened his back and took a deep breath, struck the first chords in his mind, heard the priest read the day's homily, darkness lay over the great deep, heard him start the antiphony with the congregation, *kyrie eleison*, thought it was good that all Greek and Latin hadn't been removed from the liturgy, there's still something we simply have to listen to, not understand, something we just have to allow to fill us, and he placed his fingers on the keys and pressed down two pedals and released the music, now it was his turn, he sent the music out from the gallery and down toward the pews, *laudamus te, benedicimus te*, brought the white heads up and lifted them toward the dome, *adoramus te, glorificamus te*, and darkness lay over the great deep, and above that lay the music, his music. He disappeared into the music and came out on the other side, where words did not exist, where everything was movement; he felt something stream toward him, into him, and he could look down, a long way down; there was nothing above him, only emptiness, everything was below him, a long way down, farther and farther down.

'The question is not why, my children, but for what purpose.'

Manfred woke up. Father Neumath was giving a sermon; that was unusual during a mass.

'We are in the midst of a difficult time with great suffering, a time when all of us will be asked to give up something, and many will be led into sorrow. Many are those who will ask: Why this suffering?'

Father Neumath held out a worn Bible, as if to document what would follow.

'In the Book of St. John, chapter nine, verses two and three, we read about the people who came to Jesus and asked: "Master, who did sin, this man, or his parents, that he was born blind?" And Jesus Christ replied: "Neither hath this man sinned, nor his parents: but that the works of God should be made manifest in him."

'In other words the question is not why, but for what purpose. What purpose does this suffering serve? Can it further the glory of God and His name?'

This is getting out of control, thought Manfred, it could easily take half the day.

Father Neumath raised his voice.

'Where does evil come from?'

A rhetorical pause.

'Does it come from God? Is it God who created it? Is He the source of both good and evil? Or is God battling a power that is just as eternal as He is?'

Manfred stuck his hand in his pocket, it itched abominably, had been itching for days, weeks, years; no one else in modern times had ever experienced such a cruel and lasting itch.

'In the Book of Genesis, chapter one, we read that darkness lay over the face of the deep; this may signify that evil existed in the beginning.'

Father Neumath was now red in the face, agitated.

'But for a Christian this is not enough. We Christians must see

59

something more than darkness and the deep, we must see an evil will, a rebellion against God, an "I." We find this in the Epistles of Jude, in the Revelations of St. John the Divine, and in the Gospel according to St. Luke: a fall from the world of the angels. But then God must have created angels in such a way that they could rebel, isn't that true? Does that make Him to blame?'

Father Neumath shouted these last words, upward, toward the gallery. Manfred gave a start; his finger that was scratching had produced what is called an unintended effect. Father Neumath, that man, he sees everything.

'God could have created us as automatons, incapable of rebelling, but then He could not have given us freedom. And without freedom the joy that God has planned for us will also disappear, the joy of being freely bound to Him through love.'

I have to, thought Manfred, I have to, I have to, I have to.

'Is war the price we must pay then for free will, for man's ability to choose evil just as he can choose good?'

Father Neumath's face was dark red now; he was standing on his toes and shouting at the congregation as little drops of spittle rained over the parishioners like star dust.

'Remember that we Christians do not acknowledge evil, we acknowledge only the victory over evil.'

No, thought Manfred, no, no, no. Don't, don't, don't. Think of Queen Victoria.

'And evil shall be driven out with evil. But there is a difference: We are the time of light, those over there are in the depths of darkness. We are the footsoldiers in God's army, we have been sent out to redeem the Creation. Through the Fall evil has entered into the Creation, like a parasite. We have been sent to drive it out, so that the glory of God might be revealed.'

Amen, thought Manfred, amen, amen, amen. Now we can put all this sadness and hurt behind us and move on; either we start in with a little hymn and some organ music right now or else, or else, or else. He suddenly pictured his sister as she stepped out of the bath that morning, he gasped and doubled over, tried to drive away the image, whispered: *Oh Death, where is thy sting, oh Death, where is thy victory?*

Quiet days and the sound of notes from a piano behind Rilke's door on the first floor where Manfred is sitting and practicing while Rilke gazes at him with a rather tender look in his eyes, a sad yearning. There is a way out of everything, Manfred: music. Quiet days before the war and Rilke who taught him to read music as he placed his hand on his shoulder, sometimes impatiently, as if it were urgent. Rilke taught him to walk the five floors down from his parents' apartment to another world, down to Rilke whose eyes lit up with new life every time he opened the door and the clear eyes of the young boy looked up at him inquisitively.

Rilke taught him to read music, taught him chords and intervals and harmony while he leaned over him and moved his fingers on the ivories; gave him the key to something different, five floors down from the kitchen table with his mother and father. Until one day Rilke didn't open the door himself but sent someone in uniform, someone who said no, there would be no more piano lessons.

Quiet days before the war and Rilke never appeared again, no matter how long Manfred rang the bell. And the landlord gave Manfred an envelope with his name on it, many weeks later, and said: I found this in Rilke's apartment. And Manfred merely nodded when he opened the envelope and looked at the scrap of paper with a name and address on it, nodded because he, with the swiftness of his young mind, had already grasped the message: Rilke was sending him on, Rilke knew that he would never see him again, and he was sending him on.

Later in life Manfred would ask himself how it was possible for so many to know so much without saying a word, but not then. Back then he simply went to the address on the piece of paper and found the nameplate and waited for the maestro to open the door. Gray hair, dark eyebrows, sharp eyes.

'What can I do for you?'

The maestro towered in the doorway.

'Music.'

The maestro stood there a moment, scrutinizing the little boy before he stepped aside and invited him in. Manfred felt something fall into place as he entered the small apartment, the way the picture emerges when the last puzzle piece is put in. He nodded with recognition at the piano over by the window and the crowded bookshelves, the copper engravings on the wall, and the bronze bust on a little table. He understood, without being able to put it into words, that he had found his way back to a lost time.

Later in life he did manage to put it into words, but then he chose the word 'suspended,' not lost. He had found his way back to a suspended time, or it had found its way to him. That gave him the slight nuance he needed to find an opening in the question about how it was possible for so many to know so much without saying a word.

'Who sent you here?'

'Rilke.'

The maestro nodded and looked out the window.

That was how they would talk to each other, for the rest of their lives and beyond: curt, spare, taut, as if words were of no interest to them, futile. Only once did Manfred ever hear the maestro say anything with emphasis, so forceful and coherent that Manfred had written it down on a scrap of paper, which he always carried with him in his left breast pocket, closest to his heart: Life is music. Our only task as human beings is to let it out.

That was a long time after the first afternoon, long after the maestro had asked Manfred to talk about himself and Manfred sat down at the piano and talked: *adagio*, about his mother and father who sat at the kitchen table and disappeared, and *crescendo*, about Thea; the music grew and grew until it filled everything and erased all else.

When he finished playing, the maestro sat in silence and looked at him.

Quiet days and the sound of notes from a piano behind the maestro's door. Manfred grew bigger, stronger, more solid; the maestro became smaller, whiter, but the relationship between them remained unchanged: The maestro gave something of himself and Manfred accepted it. Both did so with a feeling of reverence, both knew that this was important; in this way human beings throughout the ages have passed on music so that others might continue.

When Manfred appeared in uniform to say goodbye, the maestro did not let him in, merely stood in the doorway and looked at him. Inside himself, Manfred could hear the maestro saying that we have given the world the greatest of all music, is it time now to give this too? But in his eyes Manfred could see the maestro reply: Do you think I taught you the craft so that you would let out *this* music? For the first time Manfred caught a small glimpse of what it means to take responsibility for your own choices. The maestro stretched out his arms and embraced Manfred, briefly, before he turned him around and sent him down the stairs.

The letter wasn't even left out for him, so absorbed in themselves were his mother and father. Manfred found it under several old newspapers on the kitchen counter when he was looking for the radio schedule.

'When did this arrive?'

His mother gave him a frightened look: Is there a reproach in the question? Is there something wrong with me? His father sat behind his paper with the sports scores, muttering, not listening.

Manfred opened the letter and read the draft notice, read his name and the name of the regiment and the induction station, unable to take it in, to imagine it. His life was playing the organ in a church, and now someone suddenly wanted him to do something entirely different. He knew that others had been called up, he just hadn't thought it would happen to him; the thought hadn't even occurred to him.

Thea came into the kitchen and saw him standing there staring at the draft notice.

'What is it?'

'I've been called up for military service.'

His mother gave a start, his father kept on reading. Thea didn't say a word. Manfred looked at the letter again and pointed his finger at the date.

'I can't go that day, I'm supposed to play for a wedding.' He gave Thea a resigned look, realizing that he wouldn't be playing for that wedding. He had served the obligatory years in the youth movement, along with everyone else, and he knew what a military order meant.

'Wedding? What wedding?'

The word had managed to reach his father behind the newspaper; he peered around it.

'A wedding on the day he has to report for military service.'

That was his mother.

'Military service?'

The father looked at the son with new interest. Manfred sighed inside, he knew what was coming: his father's endless stories about the war, about the time when everything was different and everything had a meaning, a purpose. He could sense Thea bustling around next to him, searching for something in the cupboard; they both knew that their father had never been anywhere near the front. Later Manfred would understand that this was exactly the problem; it's the men who wish they had been at the front who talk the most. Their father told the same stories all over again; across the table their mother sank down a little farther. And Manfred went off to war the way boys have always gone off to war, because they have to, and because deep down his father's feelings for him were important, and his father was clearly proud of him now, elated. The only discordant note came from Thea. She stood staring at him with a look he'd never seen from her before, a look he couldn't read.

Manfred listened. He was lying face down on top of a collapsed wall and listening, a sharpshooter's rifle hugged close to his body. The planks in the wall underneath him smelled of cabbage and something else; it reminded him of something, something he could no longer manage to remember.

The façade of the building was the only part left standing; inside, all the walls, all the doors and all the stairways had been shot and blasted to ruins, just as they had in every other building along the whole street, in the whole district, the whole city. Manfred had run from doorway to doorway to check the heaps of rubble inside, run from façade to façade, thinking: If we end up taking this city, we won't be taking a city anymore but an empty façade, and that changes the war in some way, but he didn't have the strength to figure out how. The biting cold seeped inside him through his mouth and nose and eyes and ears, freezing his thoughts in midstream; *the façade war*, he thought, and watched the thought stiffen, freeze up, freeze over.

The battle for the city was moving from door to door now, from rubble heap to rubble heap, through narrow streets and cramped alleys. The time for tanks was past, the time for artillery was past, they couldn't maneuver in the narrow streets. Now it was time for snipers, time for duels.

Manfred listened. He had volunteered for a mop-up operation after the boy he was sitting and talking to suddenly exploded. The boy had asked him about Thea with a light in his eyes, more light than Manfred could remember seeing in a long time, and Manfred had smiled and started to reply when the boy suddenly exploded, and the light in his eyes was extinguished, and the top half of his head disappeared, and Manfred went over to volunteer for the mop-up operation.

Manfred listened. He had crept into the district along with five others and a corporal. The corporal had assigned each of them to a sniper, one on one, and sent them off; it's him or you, don't come back without completing the mission.

Manfred listened. There was a rhythm to the sniper that excited him, as if the Russian down there were whistling a melody; two bars rest, one bar shoot; two bars rest, one bar shoot. Manfred listened to the melody, floated into it, crept toward it.

A pale moon hung over the ruins, over the district; it was the only light they had, the tracer bullets had run out long ago. Cold was the only thing there was plenty of, it hung like metal just below the moon; cold and hunger. The hunger rose up from the ground and entered them, slicing and etching its way into their guts; the cold descended on them with the light from the moon, pressing them down toward the ground and the hunger.

Manfred listened. The Russian was taking a break, as if to change a cartridge clip or listen for a reply from someone out there. In the silence he could hear other snipers, some far off, some nearby, repeated shots and single shots, repeated shots and single shots, without rhythm, without harmony, and he thought: My sniper is the best of them all, at least he tells a story.

He listened to the story when the Russian opened fire again, two bars rest, one bar shoot; then he suddenly made a change and inserted a single shot on the one and the three in the first rest bar. Manfred smiled and listened to the story. It was about a young girl who was sitting near a still forest lake, waiting for a prince who had gone off to war. Each day she sat beside the water with her head bowed. Many years passed and the prince did not return, the young girl became a young woman and her corn-yellow hair grew long; when she bowed her head, it reached all the way to the water, and then she sat there enclosed in a little golden chamber and heard only the sound of her own tears striking the water's surface.

Manfred nodded and released the safety; he replied first with the basic rhythm, two bars rest, one bar shoot, then he inserted single shots on the one and the three in the first rest bar. After a short pause, the Russian answered with the same.

Manfred hunkered down, the shots struck the wall plaster right above his head, the Russian was good. He laughed as he waited for the rest bars, now they had a *cantus firmus*, now they could add the counterpoint. Manfred aimed toward the sound and repeated the basic rhythm, and the Russian replied with the same. Manfred no longer noticed the cold, he didn't notice the hunger, he was inside the melody now, inside a rhythm that filled the darkness and the ruins and made the light from the moon coalesce into rays. He took a step outside the ruins and added a counterpoint, repeated the basic rhythm and added a new counterpoint. The Russian let the echo of the shots die out before he replied, a certain lightness had come over his shots, like playing a piano; he too repeated the basic rhythm before he added his counterpoint, playfully, tentatively.

Manfred laughed and drew the Russian into a rondo, received a reply, led him further into a fugue, received a reply; two musicians playing for each other in the dark. They moved from Renaissance to Baroque, Manfred sent fragments of Bach out into the darkness, the Russian answered with Palestrina. Two musicians playing for each other among the ruins, closer and closer to each other, in the same district now, in the same street, in the same building.

Manfred listened. He's in there somewhere, behind one of the heaps of brick, a shadow blacker than the dark; very quiet now, one foot cautiously forward, then the other, he pressed his head to the remains of a firewall, peered out cautiously.

Manfred pulled off his shooting gloves and warmed his lips against his hands, puckered up his lips and blew warm air through them until they were so soft that he could whistle. He stood with his face pressed to a bullet-riddled Russian door frame and whistled, a slow, tender fugue about his sister. He missed her, missed being near her, missed hearing her scold him, fret over him. A cloud covered the moon and the light grew less cold. The Russian acquiesced and repeated the fugue, but as counterpoint he continued on with his own story about the young woman by the water. One day as she sat there, she heard the sound of steps, footsteps, and she parted her long blonde hair and looked up. The tears in her eyes splintered the light like prisms so that she saw four white figures, four white figures riding on the backs of four white horses; they came toward her from all directions, she rose to her feet and stretched out her arms to them.

Manfred rose to his feet too, it was his turn to reply. He returned to the basic rhythm, stepped forward from the door frame and went back to the basic rhythm, but now he was whistling the shots, two bars rest, one bar shoot. Then he added the notes on the one and the three of the first rest bar and waited until the Russian began to sprint on the four, waited until he saw the fur-clad figure take off, sprinting for the next doorway on the rest of the 4th beat, the one without a shot, and then spin around in surprise when it came all the same, spin around and stare in surprise at the glowing red bullet coming toward him, and beyond it the black muzzle of a rifle, and beyond it two eyes that looked as if they had lost something, something of value.

The conditions for the surrounded soldiers grow worse day by day, the German air force manages to fly in less than a third of what is needed. By Christmas 34,000 Germans are evacuated by plane from the surrounded area; primarily the wounded, but also 7,000 'specialists' from the special political units, partly by means of bribes.

January 25, 1943: The Russians attack Stalingrad. The 6th Army is squeezed in from all sides until the area it controls is so small that it's almost impossible to receive air drops. Cold, hunger, disease, and frostbite are about to break their resistance; bread rations are down to 75 grams a day; suicide is not uncommon among the German soldiers. General Friedrich von Paulus requests several times for permission to surrender, but is refused; it's a matter of 'saving the Western world.'

'Dieter, do you see that plane over there? Guess who's going to be leaving on it.'

'That's not true.'

'How do you know?'

They were standing in line for food; a silent, dejected food line of men wearing long coats with snow on their shoulders and collars. Most of them had no hats, some had wrapped their heads in rags, none of them had gloves; they pulled their hands up into their coat sleeves and blew warm air inside.

'I hear they're paying four thousand to buy passage.'

Dieter grew angry and raised his voice.

'That's not true. Those planes are evacuating the wounded.'

A stranger standing in front of him in line turned around and looked at him.

'What planet are you from?'

Two months since they were surrounded, sixty days, and the enemy was forcing them into an area that became smaller and smaller each day; by now it was so narrow that one of every three air drops missed. They stood and watched air drops of food and supplies land behind the enemy's positions. Twice an hour they watched planes take off from the improvised airport and head west with evacuated men. Occasionally they were shot down and hurtled toward the ground, trailing black smoke. They watched them crash without a trace of sympathy, more like envy.

Dieter, Markus, and Manfred's company had dug in under a rubble heap, a collapsed apartment building. They had dug tunnels into the piles of brick and made small rooms where they could get a few hours' sleep while others kept watch, a few hours' reprieve from the cold and hunger and smell of diarrhea, a few hours' exhausted sleep disturbed only by twitches in their face and body each time another shell exploded and more plaster rained down from the ceiling. They had made a special room for the bodies of those who took their own lives; for some reason it didn't feel right for them to be put with those who had fallen in battle, but it didn't feel right for them to be left hanging either, or lying with a gun barrel in their mouth and the back of their head blown off. They had killed any civilians they came across in the rubble heaps, but only after a time, only after they had taken out their despair and anger and hatred and terror on them, and now they knew something about themselves that they never would have believed.

'Is that all?'

Dieter was standing at the table where the food was handed out; he turned the square of brown bread over and looked at it. Markus put his hand on his arm.

'Take it easy.'

There were rumors of nighttime executions. The soldiers were on the verge of revolt at any moment and had to be forcibly restrained.

Dieter spun around and left the food table; he had tears in his eyes. His nose was white with frost. Markus and Manfred followed.

'They found a private food cache for officers in the twelfth tank corps yesterday. With wine.'

Dieter grew angry.

'You two believe anything you hear.'

'And last week four hundred men in the special units managed to get themselves evacuated by paying bribes.'

'Why would they do that? Good Lord, you're talking about the elite, the absolute elite.'

'Dieter, they know what they've done, they know what's in store for them if they're captured.'

A shell exploded behind them, they threw themselves to the ground, lay with their hands over their heads as snow and gravel and splinters of wood rained down on them. When the booming stopped and the ringing in their ears had ceased, they could hear Dieter crying.

January 31, 1943: Friedrich von Paulus, now Field Marshal, surrenders and submits to Russian imprisonment along with

110,000 soldiers. A total of 750,000 German soldiers lost their lives during the battles of the Volga, the Don, and Stalingrad.

A wind streamed cautiously over the cavalry. It carried something with it, something light, something muted. The cavalrymen glanced up, to the side, turned their faces toward the wind and closed their eyes. On the ground all around them the soldiers had lain down to rest, in groups, as if it was easier for them to rest close together. A few raised their heads to look at the wind, follow it with their eyes; others merely listened, noticing the slight ripple in a tent canvas, a latch falling shut somewhere, and the delicate notes of a harmonica far away.

The wind looked down on them and smiled, something unfolded from it, yellow, warm; both the cavalry and the infantry noticed it. They looked at each other with something new in their eyes.

They were beaten now. Defeat stared at them from every bulge in the makeshift trenches, from every brick in the collapsed heaps of rubble. It was a silent defeat, wordless. They had given their utmost for as long as they could; now the time had come to hand over their weapons. The enemy was stronger and more persevering than they had been led to believe, which spared them much of the shame but none of the sorrow, because they had lost more than a battle.

They had gone off to war with the sound of brass bands and crowds in their ears, proud; they had moved from victory to victory in the first phase of the war, certain of their cause. They had accepted the violence that gradually caught up with them, regarding it as a necessity, unwilling to see that it had also slowly changed them. Now it was too late, now they could no longer regard the violence as a necessary means to achieving a goal; now the goal had been taken from them, and they saw that it made the violence blind, without purpose.

71

Some of them asked themselves whether they might have won if they had used more violence, but most refrained because somewhere deep inside they knew that the natural counterpart was the question whether they might have won if they had used less.

The wind kept streaming over them, the notes of the harmonica followed, like something painful, melancholy, and at the same time something good, an ending. It was silent and white all around them, silent; for the first time in months they could hear the silence.

One of the cavalrymen said something into the silent whiteness.

'Did we ride all that way for this?'

No one answered.

'I didn't think victory and defeat would be so alike.'

Markus looked at the cavalrymen and thought: masks. Victory and defeat are the two masks of war, and the same pain shines from the eyes of both. He looked from the soldiers around him to the guards with the brown combat uniforms and dark eyes holding the same pain, the guards standing at intervals of several meters who had disarmed them and pulled out all those they found from the special units and led them away.

Markus listened to the notes of Manfred's harmonica and the story they told; the notes came from a rolling, green grassy hill where a young man, bare-chested, knelt with his clasped hands held up to the sky, as if offering thanks for something. Close by sat a young woman on a blanket with a picnic basket, smiling, patient. Around them the grassy hillside stretched toward the horizon in three directions before it sloped down to a small wood and disappeared. No one but the young couple was present; the horizon was empty, the edge of the forest was empty, the grassy hillside was empty. The young couple did not look around; they seemed to know that no one else would come.

The cavalrymen were familiar with death, they had lived so long in the borderland between the real and the unreal that it

had become part of their lives, but only now did they understand the very core of the nature of war, its deepest marrow. In
a war death is the rule and life is the exception; they knew that
now. And they knew that it is impossible to survive mentally in
a war without counting yourself as one of the exceptions. They
had seen enough men lose their grip to know this. Now they
could put words to the expressions on the death masks of those
who had fallen: not pain, not fear, not horror, but surprise,
surprise not to be among the exceptions after all. It was the
same surprise they felt themselves when they looked at the
guards, with rifles ready and high cheekbones, standing silently
around them.

From the distance came a shouted command, it rolled over the
rubble and the cavalrymen and the guards, reverberated, grew
stronger; another command shouted from a different direction,
then another and another, and the rubble stood up, staggering; all
around, the cavalrymen stood up, without horses, stood up
reluctantly, as if uncertain whether they should, and took a
few hesitant steps. The guards shouted, struck them; the cavalrymen obeyed, forming a kind of column, an exhausted, ragged
column with drooping heads and worn-out eyes. Dieter took a
firm grip on Markus's coat on their way to the assembly area;
Manfred came hurrying toward them from between two destroyed buildings. They looked at each other and whispered: We
won't make it if we don't stick together. The shouted commands
multiplied, grew stronger, the cavalry's own officers were forced
to give orders, no one was allowed to speak, no one was allowed
to sit down, no one was allowed to help the sick, who one by one
tumbled into the snow and stayed there.

The guards made them stand all night; they rolled out cables
and set up floodlights and made them stand there, bathed in light,
hour after hour. Their shadows stretched out toward the city they
had destroyed; surrounding them on all sides lay the winter
darkness, which in the end had broken them. When morning
came, the floodlights had burned a new truth into every single

cavalryman: Over there stand the men who won, over here stand we who lost. The light had streamed into all the cavalrymen and filled them – there stand those who won, here stand we who lost – filled them and marked them and erased all the old truths, so that when morning came, they were finally ready.

In a silent procession they slowly began to move when the command sounded. They moved the way people who have lost move: shuffling, listless; they held their eyes the way people who have lost hold their eyes, fixed on the ground in front of them. They took note of the direction they were headed, without comment: eastward, toward eternity. They knew it had to be that way, just as they knew what lay before them. The only thing they didn't know was how many days and weeks they would be forced to walk, or how cold it would get, or how deep the snow would be that they had to plod through. They did know what would happen to the wounded and the sick and the weak, and there was one other thing they knew, but none of them put it into words, none of them had thought it all the way through, they just knew.

'Emma, Emma, guess what they've started doing now.'

Half-timbered houses and cobblestones and a northern German midsummer, shrieks from the seagulls circling above the cannery and filleting hall, the sound of water and knives along the bloody steel troughs, stiff canvas aprons that puckered, and not a word from the one hundred and ten thousand Germans that surrendered at Staligrad, not a single word, just rumors, rumors, rumors.

'They've started melting down the dead for tallow candles. They boil them in big brewing vats and strain off the fat.'

They were barely sixteen and not yet women in the legal sense of the word.

'You shouldn't believe everything you hear. People say all kinds of things.'

She was petite and agile, with flawless, clear features and

74

sharp brown eyes. Her girlfriend was blonder and less clear, like a person a little out of focus.

'Emma, why would somebody make that up on purpose?'

Emma didn't reply. She pulled over another fish with her spiked hook and sliced it open with a swift incision, turning the flesh inside out and hauling out the guts. A lock of brown hair slipped out from under her white canvas hood.

'My Wolfgang as tallow candles? In a Russian sod hut?'

Her girlfriend threw out her arms in resignation.

'My Wolfgang isn't allowed to shine for anyone except me. Who knows what he'd be a witness to then.'

They kept on working, smiling, with black blood under their fingernails. Outside they could hear the sound of a fishing boat on its way in or out; they took note of it and stored it away without thinking, just as they took note of and stored away the sound of the sea. They had grown up near the sea and had the voice of the sea inside them; when it rose up, something rose up inside them, when it subsided, something subsided inside them.

'Emma, do you know what Russian women use tallow candles for?'

Emma looked up, her eyes glinting. Her girlfriend leaned close and whispered in her ear, both eager and bashful, with one hand on her shoulder. Emma listened, smiled. She turned away when her girlfriend was done.

'And Wolfgang, how much fat does he have on him? A log candle or a cake candle?'

Her girlfriend screamed and struck out at her, ran laughing after her toward the door. A foreman wearing a gray coat tried to block their way.

'It's not time for a break yet.'

They moved close to him; her girlfriend placed her hand on his arm.

'We have to, Herr Foreman. We just have to.'

Emma's hand brushed against him, he blushed and let them

pass as he cast an uneasy glance at the other workers in the hall. Then he turned around and stared after the two girls, a little embarrassed. They knew something about him that they weren't supposed to know, something that gave them power over him.

Emma and her girlfriend disappeared in among the stacks of benches. The women at the cannery had stacked them up so they formed a room with an open roof, a cave where they could sit without being seen, take a few drags on a cigarette, let the sunshine warm their faces, and dream. The foreman knew about the room but didn't dare do anything about it. Once he went inside and found five young women; he was about to throw them out and order them back to work, but something in their eyes stopped him, something in the room, something that trembled. They had merely sat there staring at him. He heard his own voice getting weaker and weaker, less and less confident, until at last he had stopped altogether. Two of the women had stood up and come over to him, very close; he felt their breath against his face. The other three had sat there watching, laughing, clapping enthusiastically when the two standing in front of him had discovered what they weren't supposed to know. The news had spread to all the women at the cannery, he could tell they knew.

Emma took out a tobacco pouch and papers. Her girlfriend climbed up on the stacked benches, craned her neck over the edge, and peered toward the shore.

'Emma, Emma, they're walking around bare-chested.'

Emma gasped and climbed up, put her arm around her girlfriend's shoulders, and looked. Down on the beach about a hundred men were building fortifications; they were pushing wheelbarrows and hauling planks and rolling rocks. Some of them wore white undershirts, others were bare-chested; they had dark skin, hair, and eyes. Armed guards stood at ten-meter intervals and kept an eye on them.

'See that one over there? The one at the cement mixer?'

It was as if the man they were talking about could hear them; he turned his head and looked in their direction. There was something cocky about the way he turned his head, as if he knew.

Emma sighed.

'Look at those shoulders. Look at those arms. Look at those hands. My God.'

Her girlfriend put her arm around Emma's waist. They stood there with their arms around each other, looking at the foreign workers, the forbidden.

'When I get married my husband will be blond, when I have children, they'll be blond; just once I'd like to feel dark hands on me, run my fingers through dark hair, look up into dark eyes.'

'Ilse was alone in a storage shed with two of them once, just for a few minutes, while the guard ran to open the gate for an officer. She says it was indescribable.'

'Ilse says lots of things. You shouldn't listen to her.'

The man at the cement mixer finished filling a bucket and hoisted it to his shoulder with a jerk; the muscles in his back tightened. Emma slid her arm down her girlfriend's back.

'So what did Ilse say?'

'One of them grabbed her from behind, stuck his hands under her blouse, and unfastened her bra.'

'But Ilse is flat-chested.'

'Not in her story.'

'And the other man?'

'Stuck his hand between her legs from in front and held her tight with his other hand on her rear.'

'My God.'

Emma took her girlfriend's hand and guided it.

'Ilse says it wasn't their hands that were the most exciting. It was the smell: of sweat and garlic; and the sight: of dark skin with dark hair, masses of hair.'

'Do they carry garlic around with them?'

'Russians never go anywhere without garlic. They say that

Russian woman rub garlic on their bodies at night so their men can find their way, even without light.'

'Don't their men know where to go?'

'To save time. Russian women are huge.'

The man with the cement bucket was back at the mixer. He stood facing them for a moment, with his hairy chest and rippled stomach muscles. He had broad cheekbones and his head was shaved.

'There was a gleam of gold in his teeth.'

'And the sun played on his sweaty muscles.'

'He took her in his arms with a tight embrace.'

'She tried to pull away.'

'But he was stronger than she was.'

'He took off her clothes.'

'Tore them off.'

'First her blouse.'

'She whimpered.'

'Then her pants.'

'She pleaded with him.'

'He didn't say a word.'

'Just pressed her down on her back on the dining table.'

'So that her ass was right at the edge.'

'Forced her legs apart.'

'And then the air raid siren went off.'

'She shut her eyes and waited.'

'Emma, Emma. The air raid siren. Pull yourself together.'

Emma opened her eyes. The workers on the beach were running toward a rendezvous spot at the water's edge. They lay down, close to each other, with their faces in the sand and their hands behind their heads. The guards jumped into half-finished bunkers and took up position. The shriek of the sirens merged with the screams of the gulls and the hammering of the anti-aircraft guns and the roar of airplane engines and the shouts of terrified, fleeing people. Emma spun around and stared at the workers on the beach one more time, one last time, then at the bombs hovering under the planes right overhead, suspended in midair; she had seen it before, it had something to do with the backwash that made them hover like that for a moment, and on the other side of the little inlet, beyond the workers, she saw the remains of the town she had once grown up in, here and there a chimney stuck up from the heaps of bricks, and over there was the church spire. In its shadow, she had been kissed for the first time, by a boy with strong hands, strong, strong hands.

Partly because of the government's policy on women — a woman's place was in the home — 5.3 million slave laborers from occupied countries and 1.8 million prisoners of war were put to work in the German armaments industry to replace all of those who had been drafted into the war. The slave laborers were transported into the country in freight trains, they worked under strict guard, and they were given very bad food. The prisoners of war had it worse.

The cavalrymen were resting at a water hole. One of them took off his left boot and tended to a sore, another lay down to sleep in the slushy mixture of grass and snow. The others sat in silence, passing around a canteen.

A figure approached, stopped some distance away, studied them with his arms akimbo under his long, open coat. The cavalrymen turned toward him, looked at him, nodded.

The stranger touched a finger to his hat in greeting and stepped forward.

'Those horses.'

The others looked at each other. The stranger sketched languid lines in the air with the forefinger and middle finger of his right hand, transforming the water hole into a saloon, the slushy snow into a worn plank floor with tables and chairs and a bar. The cavalrymen downed the first round of beers in one gulp.

The stranger wiped the foam from his upper lip and pushed his hat back from his forehead.

'Ever see a man get hit?'

The others didn't reply.

'Get hit real hard?'

The stranger ordered another round before he continued.

'It's not the sight, it's the sound.'

A brief, abrupt sound as he spoke. The cavalrymen stared at the crushed hand and the blood as it started trickling. The stranger grimaced, placed his hand in his lap.

'That sound.'

A hollow sound now, like a boot against a soft part of the body. The stranger doubled over suddenly and clutched his groin.

'The sound.'

The cavalrymen backed away, looked at each other. All movement in the saloon had stopped, all sound had ceased; only the stranger moved, was heard.

'It's enough to scare a man.'

There was a cracking sound as the ribs in his right side were smashed in, first the heavy sound of something hitting him in the side, then the sharp crack of his ribs breaking. The stranger stood all lopsided now, one hand at his groin, the crushed hand halfway up his side. He looked at the cavalrymen.

'Those horses.'

A harsh, high sound as half his face disappeared and he screamed with a gaping mouth cavity. He struggled to shape his words, his tongue searched for a palate that was missing, half a row of teeth that was gone.

'We should have had those horses now.'

40,000 of the 110,000 German soldiers who were taken prisoner at Stalingrad died during the march eastward to the prison camps.

DAY FOUR

'Allah is great. Crush the Armenian dogs. God is with us. Sever the Azeri heathens from people and fatherland.'

Markus stood next to the radio cabinet, switching between an Armenian and Azeri channel; they were only a few centimeters apart. He played with the tuner, swiftly turned the knob back and forth until the two channels merged into each other.

'History is on our side, this area has always been Azeri, if we had known what we know now we would never have allowed the Armenian cockroaches to settle here, crush them, but openness and friendliness are part of our Azeri nature, crush the cockroaches; we have our historical right, this area has always been Armenian, but we have been too trusting, it's part of our Armenian nature, we thought we had enough faith and trusted the Azeris who lived around us, exterminate them, the barbarians, exterminate every single one.'

A second-lieutenant stuck his head in the door.

'Would you mind turning down the radio? The wounded get upset, it makes their fever go up.'

The second-lieutenant smiled and left; he was a friendly youth in his mid-twenties who clearly showed that he liked the two elderly men. He was in the habit of sitting down with them whenever he had a break, listening to their conversation with attentive eyes, a glass of tea in his hand, now and then asking a question if there was something he didn't understand or something he wanted to know more about. Markus had tried to get him to talk about himself, had asked him questions, but the second-lieutenant had merely shaken his head.

'What distinguishes an Armenian from an Azeri?'

The priest didn't reply; he was sitting at the dining table reading the Bible.

'Religion? A foreskin? The shape of his skull?'

The priest kept reading, not letting himself be provoked. Markus went over to the window and leaned his elbows and forehead against the sill.

'Do you know what the very core of fascism is?'

Markus studied the garden before he continued.

'The indiscriminate categorization of people into groups. Are you listening? The indiscriminate categorization of people into groups. That's all you have to say. But it has taken me half a century to express it so concisely. With group categorization comes ranking, with ranking comes competition, and with competition comes war. Do you remember who said that war is the logical consequence of competition?'

'Bertrand Russell.'

The priest answered without looking up. Markus turned around and stared at him. Then he turned back to the window.

'During my first years here I was so locked into my own heritage that I never saw beyond it; I was a son of European fascism and that's what I would continue to be.'

Markus was speaking in a low voice now, almost sadly, and more to himself than to the priest.

'That's what I've been, I've been loyal, I've kept up the role of a son of European fascism, that's what they needed me to be, and I needed it myself. But gradually, as the years went by, the heritage enveloping me has grown thinner, frayed; now light seeps through in several places. This means that I see more than I used to.'

'What do you see?'

'The Slavophile movement, for one thing, the historical notion that Slavic culture is superior to all other cultures and must be kept pure of influences; contact with European culture, for instance, might pollute it or pervert it, as they say. The words sound familiar to me.

'Almost a hundred years after the founding of the Slavophile movement, as we were about to start our campaign against the East, we invited those who were our allies to join us. The Hungarians and Romanians came along, but not the Bulgarians. Do you know why? It was unthinkable for them to go to war against "our Slavic brothers." Take note of the expression: *our Slavic brothers*. It might be possible to find a European who once in his lifetime talked about "my European brothers," but I doubt it.'

'People say things differently here.'

'Do they think differently too? To this day we Germans are still scorned for our dream of a Great German Empire, but is there any scorn expressed here at pan-Slavism, the dream of a Great Slavic Empire? Or the Turks' dream of a Great Turkish Empire?'

A tremor flickered across the priest's face. Markus glanced at him.

'I'm sorry.'

'That's all right. It was before my time anyway.'

Markus went back to the window, the priest continued reading his Bible. It was raining outside, the clouds hung low, the colors were leaden. A truck full of wounded stopped outside on the road and backed up through the gate. It had a red cross painted on a white background on both doors of the cab. Medics came outside; they stood silently in the rain and waited until the truck had backed up all the way to the steps and the tailgate was opened. Their hair was plastered to their heads, making them look naked. The wounded lay on stretchers on the bed of the truck, packed close. Markus tried to study their wounds; he was waiting for a change. Up until now they had all been wounds from shells, artillery warfare; he was waiting for wounds to show up from handguns, close combat. That changes the nature of war.

'Do you have any opinion about Jews?'

Markus had turned away from the window. The nurse with the brown eyes had come in to eat; she looked up. The priest smiled at Markus as he replied.

'We don't use that word here. That's mixing religion and politics, and that's exactly what they want.'

'What word do you use?'

'Short-skulls.'

The nurse dropped her knife on the floor.

'Do you have any opinion about short-skulls?'

'Riffraff. Just like all the rest of the Semites, Arabs, and Palestinians. Riffraff every one of them. Not a hair better than the Russians or the Turks. Riffraff.'

The priest closed his Bible.

'The problem, Markus, is not that you Germans have the extermination of the Jews on your conscience – there are plenty of other countries that do too, and the idea of the 'final solution' was promoted for the first time as far back as 1905 by some extremist Russian nationalists. The problem is that Jews are exploiting what you did to the utmost. The extermination of the Jews was only one of the exterminations you carried out, and you must be prepared never to be forgiven, but in European countries no one remembers any longer the other exterminations: of Slavs, Poles, Gypsies, the mentally retarded, people with birth defects, the severely injured, the terminally ill. Only the extermination of the Jews is kept alive, through films and books and newspaper articles; it has even been given its own name.

'In Europe there's one question that nobody is allowed to ask, one question that may never be asked. Here we've always been able to ask it, although it has had its price; the Jews have made the world see us as anti-Semites.'

'What question is that?'

The priest steadied himself, took a few deep breaths before he answered.

'What have the Jews gained from the extermination of the Jews? They've won a country and they've acquired an historical identity that strengthens their belief that they are the chosen people, that they are the Lord's long-suffering servants in Isaiah 52–53.'

Markus did not reply. His gaze was turned inward and back.

'One of them was once my girlfriend. I wrote to her from the camp, many times, but never got an answer. I think she must be dead.'

'I don't think it's right, Rachel.'

Rachel looked at the man, his outstretched hand holding the letters.

'I see no reason why you should continue to have any contact with him.'

Rachel looked at him again; a thin man, with close-set eyes and a black beard. She always hid her eyes in his beard when he lay on top of her at night so he wouldn't see her expression; she always kept her eyes shut, but some looks are so strong that it's not enough to shut your eyes.

'I don't have contact with him. He doesn't receive my letters.'

See no reason to continue to have contact? How blind must his eyes be not to see the reason, how cold must his heart be not to feel it?

'You know what I mean.'

Rachel took the letters from him and left the room; went into the cramped bedroom and closed the door behind her. She avoided the bed and instead sat down on the window ledge, holding the letters up to the light from the window. Down on the street a flood of bicycles flowed past; the siren from the factory had just sounded. An occasional car honked, parting the stream of bicycles. In the surrounding buildings the first lamps were turned on; it was December, dark early. The heaps of rubble were gone, the buildings repaired, above three of the rooftops she could see cranes. If it hadn't been for the American soldiers with women in high heels, this could have been real and the other unreal, but the soldiers were the bridge back to the other reality.

Rachel had stared at the stranger and the letter he held out. Brown coat, gray hair, round horn-rimmed glasses, red cross on a white background, gray envelope.

She had taken the letter, read her own name, turned it over, no sender's name. The man tipped his hat.

'If you'd like to reply, we have an office in the old chancellery. Look for the flag.'

He pointed vaguely toward the red cross on his chest, nodded, and left.

'God,' whispered Rachel, pressing the letter to her face. She shut the door and stood in the dark hallway for a moment, looking at the closed doors. From one came the smell of boiled cabbage, behind another she could hear the sound of angry voices.

Rachel went into her room, lifted up a small child from the floor, went behind the sheet that divided the room in half, and sat down on the bed. Between the planks nailed to the window a narrow ray of sunlight seeped in. She moved over until the ray found her face. From the street outside came the sound of soldiers singing and shrill loudspeakers atop cars. Two buildings away she could hear the sound of bricks falling; a youth brigade was in the process of tearing down the most precarious ruins. Several years into the war and everyday life still went on, but just barely. The bomb shelters and the makeshift rubble caves were now approaching, and everyone knew it; everyone knew it, no one said anything. Only the faltering songs of the soldiers betrayed it.

Rachel opened the letter, turned over the three pages

crammed with writing, read the greeting at the end, smiled. The child reached out his hands for the letter; she gave him the envelope.

She had been so proud of him. The last Sunday before he left he came to pick her up in his uniform. They had strolled arm in arm beneath the linden trees through the cobblestone streets, promenading like miniature grown-ups. On their way back to her house she had pulled him into the partially collapsed passageway that no one used anymore, pulled him close, and guided his hands until they no longer needed to be guided.

'We are a chosen people, we have no room for the likes of you,' her father had said when he learned her secret and ordered her out.

'We can't have women who give themselves to men who are not one of us.'

Rachel had taken along her morning sickness and despair and joy and pride and moved into an endless series of rooms that came and went, smaller and smaller, while she dreamily protected the light that Markus had lit inside her and felt his hands.

She saw his hands before her now, saw them smooth out the sheets of paper, grip the pencil. She smiled as he raised his eyes and looked around for some place to start; it was so like him.

Markus decided to start with the copper beech down by the harbor, the mighty tree that stood silently staring out across the sea. He could see it from where he was sitting. Legend had it that the tree was a king who had sent all five of his sons off to war beyond the sea and across the Asian steppes on the other side, and he never saw them again. Every night for the rest of his life the king went down to the harbor and looked for the ship that would bring his sons back; every night, year after year. All life in the town came to a halt whenever the king stood there, staring; lamps flickered and went out, the prayers in the temple ceased, the sky sank. Hour after hour the king would stand there while the town held its breath, until he sighed, heavily, slowly, and signaled to his bearers. Then the town would sigh with relief, the lights would grow stronger, the sounds louder.

Dieter turned to Markus.

'What happened next?'

'One day the king picked up a stone, leaned way back, tossed it, and smiled proudly. It skipped five times: I may have lost five sons, but not my spirit. At that very moment God struck him dead and changed him into a tree; a brooding, capricious god with no sense of humor and a penchant for trees.'

Manfred looked up from the soup he was cooking.

'After all this time, and the only thing you write about to Rachel is fables?'

'Rachel loves fables. And besides, what else should I write? I'm not allowed to say where we are or where we've been or where we're going, what we're doing or who we're with or how they treat us. What if they cross out everything I write? What if she gets a letter that says only *Dear Rachel* and *Your Markus*?'

Dieter raised his eyes.

'That would be enough.'

He had tears in his eyes.

'That's all they'd need to know. Then they could post lists in the marketplace, like in the last war: These men are dead and can be forgotten, these are alive and should be forgotten.'

Markus went over to him and put his arms around his neck. Neither of them said a word. Around them were the others, sitting and lying in groups or alone, some on the bare floor, some on mattresses made of branches, cardboard, or rags. An icy wind came in through the broken windows; they had tried to put up coverings, but the guards tore them down. Markus crossed out what he had written and started over:

'Near the harbor where I am now living, there is a big beech tree. Like a giant it stretches out its limbs toward the sky; underneath, its roots are so long that they can touch the earth's heart. Every time I walk past the beech I wish I could trade places with it, wish I could be like the tree – a force, confident, secure, without yearnings or dreams, without desire to be anything else, anywhere else.'

Dieter continued:

'One day something happened. It started when people thought they heard sounds coming from the beech; some thought the tree was sighing, others said it was murmuring. The branches swayed even though there was no wind; soon the trunk began moving too. As if it were writhing or rocking. Suddenly the branches spread out sideways and the beech yanked itself free, pulling itself out of the ground with a long, drawn-out roar. Everyone fell back in terror, the beech climbed out, flapped its branches a few times, and turned into a bird, a gleaming white swan that rose up into the sky. The swan circled the town to give it a close look and then set course toward the northwest and disappeared with measured flaps of its wings. Wherever the swan flew, stars were lit and time rolled backward; whatever had been, vanished.'

Manfred took over:

'After that, nothing more happened. The white swan never came back. The hole in the ground down by the harbor was never filled in. People said sounds came out of it; some said it was the earth's heart weeping at being abandoned, others said it was the roots grieving. But either way, the hole was a good place to piss.'

Two years later Rachel cast a quick glance out the window to make sure her son was outside before she took out the letter. The boy looked up and smiled, she waved back.

The letter had arrived four days earlier. She had placed it unopened under the tablecloth, taken it out again and again, held it to her breast and put it back, unopened. Now she sat down on a chair, ran her fingertips over the envelope and the blue, rather angular script.

89

From the window came the sound of bulldozers, trucks, and hammering; slowly a nation was rising up from the ruins. In a sand pile down on the street her son was playing with two other three-year-olds, their voices singing in the summer light.

Rachel looked around the room, a small room with only one window, but it was intact; intact, dry, and warm. The bomb shelter had not been intact, part of it collapsed when the building was hit, a paltry heap of bricks and planks where the victors had found her easily, hauled her out and laughed. One of them was a Negro. He had an acrid smell and big, hard hands; the other soldiers laughed when she whimpered.

The tent camp had been wet; wet, cold, and silent. Rachel had lain awake at night, listening to the silence of a thousand people; there is nothing more to say after a war has been lost. One day she went over to the tent where the screams were coming from, abrupt, sharp screams. The rest of the week she lay with a bloody towel between her legs and listened to the silence inside her.

The barracks camp was better, more aggressive. Rachel noticed it in herself; she pushed her way forward in the food line, fought with the neighboring families over more space, determined to live.

At night she lay with the little boy's body pulled close and stared up at the ceiling; a dormitory is never completely dark, never completely silent. Rachel looked at the bulletin board with the lists of allocated living space, looked at her sleeping son, made up her mind.

Now she looked around at the room, a small room with only one window, but with a bed, a table, two chairs, and a dresser. She smiled, proud, sad.

There was a knock at the door.

'Hi, Babe.'

Proud, sad.

Rachel quickly stuck the letter under the tablecloth, opened the door, and smiled at the American soldier outside; his arms

90

were full of canned goods. She moved aside to let him in as she swiftly hung a red ribbon on the door plate, a signal to the neighbor woman to keep an eye on her son.

Several hours later she lifted the soldier's arm off her breast, cautiously, not waking him, and started a letter to Markus.

Dear Markus, she thought. Dear, dear Markus. Does a human being have a soul? If I could breathe in a light, would it find a soul inside me and light it up? Or would it find only an empty space?

The soldier stirred in his sleep, grabbed her left breast, let his hand slide down her naked belly. She followed it with her eyes, unable to stop it. Chosen. The last she had heard of her father was that he had been sent to a camp in the north. Chosen.

Rachel listened to the silence. She allowed it to flow into her, warm and calm. The window stood open; from the evening darkness came the sound of a light breeze and the sound of the sea, sounds from the other side of reality, the silent side.

Her son was asleep, she was sitting at the window with a cup of hot milk. She usually sat there for a while in the evening after he had gone to bed; it gave her a feeling of existence, of a self.

'Mama, am I a Jew? That's what the others call me.'

'No, you're not.'

'What is a Jew?'

'Someone who has chosen to belong to a special people.'

Rachel smiled at her bedtime replies; their echo touched a chord inside her, a deep powerful chord. She closed her eyes and conjured up the afternoons in the synagogue, the endless afternoons when outdoors there was dry ground, hot sunshine, and games of tag; indoors there were hard chairs, thick books, and a voice that never stopped talking.

She conjured up her parents' apartment and placed it on top of the synagogue; the gloomy furniture, the lace tablecloths, the candle holders. Markus was sitting there, embarrassed; her mother paced restlessly back and forth; her father shut him out, refused to acknowledge him, he was not one of them.

91

She conjured up the summer she had hoped something would happen. It was the summer the rabbi told them that their religion had two hundred and forty-eight commandments and three hundred and sixty-five prohibitions and they would have to learn them all by heart, every single one. Rachel wondered whether it was prohibited to have breasts; Esther and Maria already had them, she could see them when the girls jumped rope.

That summer an old man came to the synagogue; the rabbi called him a cabbalist and was angry at him; the old man was angry back. Their angry voices rose up to the clear summer sky and punctured tiny holes in it.

One day the old man came over and wanted to give them amulets. He smelled of boiled potatoes and mold. On the amulets he had written secret formulas that would protect them.

'Protect us from what?' Esther gave him a questioning glance.

'From what awaits you.'

'How can you know what awaits us?'

'Cabbalists know.'

'But if your amulets can protect us from what awaits us, how can you say that it awaits us?'

The old man gave Rachel an annoyed look. Cabbalists don't like logic.

'Religious people have always felt the need to be the chosen, to believe that God has determined a life-path just for them,' said Markus when Rachel told him about the old man. Markus with the smiling voice.

'But do they think they can influence God's decisions, make Him change His mind?'

'I assume so, otherwise there wouldn't be any explanation for acts of sacrifice, atonement, or magic. But what a thought, what a disrespectful shopkeeper's way of thinking – bargaining with your own god.'

Rachel leaned toward the cool night air from the window;

92

Markus with the big head and all those books, Markus with the big, wondering eyes.

The next day they had let the old man pin the amulets on them. Rachel stood still and looked down his shirt front as he fastened the pin with the little paper scroll to her blouse, glad that she didn't have anything he could touch the way he had touched both Esther and Maria; she had seen it in their eyes and the color of their faces. Rachel counted the long gray hairs sticking out of his shirt front; there were five, a little frayed at the ends. His mouth smelled of old age.

As soon as the slight figure in the too-small coat and too-tight hat had disappeared down the street, they opened the amulets and looked at what was written on them: meaningless words written in Hebrew letters. The rabbi grew angry when they showed him the slips of paper.

'Nothing but utter nonsense. Cabbalists spreading super-stition.'

And yet the old man continued to fasten amulets to the blouses of the three young girls for the rest of the summer. People said that he had once created a spirit out of dust – a widespread legend among the cabbalists – but that a dwarf had come and taken the spirit away from him. Now the old man spent all his time traveling around looking for it. He would know that he had found it the day he came to a place where nothing grew; the dwarf dragged a long veil of curses after him, underneath it nothing grew.

It was the summer the three girlfriends hopscotched their way into adolescence, the summer the colors grew stronger and there was a false bottom to everything. They pressed the amulet papers flat in their diaries while they giggled at the thought of what might await them when they gave up their protection. The words written on the slips of paper remained completely meaningless up until the day when Rachel opened one of them and read a question written in ordinary letters, a question that brought a blush to her face.

Esther and Maria shrieked with laughter.

'He can take a look at ours too.'

They wrote 'Behind the shed in the back yard, Thursday, twelve o'clock' on a piece of paper and slipped it to him the next time he pinned the amulets on them. Rachel was the one who slipped it down his shirt front. He gave her a brief look; she could see goosebumps on the skin of his chest.

The old man opened the piece of paper and read it five meters away from the synagogue; six meters away from the synagogue he leaped with excitement; seven meters away he danced and counted the minutes until Thursday at twelve o'clock.

Behind the shed in the back yard, where they had tried smoking cigarettes earlier in the summer and gotten sick, where they had giggled over a magazine Esther had brought along. Behind the shed in the back yard they found the cabbalist on Thursday, at twelve o'clock, with the fly of his pants open, as dead as only an old man can be.

'That's what I've always told you, never excite a cabbalist' said Markus, leaping aside.

'Maybe the dwarf dragged the veil over his fly,' said Erich Maria, setting off behind Markus. Rachel ran after them, caught hold of them, gave them a shake. They laughed and let her shake them, falling to the grass in a heap. Rachel lay on top of them and held them down. A tentative exaltation suddenly opened up inside her; the old man was not only dead, he had taken the dwarf and the spirit along with him, and the dwarf had taken the veil too, she could feel it as she lay on top of Markus.

Rachel held the image of the three of them quite still, studying it. Three young people on a lawn, happily ignorant of what was to come. She set her cup of hot milk on the windowsill and asked the silence outside:

'Is it true after all, Markus? Is there something awaiting us? Has a path been set for us that we can do nothing about?'

Somewhere outside music started playing, cautious, and calm. Rachel stood up and listened, gave a smile of recognition, stretched her hands out to the sides and danced. It was the music that her father would never allow her to listen to, what the others called jazz. Rachel had listened all the same; now she sang as she danced, sang along with Billie Holiday, 'Getting Some Fun out of Life.'

Isn't that what we're all doing? she thought. My family and Markus and Erich Maria and I? Aren't we getting something out of life?

'It happened, Rachel. Won't you join us now?'

She had sought out the synagogue when her son began asking questions. She didn't need to go there for news, there was no more news to hear, but she had a desire to show him that another time had once existed, show him that the world had roots.

'It happened, Rachel. Won't you join us now?'

Esther and Maria were gone, she knew that; almost all the others were gone, she knew that too. But it was only when she entered the synagogue that she felt the flapping wings of the terrified fledgling that had sought refuge inside her. The synagogue had been repainted after the fire, the furniture was new, the administrator was also new.

'It happened, Rachel. Won't you join us now?'

Rachel stared at the creaky old voice of the woman; she remembered her as a disgruntled harpy. History had now given her a new identity, a new mission.

Rachel stared at the new administrator with the gaunt body and the close-set eyes; he had never been accustomed to having people notice him, especially not women. The American investments had now given him a role, a power.

In the middle of the synagogue Rachel had shut her eyes and spoken to Markus:

'Markus, is there a common identity in suffering? Do other people have claims on me because we share the same fate?'

She waited anxiously, always anxiously, for Markus.

But Markus did not reply, merely followed her with his eyes

as she took her son and went home, followed her with his eyes as she opened up for the little fledgling inside her, followed her with his eyes as the administrator with the close-set eyes knocked on the door after her son went to bed, and she opened up for him too.

Rachel conjured up a picture: She was lying next to Markus and Erich Maria under a linden tree in the park. It was the middle of summer and a hot afternoon, a quiet hot afternoon; quiet the way the world is only in the middle of summer, when both the colors and the light are stronger than the sounds; hot the way the world is only in the middle of summer vacation, when it's permissible to wear light clothing and notice that you have a body.

Erich Maria lay with a notebook in front of him, an exercise book. He paged back and forth through it with awe.

'Imagine that anyone could do something like this.'

Rachel took the exercise book from him and read: ' "Immanuel Kant's Categorical Imperative" by Erich Maria Landauer, 3B. Immanuel Kant was a very short man, according to some sources no more than 147 centimeters tall, and in my opinion one should generally be skeptical of small men. He was also an obsessive-compulsive. For example, outdoors he never breathed through his mouth, only through his nose, and in my experience it's never productive to spend much time on the thoughts of an obsessive-compulsive. They will always have something compulsive about them.'

After that opening paragraph the teacher, Mr. Krause, had attacked Erich Maria's exercise book with his fountain pen; he wielded it with violent force straight through the book so that the ink splattered and the tip broke off, again and again, in wild fury, until the book ended up the way Rachel now held it in her hands: bloody, mistreated, murdered. Mr. Krause had a religious attitude toward philosophy.

Markus looked at the dead book.

'What else did you write?'

Erich Maria read:

'That Kant's philosophy could also be bad for your health. "When I press my thumb against my eye, I see two things: the starry sky above me and the moral law inside me," wrote Kant. You can't write things like that: it challenges the people of an entire nation to press their thumbs against their eyes. Aside from the fact that it would be an extraordinary sight, it's dangerous. Children could easily end up poking out their eyes in their zeal and grow up with a one-eyed view of life; elderly people might do the same in their spasms and lose a whole dimension, lose a whole dimension on life just before closing time.'

Markus rolled onto his back and laughed.

'At least then Krause would be spared.'

His hand found Rachel's, she turned her head with a smile. For Rachel, those were sacred hours: hot, pleasant afternoons with Markus and Erich Maria. She felt close to both of them. Sometimes she would rest her arm or head on Erich Maria's shoulder, and then he would sit very still, but it was Markus who came to her in her dreams at night and the other reveries she had in the daytime.

'Markus, do we have a moral law inside of us?'

'A moral law that can tell us what's right and what's wrong? I doubt it. But a pride, something upright and noble that sets limits on what we do to each other? Yes, I think we do. Without pride, I don't think life is worth living.'

Now Rachel looked over at the narrow bed in the room and thought:

Pride, Markus? Is there still room for pride in our lives? Can those who lose a war be proud? We lost this war, each in our own way, you and us, we lost ourselves.

Rachel caught herself too late. For the first time she had used the words 'you' and 'us.'

★   ★   ★

She hadn't objected when the administrator asked her to change her son's name to David, but she continued to call him Jochen. Jochen on regular days and David on holidays, religious holidays. The boy learned the rules, like a code. Nor did she object when he asked her to have her son circumcised. But every evening she would excuse herself as soon as the administrator was done, climb into the bathtub, and rinse herself with lukewarm water. In the meantime the administrator would put on his clothes and leave, as if he were ashamed of something, a weakness.

At times he would come to see her almost every evening. He read aloud to her from the holy book, he talked about his work, he told her about the camps, about the gas chambers, about the piles of corpses, and his voice would fill the room and the evening darkness seeping inside; a voice from a much too recent past that flowed toward the present, quiet as a river, filled with sorrow and above all disbelief; the river flowed past the present and on into the near future, it moved faster, more confidently, more aggressively, the way people who survive persecution often become, convinced of their historic right.

Rachel listened to his voice with a feeling of duty; this was her cultural inheritance, these stories were her story. Later she gave herself to him with the same feeling of duty; this was the man that history had chosen for her. If she had been allowed to make her own choice, she would have chosen something other than those dry lips and fumbling hands; she would have chosen tenderness. But history had robbed her of this choice, perhaps even of the right to choose; the administrator could lead her son back to what she had forsaken, he could give her son the security she wished for him, and Rachel was prepared to pay the price, the way women have always been prepared to pay with themselves for their children.

Sometimes as she lay there, she would see a shadow in the room, a figure studying her. Then she felt herself exposed. The figure took note of the tricks she had learned to get it over with quickly, watched her hands stroking the administrator's back according to script, looked for something in her eyes that wasn't there. Sometimes she would shout at the figure, resigned, and the administrator thought he was the one who made her shout, and smiled.

Every week she accompanied her son to the synagogue. Slowly it began to fill up, slowly the survivors came back. Everyone had stories to tell, gruesome, nightmarish stories, stories that intertwined with each other into a single massive story, and slowly the idea that God owed them something began to grow.

She could hear Markus shouting, indignantly, but he wasn't there; she was among her own people. It's 'us' and 'you' now, Markus, and we have made a burnt offering.

But Markus refused to give up, she could hear him shouting whether the offering was voluntary, because God accepts only voluntary sacrificial acts. And Rachel didn't know how to reply, and when the sacrifice was later used to claim the right to the Holy Land, she knew even less how to reply, and she could feel Markus's eyes upon her, inquiring, and she saw that the shadow in the room behind the sweaty, gasping breath of the administrator was herself.

It was the scripture that had sown the first doubts inside her about the religion she had grown up with. She had talked to Markus about it, glad to have someone to talk to who did not immediately raise his voice in self-defense.

'Markus, does Christianity say that those who aren't Christians are lost?'

'Yes. The doorway is narrow; those who are baptized slip through, those who aren't are locked out.'

'And if it's the parents who have neglected to baptize the children because they aren't sure?'

'Then the children must answer for their parents' sin of neglect.'

99

'What happens to children who aren't baptized?'

'Some say they burn in hell, some say they end up in a kind of limbo; they aren't tortured, but they aren't allowed to bask in the heavenly light.'

They were walking under the linden trees as they talked, arm in arm, the way they usually did on the way home from school with all the time in the world. That was one of the things Rachel liked best about Markus, just walking and talking to him, asking him about things she wondered about, and listening to him.

Rachel's father broke the bread, dipped it in the soup, and chewed.

'He's not one of us?'

Several blocks away, outside the ghetto, Markus's father poured coffee and gave his son an inquiring look.

'One of them?'

Something surged up inside the two young people. They stared at their fathers without saying a word. Outside, afternoon and late summer and joy that the country had finally managed to rise up from economic ruin and the shame of the previous war; the new war was only in its first year and still on its way up.

Rachel's father broke the silence.

'We are a chosen people, Rachel. You must behave accordingly.'

Rachel looked down and pressed her right hand hard into the left; she was not allowed to contradict him. Her father stood up and went over to the bookcase, took out the holy book without having to search for it, he could find it blindfolded. He came back to the table and opened it to a verse without having to look for it, he could find it blindfolded.

'Listen to David's last words, Rachel.'

Rachel fought back the nausea; she wanted to scream, smash something.

For is not my house established with God?
For an everlasting covenant He hath made with me,
Ordered in all things, and sure;
For all my salvation, and all my desire,
Will He not make it to grow?
But the ungodly, they are as thorns thrust away, all of them,
For they cannot be taken with the hand;
But the man that toucheth them
Must be armed with iron and the staff of a spear;
And they shall be utterly burned with fire in their place.

Her father lifted his eyes from the book and looked at her.

'Do you hear what the scripture says, Rachel? Thus it has been ordained, thus it shall be. No one touches them with their hands, no one comes near them except with iron and spears.'

The father went back to eating. An aching, tense silence descended over the table; Rachel's two younger sisters peeked at her cautiously, her older brother tried to smile at her. Her mother simply stared down at her plate.

After the meal Rachel asked her two sisters to go out and play for a while so she could be alone in the bedroom. Her sisters nodded without a word, old enough to understand a little, old enough to know that Rachel would show the way.

Rachel wrote the last words of David down on a piece of paper; she knew them by heart, her father had demanded that the whole family learn them. She took down a picture of her grandparents, somber faces with staring eyes, and hung the piece of paper on the nail. Then she got undressed and lay down on the bed in her underwear, white underwear with tiny flowers. She crossed her arms and hugged her shoulders, pressing them gently and whispering:

'Markus. Markus.'

She let her fingers slide down to her stomach, whispered again:

'Markus.'

The piece of paper on the wall began to vibrate. A sound issued from it, first low, then shrill; the paper shook on the nail, grew, bulged, swelled. Rachel turned toward the scrap of paper and watched it with something cunning in her gaze; she let her fingers slide farther down her stomach and under the edge of her panties, whispering his name again, and at that moment the paper on the wall exploded in a sudden flash, and red blood gushed into the room.

Several blocks away Markus sensed that someone was whispering his name, and something pressed on him from the inside. His father looked at him. The two of them had lived alone all these years and had learned to read each other, without any family in between.

'How serious is it?'

Markus blushed, his father gave him a look of surprise, looked away, looked down. He had known that this day would come, had expected it, dreaded it; he had never thought it would frighten him this way.

'Do you understand the dimensions of this, Markus?'

Markus didn't reply; he didn't understand what the word 'dimensions' had to do with it. He saw himself swimming with Rachel in a quiet forest lake in which the trees and sky and clouds were mirrored and the sunlight glittered in rings that rippled outward with each stroke they took; is 'dimensions' the same thing as rings in the water?

His father smiled sadly, took off his glasses, and rubbed his eyes.

'We don't live alone, Markus, like hermits. We live in a culture, with others, others who share the same values and the same world-view as we do. Around a culture there is always a fence, high enough to keep people both out and in; it's the fence that makes it possible for a culture to survive as a culture. If you try to climb over the fence you will risk two things: losing those you leave behind, and being rejected by those you try to join.'

He was a book man; when he talked it was usually in images,

not directly. Markus had learned to study his images; some of them he liked, others he didn't, but he always studied them carefully. Now he held up the image of the cultural fence and looked at it, searching for details. He saw Rachel and himself sitting on top of it, dangling their legs. She was wearing her school-uniform skirt and white knee socks; between the socks and the hem of her skirt he could see sunburned skin. Rachel stood up and balanced on the fence, reached out her hand toward him, pulled him up. They walked single-file along the fence, balancing with their arms held out to the side.

'Do you understand the dimensions, Markus?'

Markus looked around the room with the flowered wall-paper, a bookcase made of heavy, dark wood, and the nightstand covered with books next to the sofa where his father had taken to sleeping; books always grew in stacks around his father. And suddenly Markus thought that some-one who swims in a forest lake makes rings in the water, but someone who reads books doesn't, and for the first time he looked at his father with something that resembled astonish-ment in his eyes.

'No, Jochen, no!'

Rachel turned away.

He had come running in to her, his eyes full of anticipation, proud, wearing a gray uniform shirt, gray shorts, gray knee socks, and a red neckerchief with the ends threaded through a metal ring.

The years had grown colder. In the east, barbed wire and armed border guards sprang up from the ground; in the west, the speeches had grown more and more strident. Sometimes she could close her eyes and hear the same speeches from an earlier war. She had received letters from the administrator, he had gone to the Holy Land and volunteered to fight against the others, the unclean; now the land would be cleansed, and she had thought to herself that somewhere the work of reconciliation had to begin. She had signed up her son for the Young Pioneers, but she hadn't expected this.

'You don't like it?'

Jochen gave her a hesitant look.

Rachel pulled herself together.

'Yes, of course. It just took me by surprise.'

'Why?'

Rachel chose to evade the question.

'The uniform reminded me of someone else.'

She felt like a traitor, a manipulator, but it worked, as it always did. Her son grew somber and sat down.

Later she went to the leader of the Young Pioneers and asked about the uniform, cautiously, politely; she didn't want to make any trouble. And the leader assured her that no, the parents didn't have to pay anything for the uniforms, it had all been taken care of, and yes, they had talked about the uniforms at the last parents' meeting, but she hadn't taken the opportunity to attend, had she? Rachel asked quietly whether they hadn't had enough uniforms in the country by now, and she saw the glint in the leader's eyes, saw them flash with hatred, and suddenly she remembered him in uniform, before the war. They both got hold of themselves; he took her hand and said with emphasis that a uniform is an expression of collective identity, if we're going to win the battle against the intransigence in the world we must stand together, and then she remembered where she had seen him in uniform; it was with Dieter, on the way to a military review, and she tried to pull her hand out of his grasp, pull away from the sweaty palm and the moist look.

When she reached home, she found a letter from Jochen to Markus; he had left it out for her so she could send it along with her own. A sheet filled with big, carefully formed handwriting about school and the fishing expedition a week ago when he caught a big carp, and the camping trip with the Young

Pioneers when they roasted sausages on a bonfire and sang songs about all people being equal. Next to the letter her son had placed a drawing of himself in uniform, and Rachel clenched her teeth to hold back her tears.

She went into the bedroom and put the letter with all the others she had written to Markus, returned unopened, every last one of them, either by Russian or German authorities, what difference did it make? When Markus came, at least it would be out of love and not duty.

Markus, you have a surprise in store for you when you come home, she thought; I mean Jochen, our Jochen, and this pile of letters. When you read them, you'll discover various things that will no doubt surprise you, who knows, perhaps things you won't like, but you weren't here, Markus, you weren't here.

'I have to talk to you.'

Rachel looked at the administrator. He was standing in the dim hallway, a dark, almost shapeless figure against a dark background. His clothes grew darker and darker each month, as if he were systematically weeding out all pleasure, all light, in order to surrender without restraint to the darkness. He still had a way to go to the short black coat and the tight-fitting black hat of the orthodox uniform, but he was on his way, he was on his way.

'Talk to me? That's something new.'

The administrator's eyes flashed. His stay in the Holy Land had changed him, he had grown clearer, more confident.

'I won't stand for that kind of disrespectful talk in my house.'

Rachel waited until he came into the living room. He carried a book bound in black leather under his arm, another orthodox habit he had acquired, a signal. Now he held the book in both hands and gripped it so hard his knuckles turned white.

'The rabbi took me aside today. He said there's gossip about you.'

'Where?'

'Among the congregation.'

Rachel waited. She knew what was coming. Israel was in its first year as a self-proclaimed nation and its first war as an occupier. The immigrants were streaming there by the hundreds of thousands; they needed space, not critical questions.

'He told me people are saying that you're not with us.'

'In what?'

The administrator paused for a moment before he replied; in those few seconds Rachel looked down into a bottomless abyss; something lay down there, far below, something everyone could see but not everyone wanted to, a kind of collective certainty of what was right and what was wrong.

'Are you talking back to me, woman?'

And those who didn't want to see always turned away in anger.

'We are not only a chosen people, we are a persecuted people. Don't we have a right to a place of refuge?'

The administrator had fiery red patches on his cheeks now.

'Half a million of the others lived there. Don't they have a right to a place to live?'

The administrator didn't reply, but she could hear him scream: They were unclean, Rachel! He screamed at her with his black clothes and his black expression and his black book: They were unclean, that's why we blew up their houses and took away their property and forced them to flee, and Rachel looked at him and thought: Don't you understand that what we're now saying about them is the same thing that was said about us when we were persecuted? But she knew that the day she put this question into words everything would be transformed into black lava; the moment the question was spoken in the room, everything would harden, everything they were, everything they thought, everything they felt; it would all turn to stone, just as their religion already had.

'Do you want David to be hurt?'

106

Ambush.

'Do you want him to be hurt because of you?'

Pincer maneuver.

Rachel stood there feeling the pain inside, feeling the love and anger and frustration rip and tear at each other so fiercely that she was relieved when the administrator relented and started in on the absolution he had practiced.

'We may all have our opinions, Rachel, we may all think what we like about what's going on, but at a time like this it's important to stand together. We owe it to our forefathers.'

Things would have been fine if he had stopped there, but he kept going:

'We owe it to those who died in the concentration camps.'

Rachel's contempt for him grew to hatred before the sound of the sentence died out, and when he came across the room and put one arm around her waist and one hand on her left breast, the nausea welled up inside her so violently that she had to scream and tear herself loose. She took two swift steps back and flattened herself against the wall.

The administrator followed her, she turned her back on him and stood with her cheek and breasts and stomach and thighs pressed tight against the wall, but not tight enough. With a firm grip around her neck and her hair, he pulled her away from the wall and spun her around. She stood quite still and let it happen.

When the administrator went back to the synagogue, she started a letter to Markus. She wrote quickly and easily; she knew what she wanted to say, had thought it through while she was being held against the wall. Dear Markus, she wrote, dear Markus; once in my life I loved someone, only once, and it was you.

She put down her pencil and turned her head, pressed the back of her hand to her eyelids and let the tears come. Dear Markus, she whispered, dear Markus, I miss you.

107

She always had a feeling of failure whenever she tried to put love or tenderness or yearning into words; life had not given her much practice. But she thought she had got better at conjuring them up; she felt the yearning well up inside her now, warm, whole, complete, almost like a presence.

She sat there for a while before continuing to write; it was at these times that she felt like a whole person, the times when she sat down and conjured up her yearning for him, the times when she dared to hold up her life dreams against life the way it had turned out.

Dear Markus, she wrote, is it true that a victim must also seek revenge for an attack? Is it true that we must hate in order to survive as a human being after an attack?

She paused to consider, then crossed out the words 'a human being' and changed them to 'an individual,' paused, crossed out 'an individual,' and changed them to 'a culture.'

Markus peeked over her shoulder at what she had written, her hair lightly brushing his cheek. He smiled.

'Hate is like love, self-propagating as soon as it finds a target. Once you start to hate someone, there is only one way to go: more hate.'

'How do you know that?'

Sometimes she wondered how he managed to understand so much in so few years, forgetting sometimes that he had grown up with a library instead of a mother.

'What if you hate a whole world, the way we do?'

Markus lowered his eyes.

Rachel lay listening to the administrator breathe. It was hot and sultry in the room. The darkness of night had arrived several hours earlier, with a scent of spices. She had tried staying up after the administrator had gone to bed, saying it was too hot to sleep, but he told her to come to bed, sternly.

After he fell asleep, she lay and listened to his contented breathing. Cautiously she turned over, afraid of waking him, and sat up; she slipped the holy book out of the drawer in the nightstand and opened it to the Book of Ruth. She had always had a warm feeling for Ruth, the Moabite widow who was bound to a piece of land and was redeemed by a wealthy man. She had always wondered how it would feel to belong to a piece of land. Now she knew.

Carefully she pulled one leg out of bed, then the other. The administrator didn't like her to be up while he slept. She tiptoed out of the bedroom and into the living room; her son lay asleep on a mattress on the floor, breathing calmly.

Rachel took out a piece of paper and a pencil and wrote down the words from Amos that she had grown up with, the quotation her father had read before each evening prayer:

Hear this word that the Lord hath spoken against you, O children of Israel, against the whole family which I brought up out of the land of Egypt, saying:
You only have I known of all the families of the earth;

Silently Rachel folded up the piece of paper on which she had written the quote and tiptoed back to the bedroom. There she lifted up the top sheet and slipped the folded paper under the administrator's pajama bottoms, millimeter by millimeter, to exactly the spot where the spiral of dark hair grew over his belly, millimeter by millimeter until the paper bumped against something and the administrator stirred. Then she went out to the cramped kitchen and began to smash things. 'You only have I known of all the families of the earth; Therefore I will visit upon you all your iniquities,' she screamed and smashed things: all the glasses, all the cups, all the plates and bowls; they shattered against the walls and the floor. She shredded the Sabbath bread into crumbs, tore up the prayer shawls with the parchment texts in capsules, threw the Sabbath candles into the nighttime darkness outside the window. A voice shouted but Rachel kept on smashing things, swept the crocks from a shelf, tore down the shelf, pounded a little radio against the floor until it split open and spewed out its guts.

A voice shouted, Rachel turned around, it was the administrator, with a white piece of paper sticking up from his pajamas, and Rachel shouted: See the kingdom of priests and the holy people, the Lord be praised, and the administrator screamed in furious anger: You shall not blaspheme the Torah, Rachel, and Rachel laughed and kept on smashing things. Behind the administrator the terrified eyes of her son peeked out, but Rachel didn't see them; her rage was in the way, this time her rage was in the way. The administrator grabbed her by the shoulders and tried to hold on to her, but she twisted away; he grabbed for her again, she twisted away, then he slapped her in the face with the flat of his hand, twice; the first blow made everything inside her stop, the second blow made everything inside her die; she stared in horror at the hand that claimed her every night and had now struck her, and something burst inside Rachel; a wave surged up inside her and poured out of her, she grabbed a menorah and struck back, just below the piece of paper sticking up from the waistband of his pajamas, twice. The administrator howled, a long drawn-out howl, and from somewhere behind him came the sound of pounding on a door and running feet, naked running feet, but the sound never reached Rachel, she had sunk to the floor with her arms around her legs and her head on her knees and didn't seem to notice her son, who was trying to wipe her tears, or the administrator, who was doubled over with both hands pressed to his groin and a little trickle of blood between the middle finger and index finger of his right hand. The neighbors who had broken down the door tried to talk to her, shout at her, shake her, but Rachel had withdrawn now, back to a room known only to her, and only she would decide when she would leave it. She didn't leave it when the ambulance personnel placed her on the stretcher and stroked her cheek, she didn't leave it when two men in white coats began asking her questions, she didn't leave it all summer long at the sanitarium where she lay in a dormitory with eighteen others who had also withdrawn to rooms known only to them, and who screamed in the night in terror at what was happening in their rooms.

Only once did Rachel leave the room; it was toward the end of the summer, when she was rolled on a gurney into an operating room, and she stared up at the sharp light and shouted: What are you doing to me? And the anesthesiologist said: Calm down, calm down, and Rachel tried to sit up, tried to rip away the straps that were holding her and shouted: What are you doing to me? and tried to wriggle away from the mask that was placed over her mouth and nose, and shouted into it, half smothered, and kicked her legs, for a while, only a while.

The administrator came to get her when the leaves began to fall from the trees and the wounds on either side of her forehead had healed and the doctors said it had gone well; smiling, she waited for him in the dormitory with nineteen empty, carefully made beds, and held his arm the whole way in the bus. She sat beside him and smiled and said: It's probably for the best, when he told her that he had decided to send her son to a work and school collective in the Holy Land for a year, a kibbutz; she nodded and said: I'm sure you're right, when the administrator explained that now that they had acquired the promised land, child rearing must be a collective responsibility, not an individual's; it was too important for that. She said: Oh my, how wonderful, when he told her the boy had also won a scholarship to a summer camp in the Crimea on the Black Sea, a pioneer camp for children from twelve countries as a sign of reconciliation, won a scholarship without even applying; two men had suddenly rung the doorbell one day and said that her son had been selected, two Americans with business cards from a foundation, they came with the youth leader, everything would be covered, including a week's orientation at the American headquarters in Frankfurt.

She smiled and waited for him to step inside first when he unlocked the door to the apartment, and smiled when he led her into the bedroom. When he was done, she got up, put on her clothes, and went to water the flowers.

DAY FIVE

'Have you heard the story about Gregorius Illuminator, the light bringer?'

The priest looked up in surprise.

'Most Armenian priests have. But perhaps not the way you tell it.'

Outside on the road a stream of refugees was passing by; in cars and buses, on trucks, motorcycles, bicycles, and on foot, carrying wool blankets and pillows and floor lamps and TV sets. There was something biblical, something Old Testament about them. Armed guards were stationed around the house to keep the refugees away; Markus and the others were isolated, caught on an island in the middle of a broad, dense stream of people in flight, reduced to telling stories to pass the time.

'I haven't heard it.'

That was the nurse.

'It's not a story for young women.'

'All the better.'

Markus gave her a smile and began:

'Gregorius Illuminator, the light bringer, was an Armenian apostle, three hundred years after the Son of God died on the cross. This was during the time when Trdat the Great ruled here, a colorful man in every way. It was prophesied that a virgin of royal birth would be his demise. The prophet froze into a block of ice at the very instant he put his prophesy into words, that's how dangerous it was to predict misfortune for the king. Trdat was furious; he had three oxen brought in to lick up the figure, millimeter by millimeter. The figure shrieked with laughter until nothing was left of it, laughed either at being tickled by the tongues of the oxen or at the king's misfortune; Trdat never managed to figure it out. He brooded over the prophecy for three days and three nights, then he issued a command that all royal virgins henceforth and forever after, should be brought to him right after their first menstruation.'

Markus paused and let the nurse listen to the proclamation; it hung quivering in the quiet room.

'As you might guess, this was not a popular command, but Trdat was not concerned with popularity. He ordered the first ten families decapitated if they refused; after that the virgins were delivered without question.

'The ceremony always took place in the palace courtyard, in front of eager, screaming spectators. It was Trdat's way of showing his power; he took possession of the untouched girl and grew, the way a farmer grows with each hectare of virgin soil he plows.'

Markus closed his eyes and listened to the drums; they had been rolling over the town since early that morning. He looked at the hordes of people approaching the palace, some with prayer banners, others with torches, mostly men, but also women and children; they walked toward the palace with wide-eyed anticipation, shouting to each other and laughing.

Inside the palace courtyard it was already packed, people crowding around the wooden altar that had been erected for the occasion. Before the altar danced a group of women, from the market stalls came the sound of music. A young girl, bound with ropes, hung from a gallows; the rope was tied around her wrists, while her feet were bound to the altar and spread wide. She was dressed in a loose white silk robe, and she hung leaning forward with her eyes closed and her long dark hair gathered with a red ribbon.

'The crowds gasped as Trdat the Great appeared; they moaned as he approached the girl from behind, tore off her white silk robe and grabbed hold of her body; they screamed as he exposed himself – he wasn't called the Great without reason.

'A drum roll, a fanfare, a short blast on the bugles, and the sky split as a whimper escaped from the young girl and she opened her eyes. The spectators trembled, wept, shouted; a thunderclap rumbled across the town, when all of a sudden a monk wearing a brown robe and hood came toward the altar. Parting the crowd of spectators with his hands, he pitched rather than walked forward until he stood face to face with the king and the young girl in the ropes. The monk raised his right hand toward the king, splayed his fingers, and roared.

'Five lightning bolts flashed from his fingertips toward the king and the girl. At that very instant the girl was transformed into a pillar of salt, and the king uttered a piercing cry of pain.'

The nurse nodded.

'It hurt?'

'That's what pillars of salt do.'

The nurse blushed and looked down.

'The king's guards seized the monk and held their swords to his throat, awaiting orders.'

'He was Gregorius, the light bringer?'

Markus nodded.

'That was some light he brought.'

'The king went down to the monk, tore off his brown robe, and spat on him. Gregorius didn't even flinch. Then the king had him taken to the snake pit. Usually he had Christian apostles boiled, but Gregorius was not going to be allowed to get off that easy; he was going to suffer a slow, venomous death in the dark among the snakes.

'Up until then, no one had survived more than two days in the snake pit, but Gregorius lived there for nine years and longer; everyone lost count. Gregorius stayed alive, and people made pilgrimages to the pit. The king stationed guards so that no one could speak to him but only listen to his sighs and moans, and some said that light came from the pit even on bright sunny days.'

Markus took a gulp of his tea and continued.

'Then one day Hripsime came, the virgin of royal blood who was so beautiful that people went mad if they looked at her. Her father had read aloud from the Song of Solomon when he conceived her, and the concubine had sighed "more, more," and then her father read more from the Song of Solomon, and God smiled at such devotion and when He formed Hripsime He did so in accordance with the Song of Solomon. He gave her lips like threads of scarlet, a neck like the tower of David, breasts like two young roes, a mountain of myrrh like a hill of frankincense. Song of Solomon, chapter four, verses three to six. But God decided at the same time that no man would ever have Hripsime, no man would be allowed to go up her palm tree and take hold of the boughs. Song of Solomon, chapter seven, verse eight.'

The nurse leaned forward and fixed her eyes on Markus; he returned her gaze, just as steadfast, but with the hint of a smile.

'Hripsime was sent to a convent in Rome, and the cloister walls were black with crawling monks from the neighboring monastery every Friday when she bathed and let the sun dry her skin in the convent garden. One Friday the emperor came past and saw the monks. He ordered them down, whipped the truth out of them, chopped off their heads on the spot, piled their headless corpses on top of each other next to the convent wall, and climbed up to see for himself. The instant the emperor caught sight of Hripsime, he too went mad. He began twitching and his speech became incoherent; he went up there at night and whispered her name. Hripsime was warned, and she fled along with the prioress and many of the nuns. The emperor sent people out searching for her all over the kingdom. Hripsime and her entourage fled and fled, eventually with no money left, so that they had to pay with nuns, one for each night's lodging, until they came to the ends of the earth.'

Markus closed his eyes again. He studied Hripsime as she came riding through the portal: noble, proud, with long blonde hair flowing like sunlight over her shoulders. Behind her rode the prioress and two nuns; their travel funds were nearly depleted.

'The spectators in the palace courtyard turned around to face the four women, a moan went through them. The king heard it and turned around too, as did the young girl in front of him. She opened her eyes and looked at Hripsime, and a black bird flapped its wings in her gaze.

'The king began to shout. The soldiers seized Hripsime and led her to the altar, where the king stood waiting. He tore off her clothes and was trying to force her down on her back next to the young girl who hung in the ropes, still a virgin, when Hripsime struck him. She whirled around in a full circle on the altar with her naked breasts following and struck King Trdat the Great a blow that resounded from the palace walls and sent the king spinning backward, and he fell to the altar floor with a crash.

'The king shouted through the cracks between the planks of the altar floor where he had landed; it sounded strangely hollow beneath the altar, like an echo from far away. Hripsime set one foot on the king's naked body and pressed down; she had strong legs, the taut muscles of her thighs rippled as she pressed. Then she made her way through the spectators and rode off; no one dared stop her. The spectators stood and gaped after her entourage: a naked woman with blonde hair flowing behind her and three nuns dressed in black and white, riding at full gallop toward the horizon.'

The nurse sighed:

'What a romantic story.'

'It could have ended there. But the king pulled himself loose and caught up with them. He carried Hripsime in chains back to the palace courtyard and killed her using a method that no one has ever described. At the moment of Hripsime's death, the palace shook so that the walls fell, all the spectators became deaf mutes, and the king and his men were transformed into wild boars. Only the virgin in the ropes, in a manner of speaking, was kept by God as a witness, though she was not allowed to say a word.'

'How did the king remove the curse?'

That was the priest.

'He brought Gregorius Illuminator up from the snake pit and built a church where he had killed Hripsime. He spent the rest of his life building churches all over the country.'

There was a long pause.

'How did he rule the land during the time he was a wild boar?'

That was the second-lieutenant from the medical corps, asking as if just to say something, postpone something. Markus spoke in a low voice when he answered; his thoughts were elsewhere, as it appeared everyone's were.

'One grunt for yes, two for no; no one really noticed any great difference. His wives complained a little about the scratch marks, but otherwise they didn't notice much difference either.'

Silence descended. The priest, the second-lieutenant, and the nurse all looked at each other; a question hovered over them. It was the nurse who put it into words.

'And you? You, Markus? Which of them are you?'

That was the first time she had used his first name.

———————

The light found its way to Markus on a clear fall morning. It made its way through thick, blood-red, leafy crowns and flooded over him. He was standing with one hand on a ladder, his foot on the lowest rung, a tray of bricks on his shoulder, staring at the woman across the street.

Every day for a month he had seen her, every single day. At five in the morning she came walking down the street, a black, slightly sinister figure who drew the darkness to her.

An hour later she would come back with a lit candle, a stump of a candle in a tin box. Each morning for a month Markus had stopped to look at her, first when she came down the street and then when she disappeared back up it. There was something about the way she walked that touched him, something about her eyes, which she kept fixed on the ground in front of her. Those first weeks the guards had shouted at him, eventually more in jest than in anger. One day one of them laughed and said something he understood to be vulgar; he saw the woman across the street give a start and turn toward him. That was the first time their eyes met.

Two days later she stopped and looked at him.

'God,' whispered Markus and covered his face with his hands; rough, filthy hands, full of cracks and tiny cuts.

A ray of light bored its way between his fingers. He took his hands away, she was still standing there, looking at him with dark, somber eyes. Markus moved his hand and foot away from the ladder, straightened up, and pointed at himself with a questioning look. She stared at him a moment longer, then she turned around and left.

Dieter came over to him.

'Markus, pull yourself together.'

Markus looked at him: smooth-shaven head, emaciated body, grimy face, a mirror of himself. And yet. He turned around and looked at the dark figure disappearing up the street.

Three days later she brought him food. He saw her coming down the street at five o'clock, he saw her coming back with the lantern an hour later, he followed her with his eyes, followed her with his dreams. He went back to work, quieter. The guards laughed at him and said something he didn't understand.

Then all of a sudden she was back, breaking her routine. She was standing there when he came down with his first tray of bricks after the morning break. She was holding a bucket in one hand, the other she held up to stop him. Markus stood quite still. She crossed the street, spoke to the guards, held out the bucket, pointed at him. One of the guards opened the bucket, sniffed, and held it up to his mouth. She didn't take her eyes off Markus.

The guard gave her back the empty bucket and waved her on. Markus stood and watched her go until a guard struck him on the back with the butt of his rifle.

The next day she was back, this time accompanied by an old man. They talked to two of the guards for a long time, gave them a bucket and a package. The guards took the food into the guard barracks, the woman and the old man stood in silence until they came back out. One of the guards went over to Markus and scrutinized him. Markus scrutinized him in return, stared at the bloodshot eyes and the downy upper lip, a young boy, like himself. The guard signaled with a backward jerk of his head, Markus followed him over to the old man and the woman.

The old man talked some more with the guards, they raised their voices, almost angry, the man nodded and held up the palms of his hands toward them. Then he turned toward Markus and said in German:

'You have to be back before dark. Otherwise your comrades will pay for it.'

Markus nodded. During the first year of their imprisonment they had sat in total isolation, the second year the guards began hiring them out to the local populace in return for payment. The prisoners were always brought back at the end of the day, sometimes merely worn out after hard labor, sometimes with obvious marks from kicks and blows. One night a prisoner came back from being loaned out and refused to talk to the others, insisted on sitting and lying alone; another night four hired-out prisoners were found tossed outside the camp gate.

The old man and the woman began walking. Markus
followed them, a few paces behind. Manfred and Dieter yelled
something to him, he gave them a brief wave of his hand. The
woman held the old man's arm, he was wearing a long black
coat and he walked with a slight shuffle. The woman was also
dressed in black, full-length, he could barely glimpse part of her
worn boots. A dark brown lock of hair peeked out from the
scarf she wore on her head.

They walked for nearly an hour, heading up from the harbor
and northward, between the bombed-out buildings. The heaps
of rubble still had remnants of architectural shapes, he could see
traces of Russian, Armenian, Turkish, and Central Asian styles,
collapsed reminders of the city's period of greatness as the
cultural hub in a world that no longer existed.

The streets grew more and more deserted. Once in a while
the woman would turn around to look at him, as if to make
sure he was still there. Markus met her gaze each time,
expectantly. From an open yard three boys threw stones at
him; the woman chased after them hissing, the boys ran off
laughing.

They reached a partially collapsed apartment building; the
old man stopped in front of the door and took out a key. The
woman held the door open for Markus; she looked at him as he
moved past her. For the first time he was near her, for the first
time he saw her face close up. She had dark, rather meditative
eyes, high cheekbones, and a straight nose. Her lips formed a
little smile as he passed, he tried to smile back but couldn't do it.

The stairs in the entrance hall had fallen in. The old man
took a good grip on the railing and began laboriously climbing
up the planks that had been placed over the piles of bricks
where the stairs had once stood. Markus reached out a hand to
support him; the woman standing behind him grabbed his arm
to stop him. He turned around to look at her; she shook her
head. For a moment she let her hand rest on his arm before she
took it away.

121

The apartment was on the top floor, the old man stopped to catch his breath on each landing. A woman met them in the doorway, just as old as the man, stout, her skin darker. She was wearing a white apron and her hair was pulled back in a bun.

The old man took off his coat and gestured to Markus to follow him; the two women disappeared through another doorway, the smell of food coming from it. Markus looked around the room he was taken to: a cramped living room with heavy furniture and a gray rug, a lone crucifix on one wall, family photos on another. A bookcase with glass doors leaned precariously toward the floor, missing legs on one side; behind the glass lay an olive-green uniform cap with a red band and a medal. Markus bent forward to read the medal; the old man followed his glance.

'My father. He was an officer in the Tsar's army, distinguished himself in the war against the Tatars.'

The old man took him by the arm and led him out onto the balcony, crowded with vegetables planted in flower boxes. From a cage two chickens peered up at them, in another a rabbit shyly looked away.

'The point is to look out for yourself,' said the old man, leading Markus back into the living room; he offered him a spindleback chair and sat down right across from him, some distance away.

'My name is Bedelian. I'm Armenian.'

Silence. Markus replied:

'My name is Markus. I'm German.'

'I know that.'

Silence again.

Why have they hired me? What kind of work are they thinking of having me do? thought Markus, looking at the silence in the room.

Bedelian cleared his throat.

'You have a large head.'

Markus blushed.

'I asked my granddaughter to choose the one among you with the biggest head. Large heads have room for lots of things. And besides, there's something about us Armenians and heads. The head of the apostle Tadeus, for example, we're the ones who have it.'

A long silence.

'Mr. Bedelian, what sort of work do you want me to do?' Bedelian looked at him.

'Can you give my granddaughter, Sese, your language?'

'Doesn't she have a language of her own?'

'Not one she uses. Something happened to her a long time ago, something that made her speechless. I haven't heard her speak a single word since, haven't seen her write even one sentence.'

'Does she read?'

'Not that I've noticed.'

'Why do you think I can do anything about it?'

'She spoke Armenian and Turkish, two Cyrillic languages. I think what happened to her has forever removed everything Cyrillic. Your language uses the Roman alphabet; I thought it might be a way out for her.'

'You speak my language. Why can't you teach her yourself?'

'I can't read it, I don't know the letters.'

The two women came in carrying a soup tureen and dishes and beckoned them to the table.

Markus said as he sat down: 'When do you want me to start?'

Bedelian turned to the two women and translated. He pointed at Markus as he talked. Sese looked up sharply, looked at Markus, looked down.

The next morning Markus ate his breakfast at the sunlit wall. He took along his metal bowl with the greasy, rank stew and went out of the dormitory past the double rows of figures on the floor: apathetic, psychotic, wounded, sick figures; went outside and sat down on the sunlit wall. For the first time in almost two years he noticed that the sun also shines in Baku.

Bedelian had managed to find a cord of wood; he lit a fire in the apartment. Sese took off her outer garments. She and Markus sat next to each other at the dining table with an exercise book in front of them; it was almost completely used up from before. Markus printed tiny little letters very close together in order to save space. Sese had to lean forward to read them. Sometimes her arm happened to touch his. The first few times she pulled it swiftly away; later on she let her arm lie next to his for a moment before moving.

He never knew whether she understood anything. He pointed at the letters and pronounced them, one by one, a new one each day, and then started over. He put the letters together to form words, he drew or mimed what the words meant, he slowly learned Armenian, word by word as Bedelian translated, but he never knew whether she understood anything. She never nodded, never made any sign that she understood, simply followed along, attentive and reserved at the same time; when he looked down he could see her thighs swelling against the chair seat. Sometimes when she leaned forward, her breasts rested on the table, big, heavy, and he had to force himself to think about Rachel. He pondered how a language rises from the concrete to the abstract; he could explain to her that people meet each other, but how could he make her understand the feeling between them? He looked down at her thighs again and thought that she was old enough to be his mother.

Fall gave way to winter with clear skies and white light. Markus sat next to Sese and opened his language to her. Bedelian translated, Sese was silent; it was a game, a game between three realities, up until one day when Markus asked how to say 'feelings' in Armenian and Bedelian replied: 'That word no longer exists in our language and it shouldn't exist in yours either,' and Markus thought: God, this is no game.

One day he tried to explain what a phoneme was, but Bedelian was stumped, couldn't translate. Markus tried with cake and cape, cart and card, but Bedelian still didn't understand, and suddenly it occurred to Markus that he could shape her perception of reality in whatever way he wanted to – the Roman, not the Cyrillic; he could distort it completely if he wanted to by simply exchanging phonemes. He had just begun to taste the power this gave him over her when Bedelian suddenly threw himself at her across the table and screamed:

'Talk, damn it! This silence is unbearable!'

The old man reined himself in almost at once, but Markus managed to see it: A smile flickered across Sese's face.

Bedelian let them spend more and more time alone after that. His German vocabulary was exhausted, and Markus no longer needed anyone to translate into Armenian, he had learned the words himself.

The winter spread further into the darkness, the clouds hovered lower in the sky, and the light was weaker. They were done with the alphabet, or Markus was, at any rate; he had printed and pronounced every single letter for her at least a hundred times, he had put them together to form more words each time; if her language center wasn't damaged, she should now have acquired the basics of daily speech in her first Roman–alphabet language, ready for use, just as he had acquired the basics of daily speech in his first Cyrillic language.

In the camp at night he tried to secure for himself all the possible nuances; he played word games with Manfred and Dieter, they competed to think up the most possible words starting with a randomly chosen letter. Markus wrote the words down and put them into groups: verbs, nouns, adjectives, adverbs, prepositions. Her new language was not only full of nuances, it was well organized.

Yet she still didn't use it. But one day something happened. He was sitting next to her, taking in her presence, as he repeated the letter 't', enunciated it clearly and drew: a teapot, a tree; he looked down at her lap, a tent, and suddenly she uttered a sound, an inner scream, her lips pressed tight, as if she were shouting no, no no, without forming the words. She turned away from the drawing, he put his hand on her shoulder, she shook it off and ran into the next room.

Markus stayed where he was. After a while Bedelian came into the room, looked at the drawing, and shook his head.

'Now you know what you must never draw for her.'

His voice had an edge to it, like the sound of a door being closed.

A few weeks later something else happened. Markus was sitting and explaining about the Middle Ages in European history, deeply absorbed, with his hands clasped in front of him on the table, when Sese suddenly placed a hand on his arm. She let it lie there a moment, then she stroked his arm hesitantly, once up and once down, as she turned and looked at him.

Markus stopped talking, looked at her hand, followed it with his eyes, looked up and met her gaze. She moved her hand, took his hand in both of hers, kept on looking at him. Then something burst inside Markus, his eyes filled with tears, and he turned away. It was very quiet in the room, as if all the sounds were radiating toward him, vanishing inside him and becoming his; he saw a tidal wave coming toward him, foaming, black; he knew it would crush him in a fraction of a second, but all he felt was an intense well-being, a body that was pounding with light and sound and direction. Sese stretched out her arm and put it around him, placed a hand on his cheek and pulled him close; now she'll see my tears, he thought, and let himself be pulled close and down until his cheek rested on her breast and she wiped his tears with quiet fingers. She held onto his hand and pulled it closer, down to her lap and against her stomach, he spread out his fingers and pressed his palm against her thigh, as if to support himself, then he cautiously began playing his fingertips against the softness. She put her hand on the back of his and left it there, let him play. He breathed in the scent of her; from her clothes, her skin under her clothes, the juices under her skin, and understood something he had once read: that European culture is the only one in the world in which even intimacy must be odorless. He played his fingers against Sese's thigh and took in Oriental intimacy, dark, unpredictable, dangerous; he cautiously turned his head until his lips lay against one of her breasts, his cheek against the other, he pursed his lips into a soundless kiss and sensed a trace of spices, secret, and he saw himself standing at a garden gate. He couldn't see in, but he could sense the fragrance of henna shrubs and spikenard plants and myrrh and aloe, and he could hear that inside the garden there was a fountain, a spring, with running water.

That night he started a letter to Rachel that he knew he had to write but wasn't sure he would send. He sat down in a dark corner of the dormitory; the field of light beneath the lamp that hung from the middle of the ceiling was always crowded, but he didn't need light, just enough quiet so he could hear his own thoughts.

Dear Rachel, he began, dear, dear Rachel, today I betrayed you.

He shut his eyes and saw the word 'betrayed' grow, open up like an abyss.

It was more than a moment's weakness, he thought, more than a moment's weakness, because a moment's weakness has that marvelous feature that it passes, but today I felt another person's skin against mine, felt another person's breath in mine, and deep inside me, deep down inside me I can hear someone shouting for more. This is not a moment's weakness, this is a fall, a landslide that is whirling me along with it; I will see her next week and the week after that and the week after that, and I'm screaming in protest because I have to wait so long.

127

He stopped. His yearning for her welled up inside him like a sudden nausea.

He tried to start over. Dear Rachel, he thought, dear Rachel, I love only one person and it's you, I've made love only to one person and it's you, but at the same time there was a voice inside him that said: a lie, you're lying. That's where the real betrayal is, he thought, in the lie; the real betrayal is in knowing that the other person's image of you is no longer true but not saying anything about it. Rachel's image of him under the linden trees and at the library were now yellowed memories in an album; the war had changed him, prison life had changed him.

He tried once again. Dear Rachel, dear Rachel, but he couldn't get any farther, he saw her eyes and couldn't bear to meet her glance; he saw her grow uncertain, questioning, as if she noticed that the closeness between them was no longer theirs alone, and suddenly he understood what's at the heart of the nature of betrayal: You rob other people of security.

Markus turned toward the country for which he had gone to war, he turned toward the country against which he had gone to war, he took turns looking at them and wondered how many people he had robbed of security. Then he lay down on the floor, rolled over on his side, tucked up his legs, stuck his hands between his knees, and whispered into the darkness: It would have been so good to stay faithful to you, Rachel.

When he went to her the following week, he knew that something was imminent. He noticed it in his own footsteps, heard it in his breathing, sensed it in the dark stairwell; something was present in the room, something imminent.

Sese knew it too. He saw it in her glance when she opened her eyes, they were more somber than usual, darker than usual, more Oriental than usual. She paused for a moment with the door cracked open before she let him in; studied him, measured him, weighed him, as if she had decided on something and was nervous.

She placed a hand on his arm and leaned toward him slightly when he stepped into the hall, just briefly, but enough to fill him. He stood motionless, wanted to stretch out his arm and touch her, but didn't dare, dared only to stand motionless and hold his breath.

It was quieter in the apartment than normal, now he noticed the absence of something just as strongly as the presence of something. Sese looked at the empty pegs on the wall, led his eyes to them, then she nodded toward the door; they're out.

She grabbed his sleeve.

One day Markus was working on the beach when a group of people appeared carrying a white cloth. The wind, which was blowing in from the sea, seized hold of it, shook it, tugged at it, as if wanting to try to stop it. The cloth fluttered stubbornly. Markus paused and watched in wonder, turned around to call to Manfred and Dieter, didn't find them, turned back to the cloth. It was many meters wide, sewn together from white sheets; in places roughly stitched, in others overlapping. On the beach stood eight men holding the cloth between them, in the water three boats slowly rowed away with men in the stern holding onto the cloth; little by little it spread out over the water. More boats approached on either side and held the cloth up, the white fabric grew and grew outward from the beach until it lay fifteen meters long and ten meters wide just above the surface of the water, and the men on the beach got into boats and followed it out.

More boats appeared, boats full of weeping women and silent men, it was as if the huge white rectangle were drawing them along. Markus counted twenty boats altogether, all of them rowboats; long, painted wooden boats.

The procession rowed out toward the low afternoon sun until Markus had to shield his eyes with one hand to see them;

they were no more than silhouettes now, black silhouettes against an enormous white patch. The white patch settled on the water, the silhouettes sprinkled dots on it, with the wind came notes from a flute.

Markus sat quite still, he knew that he was witnessing a religious ceremony, something sacred, but he didn't understand what it was. The white patch in the distance gradually began to sink, rocked calmly back and forth in the water, got smaller and smaller, vanished into the deep. The people in the boats stood still and watched the white patch until it was only a white trace that disappeared.

Markus watched the boats until a guard shouted and he had to go back to the troop of prisoners; he saw the silhouettes sit down and row back, infinitely slowly, as if time was all they had.

Later he told Bedelian about the procession. The Armenian nodded somberly.

'That was a funeral procession. A ship with recruits was bombed and sank not far from here; very young boys, straight from the school bench. None of them was ever found, it's said they were locked in the cargo hold when the ship sank. The white cloth is their parents' prayer to the water spirit to set their souls free. The dots you saw were flowers and stones; flowers to please the water spirit, stones to sink the cloth.'

'Do people here believe such things?'

Bedelian's voice grew sharp:

'Don't talk like that. People believe whatever they have to in order to survive.'

'It can't be true.'

Dieter looked at the other two. They stood lined up with a hundred other prisoners in the yard in front of the barracks. A white sheet was stretched out as a screen, and a film projector had been placed on top of two stools. The apparatus aimed a thin flickering beam at the screen, as if it couldn't quite decide whether it wanted to show the images it had inside: heaps of dead and dying people, skeletal, half naked, and naked.

Next to the screen stood a Russian instructor with a pointer, speaking. Most of the prisoners had learned enough Russian to follow along if they wanted to. Some chose to listen to the droning of the projector's motor and the rattling of the reel, some managed to look at the film without seeing, but most followed the images on the screen with silent, thoughtful eyes.

'It can't be true.'

Dieter whispered louder, a guard turned around and stared, Markus and Manfred kept their eyes fixed on the screen.

The instructor had a map on which the largest concentration camps had been marked with numbers underneath. The prisoners followed along attentively, somehow realizing that if this was true, the map of their country had been changed forever.

'This is the truth about the ideology you went to war for.'

The instructor was a political commissar, but not the worst of the lot, and in any case far better than the re-education leaders on Tuesday and Thursday evenings; he left out the most hackneyed Party rhetoric and instead talked about what the pictures showed.

'The prisoners arrived at this platform in trains. Under the direction of a doctor, they were divided into two groups: those who were fit for work and those who were not. Those who were not were immediately led away to be executed.'

The images kept on flickering, past heaps of eyeglasses and shoes, into a barracks. Everywhere starving, silent prisoners stood and sat and lay, staring at the camera, as if there was something they wanted to say but couldn't put into words.

'In the beginning the executions were carried out individually. The prisoners had to dig their own mass graves, strip off their clothes, and line up along the edge. They were executed with a shot to the back of the head.'

The camera lingered on an open, mass grave filled with

131

human remains in contorted positions. In the background stood the men whose job it was to uncover the grave, a group of young workers with long shovels and wearing uniforms. The prisoners of war in front of the screen gave each other swift glances; they recognized the uniforms of those who had opened the grave.

'After a while this type of execution was abandoned; it was both too slow and required too much manpower. Now the prisoners were killed with gas. The simplest method was to crowd them into covered trucks and run a hose from the exhaust pipe into the vehicle.

'But after a while this type of execution was abandoned, it also turned out to demand too much time. Now special gas chambers were built instead with room for many, and the prisoners were killed with gas from prussic acid instead of carbon monoxide, it worked faster.'

The images on the screen grew darker, heavier; they showed a narrow room with pipes along the walls and an open hatch above in the ceiling.

'The prisoners were forced naked into gas chambers like this one until it was so crowded that it was almost impossible to close the door; then the gas was released from a hatch in the ceiling. It generally took fifteen minutes before the screaming stopped.'

The Russian instructor switched off the film projector and rolled up the map.

'A Western philosopher once said that war is the logical consequence of competition. Competition is in turn the very foundation of the capitalist system. In other words, you have now seen the logical consequence of the capitalist system. Dismissed.'

The prisoners went back to their barracks in groups of three and four. It was a warm summer evening with soft light and a gentle breeze, which now and then rustled through the foliage. A few sporadic words were spoken, but in low voices; most of the men walked with their eyes fixed on the ground in front of them.

Markus found Manfred and walked beside him, close to him.

'What is there to say?'

Manfred didn't answer. Instead he started humming a melody, sad and resigned. Markus looked at him and listened, listened for the story in the melody; Manfred had taught him that, but this time he couldn't do it, this time he saw only pictures. He saw a little boy who went out to a dark garden from his parents' house, hesitantly, frightened, looking over his shoulder the whole time to reassure himself that the light from the house was still there; farther and farther into the darkness, more and more frightened, until someone suddenly turned out the light in the house behind him and everything was dark.

'Will we ever see him again?'

Manfred had stopped humming.

'Not until someone turns the light back on.'

They reached the door of the barracks and went inside, walking between the rows of wool blankets on the floor and the ropes hanging from the ceiling with personal possessions attached, into the same picture they had now inhabited for four years, but with a different feeling this time, a feeling of something heavier, as if something had been taken from them, the image of something else, the image of what they had come from and hoped to return to, the image that had made them regard the barracks as temporary, something that would pass.

Dieter sat down near Markus and Manfred.

'It can't be true. The Russians have lied before.'

'Why would they make this all up?'

'There's no "why" here.'

A face turned toward them from a group nearby.

'Dieter, did you hear what he said about logical consequence?'

Dieter gave him a measured look.

'What about it?'

'What the film showed was the logical consequence of the system our parents chose.'

Silence abruptly descended over the room. A hundred faces turned toward Dieter and the others, expectant, tense. Dieter noticed it, exploited it. He lowered his voice and grew more dangerous.

'The logical consequence of what?'

The other man smiled sadly. He was slight and wore round, steel-rimmed glasses.

'We come from a system that openly divided people into groups and ranked them according to worth. The groups at the bottom of the ladder didn't even have the status of humans, so we were deprived of the possibility of identifying with them; they were merely presented as a threat. Then it's logical to exterminate them.'

'Do you mean to sit there and tell me you believe the Russians?'

'I believe what people said before we left, I believe what the reinforcements said when they came east, I believe what the men who went home on leave said when they came back. Where have you been, man?'

Dieter paused before replying, he noticed the tension in the room rise and wasn't sure who the others were siding with.

'If you knew about this and thought it was wrong, why didn't you say something?'

The boy with the glasses hesitated. The others looked at him in surprise, waited for his answer. It never came, and the others knew why. It would have been impossible for the boy with the glasses to say anything about the concentration camps without at the same time admitting that their own assaults during the campaign were links in a system and not random; and for most people there is a sharp moral borderline between random and systematic violence. All this they knew, deep inside their guts, but still they sat there and waited for the boy with the glasses to respond, to remove a burden from them.

Dieter thought he had the upper hand. He stood up and slowly walked over to the other boy.

'It was war, man. The Russians say that we lost one and a half million men just in the battles of the Volga, the Don, and Stalingrad. Even if only half of it is true, it was war, a life-and-death war. Then it has to be permissible to defend ourselves by any means, also against groups that threaten us from within, from behind.'

'And how did they threaten us?'

The boy with the glasses looked up at him, unafraid. Dieter didn't speak. For some reason he couldn't make himself haul out the arguments they had been inculcated with in school; they were too far away. He turned around and went back to Markus and Manfred. A sigh of relief streamed through the room, as if something had been fended off; as if the prisoners understood that they had almost been forced to look into a darkness that would have destroyed the remnants of what had once been their self-esteem.

Markus stood at the top of a scaffolding thirty meters high and looked out over the sea. On the other side of the horizon, far away, he knew that the Asian steppes began, the ones that slowly undulate toward the outskirts of the human universe. Markus looked toward them with dreams in his eyes.

None of them knew what they were building; no one told them anything, no one asked. Each morning in the gray light of dawn they walked *en masse* the three blocks from the town gate to the building site; nearly a thousand prisoners in their camp now, twice that before the onset of hunger and disease; a thousand young boys with grown-up leaders, organized into companies, each with its own tasks.

They worked until darkness fell, sometimes in icy wind, sometimes in scorching sunshine. Slowly a foundation of yellow-white sandstone rose, sixty by a hundred meters with nothing between it and the sea, only a large open square.

One hundred and ten thousand men when they were taken prisoner, one hundred and ten thousand who surrendered and were marched eastward. Everything, everything among them; everything a man is or thinks of becoming: schoolboys, teachers, doctors, dentists, engineers, architects, authors, artists, priests, everything. They carried with them an entire culture and were led into another, carried an entire universe with them into another.

The foundation grew; they built steps, gates, grandstands. Still no one said anything, but occasionally they could see some of the grown-up prisoners huddling over large white sheets of paper that they unrolled and spread out, the way the weeping people on the beach had held out the great white sheet between them.

'Are we building a monument?'

Markus turned to the others.

They had been led into a culture where people built monuments to their grief if they could. A short distance from the building site, several hundred years earlier, a king had built a tower in memory of his daughter who was so beautiful that he decided no man would ever touch her. When she drowned herself out of longing and despair, the king had a monument erected to her at the water's edge, a round tower ten meters wide and thirty meters tall, made of fired bricks, which rose up out of the water, an enormous symbol.

The foundation continued to grow, the young boys cut sandstone, extended the scaffolding, climbed up with the stones, climbed back down and got more. Their leaders knew all along how it was supposed to proceed; each morning they issued instructions, new instructions for each day. They received the instructions from somewhere, but the young boys didn't ask where; they were content as long as they had the strength to work, because the building site meant food and drink and a kind of solidarity; being sick in the barracks meant hunger and thirst and loneliness.

The prisoners built without thinking about what they were building, just as they endured from day to day without thinking ahead; it was best that way. Gradually, as the mixture of rumors and news seeped through the stones in the town wall to them, they understood that they would be staying there a long time. Markus touched the cobblestones leading to the gate and knew that he had thirteen hundred years of culture under his feet; there was nothing special about his war, and prisoners of war have always been taken, they are part of the nature of war and are regarded as compensation for destruction; in this way they disappear from history as statistics, not people. They were one hundred and ten thousand men when they were forced to surrender; that was a large compensation, but gradually they understood that the balance of accounts was even greater, much much greater.

The foundation grew and grew and grew; one story, two stories, and the prisoners kept on building without asking questions. Like industrious ants they crawled up and down the scaffolding; tiny black dots against an enormous edifice, never at rest. Now and then groups of local people would gather at the building site and shout angrily at the prisoners; an old man tore off his jacket and shirt and beat his chest bloody as he screamed; two old women threw stones, weeping. The guards let them rage for a while, turned a deaf ear and blind eye, but only for a while; then they went across the street to the grieving people and sent them on their way, kindly but firmly. Some of the grieving people would turn around one last time to look over the shoulders of the guards, not toward the prisoners but toward the edifice, and there would be something different in their eyes, something questioning.

Gradually, as the structure grew, the local people stopped shouting at the prisoners. They still came to the building site, but now they just stood and watched them work, looked at the enormous edifice that was growing and growing, three stories, four stories, balustrades and ornamentation and monumental staircases; the local people stood for a long time and watched before they turned and left, in silence.

On the scaffolding the prisoners noticed the change and worked even harder.

Summer came, the structure kept growing toward the sky. From the top of the scaffolding Manfred claimed he could see all the way to the opposite shore of the Caspian Sea. He saw a plain with herds of galloping white horses; they crossed the green eternity with calm, confident strides. And along the water streamed low pink clouds of flamingos; they were mirrored in the surface of the water, making it glow. Markus laughed and climbed up to him to see; Dieter sullenly kept on working a little farther down on the scaffolding.

Manfred and Markus sat on the top of the scaffolding with their arms around each other's shoulders and gazed at eternity; for the first time in four years they were able to let their souls go and allow them to breathe. Around them lay the town with its hodgepodge of Azeri, Persian, Armenian, and Russian architecture; before them lay the bay with its hodgepodge of drilling rigs; below them stood the edifice, which they now knew was more than just penal labor.

Summer turned into fall, the clear blue sky turned white, the colors of the leaves became deeper, purer. The edifice kept on growing: five stories, six stories. At every corner appeared towers that stretched upward. The leaders with the white sheets of paper were there almost all the time now; they rolled up the papers and pointed and looked at the edifice, pointing and gesticulating to each other and smiling, and their smiles were transplanted to the scaffolding where the prisoners looked at each other and smiled, and one would move a little faster with the wheelbarrow, and another would shout something to him, and the laughter would cautiously shake the precarious scaffolding — just for a moment, a brief moment of laughter; then the prisoners would stop, frightened by the unusual sound, until someone else began shouting, at the very bottom of the scaffolding, and the laughter would burst forth again, more confident this time. Like the beating wings of a big white bird, the laughter rose up through the scaffolding until it reached the top and launched itself from the edge with a smile and a glide. In town, people stopped and turned around toward the laughter, astonished, giving each other searching glances, uncertain. It was one of those moments when history is open and everything is equally possible: a mere shrug of the shoulders or a raging storm against the prisoners; it was one of those moments when the first move decides, and the first move came from an enormous woman wearing a black scarf and red knit woolen stockings. She tilted her head back and laughed so her colossal breasts shook; people looked at her and smiled, tried to restrain themselves but couldn't. Her deep laughter was infectious, racing across streets and marketplaces and into back courtyards until the whole town was laughing, and many places the laughter was mixed with tears, but that didn't matter because it almost always is, and it was the laughter that now had the upper hand, the laughter that rose up first toward the white autumn sky, both from the scaffolding and the town.

Peace came to the town the way war had come, with horn music and flags and military parades and trucks filled with singing youths and people in the streets, although fewer people, much fewer; there are always fewer people in the streets after a war than before a war, and they are quieter.

Now the prisoners were to be put on display. While the battles were still raging, they had been a symbol of war; now they were a symbol of victory. In front of the monument the prisoners had built, viewing stands had been erected, where the officers, wearing dress uniforms, sat and waited for them; on both sides of the parade grounds the spectators stood crowded together and waited for them. A military band played, every other melody a funeral march; the country had paid dearly for

139

victory, very dearly. The sun flashed on the medals adorning the chests of officers and spectators alike.

In a side street off the esplanade the prisoners stood in drill formation. They had been groomed, their heads newly shaven, the rags they wore replaced by matching prison garb of rough cotton.

Markus and Manfred and Dieter tried to stay together; they were uneasy about the parade, uneasy about what awaited them. They managed to maneuver their way to a spot in the middle of a company, as far away as possible from the spectators, as far away as possible from the guards.

The guards seemed nervous, as if they weren't entirely clear about their role any longer: Should they hand over the prisoners to the victors or keep watch over them?

It was a beautiful day, just as radiant as the day the war began. A breeze blew in from the sea and cooled the spectators, who had been in position since early that morning; the trees were in full foliage, the lawns bordering the esplanade were already a deep green.

The parade started at twelve noon. A warship in the harbor fired twelve thunderous salvos from its cannons; almost all the spectators and many of the officers cringed as the sound of the first shot boomed. The memory of the war had not yet subsided. Shells exploded in the air in clouds of colored smoke: red, blue, yellow, green; and the youngest among the spectators shouted excitedly and clapped their hands, while the eldest smiled and nodded, and the officers looked at each other with pride in their eyes.

Two planes flew over the parade grounds at a low altitude and released white rain; millions of tiny paper stars floated down over the spectators and officers, drifted down, whirling in the air currents from the propellers.

Then someone shouted. No one heard the words, but everyone knew what they meant, and a tension seized hold of the parade grounds and pulled taut so that the people fell silent and craned their necks to see. At first they saw only the sound, the sound of drums that punctured holes in the silence and released another sound: the sound of children singing. Among the spectators, heads were bowed and shoulders shook, and suddenly the children came around the corner and caught up with the sound. Hundreds of children in national costumes from all the republics of the union, some with standards, some with flags, some with placards, and some with banners, machine-stitched red banners with yellow letters and exclamation marks, but all of them singing, singing and singing, in all the languages of the union.

Behind the children came the drummers, stately soldiers in parade uniforms and white gloves; they kept their eyes on the children in front of them and smiled proudly as they drummed.

Behind the drummers came the tanks; brown, ominous steel hulks on caterpillar treads with little human heads sticking up from the armor. The rumbling from the treads against the cobblestones gave a deep, ominous undertone to the children's song and the drums.

Behind the tanks came the soldiers, specially chosen and erect, with clear eyes and shiny polished boots; behind the soldiers came the cannons, behind the cannons came the rocket launchers, behind the rocket launchers came the armored cars, and behind the armored cars came the prisoners. Something settled over the spectators. Behind the armored cars came the prisoners, the ones in front walking with their eyes fixed on the armored cars, the rest staring at the backs of those in front of them, not stiffly, but as if needing to hold on. Something else settled over the spectators, something even quieter.

The sound of the children's song and the drums had almost faded now; it was carried by the breeze along the esplanade, like a memory. The sound of the tanks and ten thousand boots in step against the cobblestones was still there, but changed; now it had become a landscape into which the prisoners entered, came home.

The parade grounds approached the prisoners, pulled them forward, the parade grounds with the crowds of spectators and packed viewing stands, the parade grounds with the sea on one side and the prisoners' monument on the other. The parade grounds reached out for the prisoners and grabbed hold of them and spread them out, pulling on the ranks from each side until they filled the entire grounds and each prisoner was suddenly walking alone, with uncertain eyes.

The guards, who walked at intervals of several meters on either side of the prisoners, knew what they had to watch out for now; no one had told them about it, but they knew it the moment they entered the parade grounds and saw the spectators stiffen. Here stood the ones who would pay the price of victory, here stood the ones who would live the rest of their lives with grief and loss, unfathomable loss. And the guards knew without having to be told that the first old woman to lose her head and throw herself at the prisoners would release an avalanche, a bloodbath. It wasn't necessary to see her dig her fingernails into the eyes of one of the prisoners and rake her fingers down his cheeks with a scream; it wasn't necessary to see the blood spurt between her fingers and hear her sobbing shouts. When she threw herself forward, a guard took two running steps, handed his gun to someone, spread out his arms, and caught her, put his arms around her, hesitantly stroked the back of her head with his hand. The woman collapsed in his arms, shaking with sobs, and the guard stood there holding her, stood motionless and held her, while next to them an old man stood silently holding the guard's gun, gazing at the two of them.

Farther forward an old man tried to throw himself at the prisoners and landed straight in the arms of a guard and broke down, and farther back two women clung to the arms of two guards, and over there was a guard holding onto a spectator, and over there another, and there another, and soon there were no guards left to escort the prisoners. On the viewing stands one officer leaned toward another and pointed at the prisoners, and a man in a dark suit leaned forward to look, and another tilted his head to listen, and they saw that the prisoners had folded their hands and were moving their lips, and a low murmur from thousands of voices rose up toward them, dark, quiet, in unison; they didn't understand the words, but they knew what a prayer was. Row after row, the prisoners of war surged across the parade grounds, past the monument they had built, and the prayer grew in strength, rose up toward the sky, higher than the towers on the monument, higher still, turned around to stare at the silence on the viewing stands, the silence among the spectators, turned again and rose even higher. The breeze from the sea paused down on the beach and held its breath and waited, looked at the spectators and waited, waited until one of them whispered the *shahada* to the prisoners, the first thing to be whispered in the ear of a newborn and the last thing to be whispered in the ear of the dying; the whisper traveled to other spectators, spread out, rose up, and the breeze sighed with relief and continued, gathering up the whispers from the spectators and blowing them carefully into the ears of the prisoners.

Markus met the spring somewhere between one hundred and one hundred and twenty kilometers south of the capital. He was on his way to the Iranian border in a beat-up old truck when he noticed it, a sensation of something new. Perhaps it was the newness in his own life that made him open up; the Russians had released him and given him a job as a traveling inspector of collective farms. He was fluent in Armenian, Azeri, and Russian; they needed him.

The flat landscape stretched for dozens of kilometers in all directions, broken only by brown mountainous plateaus, biblical heights on the horizon. Before him the road headed straight as an arrow for as far as the eye could see. Markus studied the landscape; there was something timeless about it. A flock of brown sheep crossed the road, they had just lambed; a horseman with woven saddlebags and a red vest was herding the sheep.

Markus turned around to watch the sheep and horseman pass and suddenly registered that the ground beneath them was green. Next to him in the cab sat a sullen Russian wearing a hat that was too small; he tried to say something to him, but the Russian wasn't interested.

Markus leaned forward and looked around; now he could see birds with red and blue stripes, stork nests on the electric pylons, turtles in the puddles. In a small grove four horses were grazing under the trees, in the middle of the road stood a donkey and foal, staring at them.

It occurred to him that it had been fall and winter for as long as the war had lasted, fall and winter, the proper seasons for dying. Now that the war was over, it was time for living. In the midst of the black-and-white war landscape a stallion suddenly danced on three legs in front of a mare and asked: Shall we snuggle up together under that tree over there? And the mare answered: Yes, let's do that, but don't make a big fuss about it. And the birds screamed when they saw what the horses were up to, and several frogs came hopping over, and everyone wanted to do it, and an element of time had now entered into the timeless landscape, new time.

Markus looked at the horizon, there was nothing between it and him, only the straight-as-an-arrow road and the flat green plain, and once again he had the feeling of being insignificant. He had been raised like most Europeans to believe that life was something important, something he had to protect and try to save; now he had the feeling of being insignificant, a ripple in the grass, gone in an instant, forgotten before the next gust of wind.

Villages came and went, horsemen along the road became more numerous and darker, their cheekbones higher and their eyes narrower for every ten kilometers south he went. He looked at the horizon and tried to imagine what waited beyond it: The other, the Asian. He pictured an enormous mask, indistinct, with a pair of eyes staring from it, indistinct, and he thought: We can go to war against the Asians every single day for a hundred years, every single day; we can kill them and wound them and humiliate them, and when the hundred years are over, a little scratch in the mask is all we will have accomplished, a tiny little scratch in the Asian mask.

Somehow the feeling of being insignificant also brought a feeling of freedom, of less responsibility; he stopped the car and gave the wheel to the sullen Russian. He climbed up onto the truck bed, stood among the sacks of sowing seed, and sang into the wind, an aria, to Rachel.

Markus was awakened by Sese talking. Her voice floated through the dark room; hoarse, unused, sore, it sounded as if she ended each sentence with a question mark, as if she wasn't quite sure what she should believe.

Markus turned to face her and wanted to take her in his arms, but something in her voice stopped him. Cautiously he turned his head to hear better, to see the sound of her voice better.

'Markus, can you make me a stage?'

He stretched out his hands in the dark and shaped a theater hall, slanting slightly around a small stage with scattered chairs covered with yellow-and-red velvet. The lights were out, he could hear an expectant buzzing in the theater. Sese touched him lightly.

'Thank you. Some stories must either never be told or be told only the way dreams are told.'

A cane was pounded hard against the floor three times, the buzzing in the audience subsided. Light from ten spotlig slowly came up and gave warmth to the small space on stage. I the middle of the stage stood a low crate, off to the left stood a piano and a stringed instrument as tall as a man; otherwise the stage was devoid of sets, merely framed by a dark blue backdrop.

Four musicians entered from the side where the stringed instrument stood, one of them sat down at the piano, one took up the stringed instrument, the other two had brought along a drum and a clarinet. From the other side came a young woman wearing a man's dark pants, wide red suspenders, and a long-sleeved white cotton shirt; she wore no bra, her nipples were clearly visible through the white cotton fabric. She cast a questioning glance at Sese, who leaned forward and whispered:

'Ladies and gentlemen.'

'Ladies and gentlemen!'

A drum roll.

'Listen to the story about the final solution.'

'Listen to the story about the final solution!'

'To the Armenian question.'

'To the Armenian question!'

Markus shuddered. He had heard something similar before.

The young actress shook back her long black hair as she shouted her lines; she had a lovely smile and almond-shaped eyes. Her lines caused uneasiness in the hall, Markus scanned the audience and saw Kemal Atatürk on the front bench, the leader of the Young Turkish movement, along with Baron Wangenheim, the German ambassador.

The orchestra began to play, a rather plaintive, atonal melody; the clarinetist came in with the voice of the melody, undulating, quiet; the stringed instrument and the drum came in with the rhythm. The narrator climbed up onto the low crate. She looked out at the audience with a proud, angry expression:

'The summer of 1915. The lights are out all over Europe. In the Levant the Ottoman Empire is approaching its end after six hundred years as a great power.

'Turkey is ruled by the Young Turkish movement with the sultan as its straw man. The Young Turks are preparing to enter the war on the German side against the Russians, and they ask the Armenians to join them. The Armenians refuse; they have never forgotten that it was the Russians who welcomed them in 1896 and 1909 when they fled from the butchery of the

146

Turks. The Young Turks are furious and decide to solve the Armenian problem once and for all.'

A messenger comes on stage with a letter, the narrator takes it, opens it, and reads:

'In a letter to the Syrian dictator Djemal Bey, a member of the Young Turks' central committee writes, "the central committee has decided to free the fatherland from the imperiousness of this cursed race and to take onto its patriotic shoulders the responsibility for the shame that will fall upon Ottoman history by doing so. The committee has decided to annihilate all Armenians who live in Turkey, without allowing a living soul to escape." '

The music stopped playing to give the last words room: 'without allowing a living soul to escape.' They hung suspended over the stage like a darkness, a flashing raw darkness. Two stagehands came running in with a covered statue on a cart; the orchestra played a fanfare, the narrator unveiled the statue with a swift tug: It was Sultan Mehmed the Fifth, a stooped, compliant man wearing gold-embroidered attire. He stared out at the audience, squinting slightly, looked around at the stage, almost fearfully, then raised his clenched right hand with his index and middle fingers stretched out and drew a vertical line in the air, the sign of approval.

The narrator threw the white sheet back over the statue, the stagehands came to get the cart, the narrator stepped forward to the first rows as she spoke:

'Ladies and gentlemen, you just saw the signal being given to kill one point eight million people. Now the lights will also be put out in the Levant, they will not be lit again in our lifetime.'

The loudspeakers behind the stage began emitting a sound, a low, indistinct rumbling. The sound gathered force and became clearer, it was the sound of a crowd of people approaching, a shouting, agitated crowd pounding on something, blowing car horns, shattering glass. The narrator gave a sign, the sound vanished, she continued:

147

'The massacre was planned with ice-cold thoroughness. The authorities called in Muslim recruits and gave them guns, put together special units of murderers and assailants brought in from the country's prisons, and notified the Kurds that from now on all Armenians were fair game.'

The sound returned, but different now, more metallic; sparks flew from the axes being sharpened, rifle bolts being checked. Four actors came on stage, two women and two men, youths, wearing the same stylized costume as the narrator. They pulled out the low crate, turning it into something resembling a bed. Two of the actors lay down on it with their arms around each other, the other two sat down at the foot. The narrator moved to the side, the lights were dimmed, nighttime. A silent tension spread over the theater, the audience leaned forward in their chairs.

The sound of boots came from the loudspeakers, many boots, and a car. The car stopped, a car door slammed, someone pounded on a door. One of the actors sat up in bed, took the other's head in his arms and pressed it to his chest; the two at the foot of the bed took each other's hand.

The pounding on the door grew louder, a voice shouted something, angrily. The four actors looked at each other, questioning, uncertain; stayed where they were. The pounding on the door changed, as if a stick were striking it, over and over again; the orchestra fell in with the beat, rhythmical, rising in force, slowly, until the door was smashed in with a violent, crashing sound.

Suddenly actors were streaming onto the stage from all directions; from the wings, from behind the backdrop, up from the audience. They wore the same stylized costumes: black pants, red suspenders, and white shirts, both men and women, but with heavy boots and black masks that they held on sticks in front of their faces. The masks were full-face, cast from plaster, and painted, a perfect impression of the faces of the actors carrying them, but without expression.

The attackers surrounded the bed with the four actors, the music stopped, all was quiet. Slowly the attackers raised their right arms to strike, the four on the bed stared at the clenched fists, as if to be ready when the blows fell. One of the attackers whispered something hoarsely, and they all struck at once, they all struck at once as the light was put out and a sound exploded over the loudspeakers, the sound of something hard hitting something soft.

The lights rose, the stage was bare except for the narrator, who paced back and forth as she spoke:

'It will always be possible to explain a massacre, afterward it will always be possible to lay out the reasons in neat rows and say what led to what. It's another matter altogether to understand a massacre; it assumes that we open ourselves to what resides inside human beings: both violence and submission, and perhaps it would be better if we ceased doing that? Perhaps it's best to go on living in the belief that we are civilized, that massacres are something that others commit, those who are not civilized.'

Uneasiness spread through the theater, people leaned toward each other, whispering; way in the back an angry voice was heard. The narrator swiftly continued:

'Regardless, after the first rounds of butchery, two things happened: The Armenians resisted and Russian forces crossed the border. With that the Young Turks thought they had the excuse they needed to be rid of the Armenians once and for all. It was resolved that for reasons of military security, all Armenians should be deported from the war zone, which in practice meant the entire country.'

From behind the backdrop came the sound of crackling loudspeakers mounted on cars and sharp voices repeating something over and over again. At regular intervals single shots were fired, as some kind of warning. Once again actors came on stage from all directions, walking backward, as they stared at what they were retreating from, terror-stricken. The actors bumped into each other, gave a start, clustered together to form a writhing, frightened statue.

Now the other actors also entered the stage, the ones with the masks and boots; they took firm, steady strides, and something had happened to them, they had put on makeup so that their faces looked exactly like the masks they held in front of them.

A whip cracked, the human statue cringed, a rifle butt struck, a young boy put his hand to his head. A voice shouted a command, and the statue began moving, surrounded by the expressionless black masks. Almost imperceptibly the orchestra slipped in with a low melody, to the beat of footsteps; the statue and the masks found the rhythm, fell in, walking around and around the small stage. The narrator moved among them.

'In every single town and village the Armenians were gathered up and driven out, from Kilikia, Anatolia and Mesopotamia; by the tens of thousands they were rounded up and forced out, driven toward the south, with nothing but the clothes on their backs. The processions met and merged into hundreds of thousands, hundreds of thousands heading for the Syrian desert.'

The light on stage changed to yellow and yellowish brown, from the loudspeakers came the howling sound of wind. The human statue started having trouble walking, it stumbled, fell, was beaten, stood up, trudged onward.

The narrator left the stage and went out into the audience, moving back and forth in front of the first row as she spoke:

'If you had sat here the way you're sitting now and watched the procession of condemned Armenians walking past, how long do you think it would have taken?'

The narrator stopped and looked at the stage as she waited for an answer, then she turned around and said:

'Twenty-six days. For twenty-six days, every single hour, around the clock, the flood of Armenians would have passed by you; while you slept, while you were awake, while you ate, while you drank; every single hour for twenty-six days the procession would have passed by you, and I haven't allowed for any breaks.'

The narrator paused for a moment as she looked out over the audience.

'Because there were breaks. Like this one.'

One of the masks walking in front of the statue turned around and held up a peremptory hand. The statue stopped, slumped forward, sat down. The mask turned toward the audience and waved, three actors with red masks came running, prancing, howling from among the seats and began a war dance around the human statue while the black masks looked on passively.

The dancers came nearer and nearer to the statue, the actors forming the statue tried to press closer together, holding their arms over their faces. One of the dancers bent down and struck, another slashed with a knife. One of the actors in the statue put a hand to his breast. The dancers continued their circle dance, more and more aggressively, the orchestra gained force. All of a sudden both the dancers and the music stopped; the dancers approached the statue with their hands held out. The statue stiffened in terror, the dancers grabbed a young woman, began pulling her out, the statue tried to hold onto her, the dancers struck, the statue let go. The young woman wept with her hands clasped, the dancers dragged her out onto the floor and held her between them. One clutched her breast, another grabbed at her crotch, one stuck the fingers of his right hand into her mouth and clamped down with his thumb. The woman screamed, half-choking, as she was pushed down to the floor; the three dancers lay down on top of her until they covered her completely, only her muffled screams could be heard under the heap of bodies. The drummer began playing rhythmically, the human statue stared at the pile on the floor, the narrator stepped forward again:

'The guards turned bands of Kurds and newly freed

151

murderers on the Armenians; they were allowed to kill and rape as much as they liked, afterward they could take as many young women and girls as they wanted.

'In places along the route, where the local Muslim populace had gathered, the guards would stop and hold a sale: twenty piasters for a girl who had not yet been raped, five piasters for one who had.'

The narrator stepped forward to the first row and stopped in front of the German ambassador, Baron Wangenheim:

'Was this what you had in mind on May 31, 1915 when you sent a telegram to Berlin stating that the deportation "certainly means great hardship for the Armenian people; it is my opinion, however, that although we may be able to mitigate the form of their tactics, we cannot stop them in principle"? What type of principle was the baron alluding to?'

The German ambassador turned red in the face and his expression grew rigid. He got to his feet, bowed to Kemal Atatürk, and headed for the exit in the back of the theater.

Kemal Atatürk also stood up and walked toward the narrator:

'It doesn't matter what he thought, we wouldn't have listened anyway; the Germans are not the proper ones to teach humane behavior.'

Then he left the theater.

On stage the young woman had stuck her head out from the heap of men to watch. The human statue had all its faces turned toward the audience. The narrator clapped her hands, the actors were startled back into their roles. The narrator walked onto the stage in front of them.

'All summer long the death marches continued toward the Syrian desert; all summer, all fall, and all winter. Example: Out of a procession of nineteen thousand, only two thousand five hundred survived; women and young girls were sold to the Bedouins along the way, the rest died of hunger and thirst. Those who survived were gathered in a camp without food or drink and kept there until they died. To clear out the camp, bands of murderers were paid to kill the prisoners; they managed to take the lives of between three and five hundred a day. In other places the prisoners were forced to walk in circles in the desert, without food or water, eventually naked, day in and day out until they died.'

The human statue crawled on all fours now, dragging itself along while the guards with the masks beat and kicked the prisoners, round after round. With every circuit they crawled slower and slower, sank lower and lower to the ground. The lights were dimmed, the clarinet sounded a note in the semi-darkness, the drum joined in. The prisoners started singing, softly, louder:

> Pack up your troubles in your old kit bag
> And smile, smile, smile.
> While I've a Lucifer to light your fag,
> Smile boys, that's the style.
> What's the use of worrying?
> It never was worthwhile.
> So pack up your troubles in your old kit bag
> And smile, smile, smile.

A young boy in the very front of the procession fell, his face grazed the floor of the stage, he lay on his cheek with his eyes toward the audience, empty dead eyes. The rest of the procession crawled over him, fell over him, was driven onward.

From the audience came a scraping sound, a chair was shoved back and someone stood up, another chair was shoved back, and another and another, and suddenly everyone in the theater was heading toward the exit with a cloud of anger and face powder trailing behind. The actors watched them go, looked at each other, smiled a bit uncertainly. The narrator went over and put her arm around one of the three dancers, he grabbed her around the waist and pulled her close. The woman

153

on the floor got to her feet and brushed off her pants, the human statue dissolved, the guards put down their black masks and breathed a sigh of relief. The dancer embracing the narrator cautiously began to caress her underneath her white cotton shirt; she pushed his hand away with a laugh. The musicians picked up their instruments and left; only the stringed instrument remained. The actors hesitantly followed them, individually and in groups, as if they weren't quite sure whether the performance was over.

Markus turned toward Sese.

'Is there more?'

Sese nodded and pointed. Markus looked at the stage; it was now deserted, except for a small figure center stage. The lights in the theater were off, the spotlights had been turned off. Markus didn't understand how he was still able to see the small figure; it sat in a faint blue light that shone diagonally from above, as if someone had forgotten to shut off one spotlight. The figure lifted its head, Markus leaned forward to see, far forward, out of the dream and into the nightmare; it was Sese sitting there, Sese as a little girl with her thick brown hair pulled back into a bun at the nape of her neck, and wearing a black, ankle-length dress. Markus tried to look away, the adult Sese lying beside him in bed put her hand on his arm and nodded at the stage; Markus kept on looking.

The little girl stared at the darkness of the theater, looked over each shoulder, as if watching for someone. She clasped her hands and moved her lips. Markus moved his gaze to the dark theater; it was no longer empty, someone was there. He glanced over at Sese next to him in bed; she met his eyes. Markus looked back at the theater, he could see vague outlines now: cloaks, cord belts, sandals. The figure on stage stared with frightened dark eyes at the theater, the outlines took shape: faces, hands, the glint of gold teeth. Someone shouted something, someone else replied, laughter. Another shout, another reply, more laughter. The girl on the stage cringed. The shouts from the theater grew fiercer, a sharp voice cut through them, once, twice, three times, a hammer pounded. In the middle of the theater a cloak-draped figure stood up and walked toward the left side of the stage, coins jingled, then the figure approached the little girl on stage. It was a Bedouin, wearing dark desert attire and a black headdress; gaunt, bearded, with desiccated skin. The girl tried to crawl away, the Bedouin laughed and grabbed her by the ankle, lifted her upside down in the air so her dress fell over her head. The new audience in the theater shrieked and stomped their feet. The Bedouin laughed along with them, smiled proudly at the hooting spectators, tossed the girl over his shoulder, and headed for the exit.

Sese turned toward Markus in bed and moved away a little.

'He carried me to his tent and took me. Afterward he gave me to his brothers, who passed me on to their sons when they were finished. They kept me for eight grazing seasons and sent me around every time we pitched camp for the night; I walked alongside a camel all day long and followed the sun, each day's march was from sunup to sundown, I made myself a little stick with notches on it that I could use to measure the height of the sun and counted the notches, closer and closer, every single day. After eight grazing seasons some Christian missionaries bought my freedom; the first thing they did was wash me with holy water down below, as they said, 'down below.' The water turned black as soon as it touched me, as soon as it touched me; the missionaries screamed and dropped the bowl of holy water, it ate a hole in the floor, so don't come and talk to me about that, Markus; talk to me about anything at all, but not that.'

Sese lay down and closed her eyes. Markus knew that he had heard her speak for the first and last time.

DAY SIX

Markus took out his notebook, leafed through a few pages, and looked at the priest.

'Who said this?'

He started reading.

'"We must eliminate all traces of sentimentality and day-dreaming and focus all our attention on what are the most urgent goals of our nation. We must stop talking about vague and unrealistic goals such as human rights and improved standards of living and democratization. The day is not far off when pure power will be what matters. The less we are hampered by idealistic slogans, the better."'

The priest thought about it.

'Ribbentrop?'

Markus shook his head.

'Molotov?'

'No. It was the American Secretary of State George Kennan in a "top secret" memo from 1948, only three years after the war was over, three years after "the free world" had won the battle against totalitarianism.'

They had stayed at the table after breakfast; the young second-lieutenant and the nurse had come in to join them. Markus and the priest switched to speaking English, the nurse knew only a few words of Armenian.

From the corridor came the sounds of furniture being moved, crates and beds banged against the walls and banisters. The house was being evacuated, the front was on the move, the soldiers in retreat. Markus had refused to leave, the commander of the field hospital had given his word that the house would not be blown up or damaged as part of the evacuation. The priest had chosen to stay with him, without saying a word; had simply stayed. The other two would be leaving after breakfast.

Markus went on:

'I made it a rule during the Cold War not to believe anything the Russians said about the Americans. Not that I thought they were lying, but I didn't think they were telling the truth either; I put parentheses, so to speak, around everything they said about the Americans and adopted a wait-and-see attitude.

'Since the collapse of the Russian empire in 1991, I've had access to practically everything I want of books and journals and newspapers from all over the world. I've read and read and read, evening after evening, night after night. I've always been a book person, and gradually I've had more and more time to myself.

'I think I understand how the Europeans must have felt when the mechanistic world-view emerged in the seventeenth century, a complete overturning of all truths. That's how it's been for me. At first I had trouble believing what I read, but as I gradually came upon one source after another that said the same thing, there was no getting around it. And it struck me that the Russians could have made do with telling the truth about the Americans; they could have skipped all that propaganda nonsense and simply told the truth – that would have been enough.

'Since 1945 the Americans have supported, subsidized, and in some cases put into power every single right-wing military dictatorship in the world. These military dictatorships have liquidated a total of one million people, more than double what the Americans lost in the Great Patriotic War, all in the name of freedom.'

The priest looked a little embarrassed and reached for his Bible, as if Markus had said something he really should have kept to himself. A truck backed into the yard, the second-

158

lieutenant and the nurse left the room, Markus followed, casting a glance at the priest.

The nurse was standing alone next to the fountain, smoking a cigarette, as she watched the wounded being carefully lifted onto the truck. He went over to stand beside her.

'This is your first war?'

'The first as a nurse.'

'Where are you from?'

She tossed her cigarette to the ground and stepped on it before she ran to help move a stretcher onto the truck bed.

They were managing just fine with all the other stretchers, but that one they needed help with, thought Markus.

He stayed where he was next to the fountain until she came back; he could see her giving him a sidelong glance. He usually ran into her several times a day; sometimes she would ask him a question or ask him to get something for her. There was a natural familiarity about her relationship to him that touched him, as if they had been friends a long time. She looked him straight in the eye as she came back to the fountain, as if preparing herself for something.

'Are you Israeli?'

She nodded.

'Yes.'

'Why wouldn't you tell me?'

'It's not something to shout about.'

'Are you a Jew?'

'No.'

'Why are you here?'

'Because I feel we have something to make amends for back home, but it's not yet time to do so.'

'Make amends for what?'

'The same as you, only on a smaller scale. Have you managed to do it?'

Markus studied the fountain and felt something well up

inside him, something that almost overpowered him, something that was both good and bad; joy at having someone to confide in, sorrow at looking into another darkness. He took two steps toward the edge of the pool and sat down.

'We tried, each in his own way. We were from the same town, the same reality; it turned out that we even belonged to the same church. Dieter was the one who knew most clearly what he had to do, but who knew least about what he was heading for; I'll show you his letters some day.'

———————————

The room was hot and close. The prisoners sat crowded together, with water vapor rising from their clothes; over by the back wall a stove crackled. Markus, Manfred, and Dieter made sure to get places next to each other, they held tight to each other as they were pushed into the crowded classroom. The transition from the cold night air outside to the stifling air inside, nearly devoid of oxygen, was paralyzing, brutal; at the end of each row of benches stood a guard who hauled out anyone who fell asleep. Markus, Manfred, and Dieter took turns keeping each other awake; they knew what was in store for them if they didn't.

The lecturer was short and stout, with heavy Slavic features. He was in his mid-forties and spoke Russian with a confusing accent; his vowels were nasal, a Polish trait, but at the same time he consistently put the stress on the first syllable of each word, a Czech, Slovak, or Sorbian trait. His uniform was wrinkled at the crotch, he moved slowly and stiffly, like a man with no awareness of his body; his hair was combed over from the left side at the back and meticulously spread over his white pate. He cleared his throat and began:

'Comrades and re-education friends, welcome. The topic this evening is: Causes. An important topic for anyone who wishes to understand.'

The lecturer fiddled with a pointer.

'If we are to attempt to explain or understand something, we must usually look for the causes. We ask: Why did something happen? Since the seventeenth century we, or at least you from the West, have been taught to accept mechanistic explanations, meaning explanations that merely present the outward causes. Example?'

The lecturer surveyed the slumping, drowsy audience with dark eyes.

Silence.

'Example: "The window broke because it was hit by a rock." Comments?'

More silence.

'This way of explaining phenomena merely describes a sequence of events and then inserts a nexus of cause and effect between the events.'

The lecturer paused again, slapped the pointer against his left hand, and lowered his voice.

'If we apply this explanatory method to the Great Patriotic War, we can use the peace treaty after the previous war as our starting point. The Treaty of Versailles from 1919 was viewed by many as so humiliating to the German people that in reality they had no choice but to go to war again.

'The American president, Woodrow Wilson, was perhaps the one who expressed it best when he said: "This is not a peace agreement, it's a twenty-year armistice." It turned out that he was right, almost to the day.'

The lecturer's voice sounded friendly now, sympathetic, as if he wished to meet them halfway, initiate a dialogue with them.

Thaw us out, thought Dieter, thaw us out.

'But there's another kind of causal explanation besides the outward, mechanistic one, comrades; there are also internal causal explanations. Aristotle called them formal, attributable, tangible. Concretely: Is there something in the nature of an object that can explain what happens? Instead of saying that the windowpane broke because it was struck by a rock, can we say that it broke because the rock was hard, or because the pane was fragile?'

A tremor passed through the room, uneasiness. The lecturer took his time, balancing the pointer in his hand for a long time, looking at the prisoners, studying them before he put his question into words.

'Is there something in the nature of the German people that dictates that you would be the ones to go to war again?'

Markus, Manfred, and Dieter looked down during the silence that followed. Not a thought moved in the dim class-room, not a glance. The prisoners sat with their eyes fixed on the bench in front of them while the lecturer waited. He had time to wait, all the time of the twenty million people of Slavic origin who had paid with their lives for this war, the twenty million who were the true winners and losers of the war; not the seven hundred thousand American and British casualties, as the Western powers claimed, but the twenty million who were killed after the cavalry began moving east.

Not a thought, not a glance, just sit motionless with your eyes on the bench in front of you and wait, listen to the lecturer, who at two-second intervals was striking the pointer against the palm of his left hand, two-second intervals, count the seconds and don't look up, don't meet the eyes of the lecturer and have to answer his question, because the first one of us who admits that yes, there is something special about us Germans, will take on an inhuman responsibility; the first one of us to put words to the possibility that we are the power of darkness, not the others, will take away from us the little we have left of light, and without light it is impossible to see hope in a place like this, impossible to see anything at all.

'Is there something in the nature of the German people that dictates you would be the ones to go to war?'

The lecturer kept on striking the pointer against his left hand as he spoke, accentuating each word, every single word; a little smile played at the corners of his mouth, he was enjoying this, enjoying the rhetoric; he knew that he was sowing seeds, that they would sprout, and he knew that many of the plants would grow so tall that they would slowly suffocate the prisoners down there. He enjoyed the thought, enjoyed imagining how the certainty of being evil would settle like a weight on many of the prisoners, heavier and heavier with each year; the lecturer enjoyed thinking about how in their long, sleepless nights the weight would first press out all joy and then all excess – press it out of them, not tear it out of them, the way it had once and for all been torn out of himself when he returned to his village toward the end of the war.

'No one wants to answer? No one dares say whether there's something in the nature of the German people that dictates you would be the ones to go to war, you specifically, the people of the poets and philosophers?'

Dieter drew in a breath, *you damn bastard*, he dug his fingernails into the underside of the bench and held on tight; one of the guards looked at him, he tried not to breathe, don't breathe, don't breathe. *Is there something in your Slavic nature that dictates you would be the ones to be the victims, is there something about your cringing, feeble submission, your irksome passivity that also makes you responsible for what happened? Or is there something in the nature of the chosen people that dictates they would be the ones to be annihilated, their nauseating conceit and their vaunted suffering?*

'Because it's not possible to attribute to us Germans a national character without admitting our right to do the same; if we have a national character, then the Slavs have a national character and the Jews have a national character.'

Dieter was now screaming at the top of his lungs, two hours later in the barracks; some of the other prisoners tried to turn away from him, some pretended not to hear him at all, while others sat motionless and looked up at him, following his words.

'Dieter, calm down.'

Markus stretched out a hand toward him, but Dieter refused to be stopped.

'The Treaty of Versailles practically eradicated us as a nation; they took from us Alsace, Lorraine, Posen, West Prussia, Upper Silesia, Bohemia, and Austria, they took from us all our colonies, they took from us all we had of property and goods abroad, they took from us our entire merchant fleet and put our coal mines under the control of the French, may God comfort and save us all, French control, and then that bastard stands there and asks if there's something in the nature of the German people that dictates we would be the ones to go to war. Name a single nation with respect for itself that wouldn't go to war after such an edict.'

Dieter took a breath and lowered his voice, making it deeper, more intense:

'But what they took from us wasn't the worst part, the worst part was what they forced upon us: war guilt, that hated, suffocating war guilt, that damned, murderous war guilt, which they demanded be included in the treaty. If there's anyone out there in the world who wonders what it's like to grow up in a pool of guilt, just ask us. We know.

'We could easily have managed to live with the demand for restitution, one hundred and thirty-two billion gold marks isn't the whole world, after all, we are Germans, and the Allies demanded no more than was proper and reasonable. The Belgians demanded more than their entire country was worth, but that was nothing, a mere trifle. The French wanted not only their war losses covered, they also demanded that the expenses for their own war operations be paid, along with military pensions and national health insurance for all those who participated, but those were also trifles. What wasn't a trifle was the war guilt: that we were forced to sign a treaty stating that we were to blame for the war, that we were the ones who had subjected our continent to a war that had cost fifteen million people their lives.'

Dieter's voice was shrill now, shouting at the walls and windows.

'Germany didn't start the previous war, that was a lie, a lie that forced us to strike back, that would have forced anyone to strike back. It's a matter of self-respect; when you're caught up in a net of lies, other people's lies, when you feel spat upon and trod upon, then you have only one choice: Either you break out and strike back, or you're lost.'

'So what about us?'

Dieter stopped in mid-sentence and turned to face the prisoner who had interrupted him. It was a young, slightly heavy boy with reddish hair and a lingering gaze.

'What did you say?'

'So what about us? Did we regain our self-respect or are we lost?'

Dieter was expecting something else. He wasn't sure exactly what, only that he was expecting something else. When the barrier at the border was raised for the train, and the released prisoners saw the first signs in their own language, everyone fell silent in the coach; no one shouted, no one sang, they all just stood and looked out of the window. Dieter noticed that many of the others were holding each other by the hand, by the arm, around the shoulders.

The train rolled on past rippling fields of grain and newly built houses and new roads and new cars; it was as if everything were new, even the blue sky and the green grass seemed new, and suddenly Dieter understood what was missing: Entering this fine new country was a train carrying something old, something that had left thirteen years earlier, when it was a different country.

Dieter sat down and tried to figure out what he had been expecting; he pictured a welcoming committee just on the other side of the border with banners and smiling children and maybe a band; he pictured representatives from the authorities who hung something around the prisoners' necks and shook their hands; he pictured weeping relatives who had learned they would be coming and had taken off from work and come to the border crossing to be there when they arrived.

He didn't want to admit it, but he pictured something else as well, some sort of monument, a kind of thank-you from the country for the campaign they had participated in and the years of imprisonment they had endured, something that might repay them a little, just a little, for all the humiliation, a formal unveiling with somber speeches. It wasn't too late yet, but during the first half hour after crossing the border he realized something that he never would have imagined before: No one builds monuments to soldiers who have lost a war.

The train rolled on with silent faces pressed against every single window and thoughtful eyes searching restlessly for something they couldn't find, not even on the platform where they were supposed to get off, in a sleepy little country town that most people had forgotten. The platform was cordoned off with barricades, and at intervals of several meters stood soldiers wearing uniforms they had never seen before, and the released prisoners peered around in confusion as they were led through the station building and outside. From a café inquisitive eyes stared at them, at a newspaper stand the owner and two customers turned around to look at them, but no one waved, no one shouted anything.

They were led in ranks of five to a tent camp, and a man wearing a white armband with a red cross stepped forward and welcomed them; he was the first one to welcome them, and he didn't use many words to do it, but at least he did welcome them, and the released prisoners looked at him with something new in their eyes. The man called the camp a transit camp and said they would be sent on as soon as they were registered and some information had been taken down. Dispersal of plates and cups and forks and knives, and distribution of food and woolen blankets, and twenty in each tent; we'll start dividing up on the

166

right – and the released prisoners looked at each other with something indeterminate in their eyes.

Dieter had expected that he would have trouble sleeping on the first night he was back, he had expected to be too wound up, but he fell asleep almost at once, after he had unrolled the blanket and lay down; it was quiet in the tent, the released prisoners had no more to talk about than they had when they arrived, many of them looked as if they had something to think about.

The next morning the registration began; civilians wearing armbands sat at a long table under a tarp canopy and took notes as the line of released prisoners snaked past; in the background sat officers wearing the same unfamiliar uniforms as the guards on the platform, studying the prisoners. Someone whispered that they were Americans, and others whispered: What the hell are they doing here? It was the Russians who won the war. And most of them didn't know what to think when they were led in one by one under the tarp canopy into the tent where two American officers sat with an interpreter.

The two Americans were both in their forties, both had a bulging, almost arrogant corpulence. They were leaning back with one leg crossed over the other, documents in front of them and a file cabinet behind.

Dieter said his name, one of them leaned over the cabinet, searched for his paper, found it, read it, showed it to the other, who also read it, and Dieter had a sinking feeling in his stomach when the two Americans exchanged a glance. One of them said something to the interpreter, who listened attentively and translated:

'They want to know which camp you were in.'

Dieter took a deep breath. Not how are you feeling, or it's so good to see you, or how does it feel to be back, but which camp were you in?

'Sumgat.'

167

The interpreter translated and listened to the reply and turned to Dieter:

'Which block and which cell?'

Dieter looked down. Not how was the food, or how were you treated, or what kind of medical attention did you get, but which block and which cell?

'Block B, cell thirteen.'

'Was everyone from your cell on the train?'

Something settled in the pit of Dieter's stomach, something cold, heavy, sinking.

'Was everyone from your cell on the train?'

One of the Americans was leaning forward slightly.

Dieter listened to the sounds from the tent opening. He could hear the others being called up and sent off on buses, four buses in the morning and four in the afternoon, with the destinations printed on a white sheet of paper in the front window; eight buses every day for a week until there was only him and a handful of other released prisoners left in the camp, him and a handful of others, and the Americans who arrived in open jeeps every morning, with sunglasses and pistols on their belts, and summoned them to the tent for more interrogations, one by one.

'Everyone except two.'

Dieter lay on his woolen blanket, alone in the big empty tent, and stared at the ceiling. He held his right hand up in front of him and meticulously counted his fingers; then he held his left hand up in front of him and meticulously counted his fingers. After that he clasped his hands and tightened his grip. There was a tapping on the pole at the tent opening, a ring striking lightly. Dieter didn't bother to answer.

A figure came into the tent, a light figure wrapped in fragrance. Dieter looked at the figure, a nurse in white, in the middle of the light from the tent opening; she took the few steps over to him and squatted down next to him, he turned away from her and stuck his hands between his knees, pressed them together and curled up in a fetal position.

She stayed sitting there behind his back, put a hand on his shoulder. Dieter tried to jerk his shoulder away, the hand held on.

'What's wrong with you?'

'None of your business.'

She spoke German. Too bad, he would have preferred a seduction scene with an interpreter, they're always more exciting than seduction scenes without an interpreter.

'That's not very polite.'

Dieter didn't reply.

'Where are you from?'

The hold on his shoulder grew firmer, she pulled him around until he was lying on his back and looking up at her. She was blonde, with green eyes and a little scar on her left cheek. Dieter tried to look away.

'Where are you from?'

Dieter waved his hand in annoyance.

'I've already told them. Every day for two weeks now I've told them where I came from. Town, camp, block, cell; town, camp, block, cell.'

'I mean here, here at home.'

She took his hand and began feeling for his pulse. Dieter closed his eyes and thought: God, no, not that, while he breathed in the scent of her and took in the image of her skin under the white uniform, the underwear he had caught a glimpse of when she squatted down, and he saw Markus and Erich Maria standing with beer steins in their hands at the bar in Händel's after training on Friday night, and someone started singing, and he looked at Markus and Erich Maria smiling as they sang, and in their smiles he saw a face, a third one, and as he cautiously reached out his hand toward the nurse, a voice whispered inside of him *Rachel* and he gave a start, and the voice whispered *if you give them*

Rachel they'll have something to use against him, and he gasped as the nurse brushed against him.

Dieter studied the supply sergeant who brought out his things and crossed them off a list: pants, jacket, shirt, undershirt, underwear, socks, shoes, a hundred marks; thanks for your effort, it was a splendid war, too bad you had to be taken prisoner.

'Do you know what's waiting for you out there?'

Dieter thought for a moment before he replied.

'I only got one letter, from my mother. She wrote mostly about family matters.'

'Newspapers?'

'Only Russian.'

The supply sergeant handed him the list and a pencil to sign the receipt.

'We were given instructions before all of you got here.'

Dieter signed his name and waited. The supply sergeant looked embarrassed.

'Yes?'

'We were told to prepare you for the fact that we're still under occupation.'

'After so many years?'

'After so many years.'

'What did the others say?'

'You're the first one I've told.'

'Those were some instructions.'

'I couldn't make myself say it when everyone was standing in line: clothes, money, sign here, we're still under occupation; clothes, money, sign here, we're still under occupation.'

'Who's occupying us?'

'Mostly Americans.'

'Is it bad?'

'You'll find out. This envelope is for you too; someone delivered it this morning.'

Disconcerted, Dieter accepted the unmarked envelope and quickly stuffed it in his pocket. He said goodbye to the supply sergeant and walked out of the camp, out of the camp and back the same way they had come three weeks earlier, past the rolling fields with scattered dwellings and into the sleepy station town.

At the station he got himself a ticket on the first train north and bought a newspaper; when he was done reading it he bought another one and read every single little paragraph, and after that another and another, and his train left while he was still sitting there reading until he had used up all hundred marks and read every single newspaper and every single magazine in the little stand. Then he raised his head from the stack and stared into space with eyes that didn't see, and he stayed sitting like that for the rest of the evening and all night long while the guards and cleaning staff walked in wide arcs around him.

Dieter bent down and let his fingers glide over the letters on the stone. Behind him light flooded through the dense foliage of the trees into the quiet cemetery and merged with the bird song and the sound of his own heart. From far away came the sound of traffic, but faintly, like the sound of something unreal. He read his mother's name with his fingers, then his father's, straightened up, stood still, and looked at the stone, turned around and left. At the gate he turned around and looked back one last time.

Beyond the cemetery lay the town with its cobblestone streets and linden trees and medieval buildings. Some of the streets were paved now, and many of the trees and houses were gone, but Dieter had no trouble finding his way; he took long strides, as if in a hurry, until he was standing in front of a modern office complex made of glass and concrete, where the high school had once stood. He hurried onward to Händel's and found a cooperative with advertising posters outside, he dashed onward to the library and found Markus's father.

'What can I help you with?'

171

Markus's father peered through thick glasses from behind the library counter. He had become an old man, his face had fallen in and dried up. He smiled at the figure standing before him, a tentative, slightly sad smile, and then something seemed to strike him, he took off his glasses, rubbed his eyes, and squinted.

'Dieter?'

Dieter nodded.

A silent scream exploded in Markus's father, a silent scream full of tears that for a split second welled up in his eyes.

'Dieter. My God, Dieter.'

Markus's father stood up, trembling, shuffled into a book vault, came back out with another librarian, got his jacket and shoes from the cloakroom, took Dieter by the arm, and led him toward the door.

'Come on. Someone will take over for me for a few minutes.'

They walked down the steps and out to the little square in front of the library; it was peaceful there, it faced away from the street, toward an open lawn.

'When did you get back?'

'A few weeks ago.'

'How are you?'

Markus's father had never liked Dieter, but he had accepted him as one of his son's friends.

'Fine, considering the circumstances.'

Dieter could see a question taking shape in the frail, stooped body of the man; it forced its way out from inside, burst, billowed: Markus, Markus, Markus.

'Markus sends his greetings.'

The father's body froze.

'Sent his greetings? He didn't come with you?'

The voice was toneless.

Markus's father sat down on the lowest step, as if his legs had failed him. He folded his hands and looked out at the lawn. Dieter sat down next to him.

'He asked me to give you this letter. The censors allowed me to bring it with me since the camps were going to be emptied anyway.'

Markus's father stared for a long time at the letter offered to him before he took it; there was dread in his eyes, as if he knew that from now on life would be divided into before and after this letter. He turned the envelope over and read the back, studied the handwriting on the front, opened it with shaking hands and started to read. He read slowly and carefully, moving his lips as he read, stopping after each sentence. It was a long letter. When he came to the words *Your Markus* at the bottom of the last page, he folded the letter.

'Make amends for what? What has he done that it takes more than thirteen years to make amends?'

Dieter closed his eyes and listened to the sounds in the darkness, the sound of drums and roaring crowds of people and shrill loudspeakers and horses' hooves and shots and flames and screams.

'Have you met this woman?'

Dieter nodded.

Markus's father collapsed a bit, the way fathers always collapse a bit when their sons grow away from them. Dieter gave him a sidelong glance. They sat for a while without saying a word, then Markus's father stood up, thanked him, and walked up the steps with the letter from his son in his left hand, held a little out to one side, as if he had forgotten that he was holding it. Inside he was screaming to know more about Markus, but he didn't want to hear it from Dieter.

Dieter watched him go, with his fingertips on the unmarked envelope in his inner pocket.

The fields around the town turned yellow and the leaves on the trees turned red, and Dieter rented a room from his old aunt, who had been widowed like so many others; he reported to the unemployment office and was sent to an undertaker who was in need of pallbearers. He liked it there from the start, it was a job that suited his mood: melancholy gravity, ponderous solemnity, organ music, a strident soprano solo from the gallery, and on the wreaths 'thank you for everything.'

The fields were harvested and the leaves fell to the ground, and Dieter carried caskets, and along with the Danish philosopher he thought: Who will be so unfortunate as to be the last one alive to throw the last three spadefuls of earth on the last of the dead? And suddenly he heard Markus ask: Who will be so unfortunate as to be the last leaf to drop from the last tree? And from inside the casket the body said: If this is going to get any more depressing, I'm going home. And Dieter turned his head and saw that Markus and Manfred were walking along as pallbearers beside him, for a brief moment, long enough to give him a smile, and for the first time Dieter felt a yearning inside him for something that once had been.

He did his best to be an exemplary pallbearer, he joined in singing the hymns, folded his hands during the prayer, listened attentively to the sermon, looked subserviant and somber when he carried the wreaths forward to the bier, but at the same time confident and firm so that the bereaved would have something to hold on to.

One day one of the bereaved on the front bench let her eyes linger on him, a young woman; he could feel something stirring under the hymnal he was holding on his lap and whispered Ave Maria, Ave Maria, and heard Manfred answer: Why not give it a try? Another day the regular priest was sick and Father Neumath filled in for him, Father Neumath from Dieter's boyhood days; Dieter looked forward to talking to him after the burial and listened more attentively than usual to the sermon; he had always liked Father Neumath. Now your sin is forgiven, said Father Neumath, now you can rest in peace, at the grave all discussion stops; Dieter looked up, what sins, what discussion?·and saw the black iron cross that lay on the white casket.

174

He waited until the casket was lowered and the three spades of gray earth had struck the lid, he waited until the farewell hymn had been sung and the weeping had stopped and Father Neumath had taken the hand of every single black-clad person and said something in a low voice, he waited until then to step forward:

'Father Neumath.'

The priest looked at him in surprise. His eyes had become smaller, as they often do in elderly men, but not enough to hide the sorrow.

'Wolfgang?'

'Dieter.'

The priest nodded apologetically.

'You're getting more and more like your brother.'

'I have no brother, Father.'

'Is he dead?'

'He was never alive.'

'So sad. So sad for all those who were never alive.'

They walked among the stones in the little cemetery, walked with cautious steps between the sound of life far away and the silence of death right behind them; more mourners came over to thank the priest and say goodbye, and he took their hands in both of his and said: God bless you, my child, and each time he said it, a bird song trilled lightly over the words.

'What was the sin that he was forgiven back there?'

'It's over now.'

'But what was it?'

'He chose the wrong side.'

'Wrong side?'

'Let him rest now, Siegfried.'

'Dieter.'

'Excuse me. God bless you, my child.'

'What was the wrong side he chose?'

'He went along with those who led the country into darkness.'

The bird song stopped.

'Was that wrong?'

Dieter suddenly had tears in his eyes.

'Was that wrong, Father?'

'God is the light, my child. It is always wrong to go toward the darkness.'

Father Neumath said goodbye and left; a little cloaked figure tottering down the slope of the cemetery and growing smaller and smaller. Dieter stood and watched him go and heard his voice eighteen years earlier, at a lectern, in a classroom; the priest was taller back then, imperious; he said that the Catholic church looked with benevolent neutrality on the new regime, benevolent neutrality; the church was prepared to submit to the state in all matters as long as it was allowed to act freely. A boy raised his hand and asked how that coincided with Christian teachings, and Father Neumath had told him to mind his own business. Dieter stood looking at the frail old figure; he had an urge to run after him and ask whether the Catholic church already knew back then that the regime was leading the country into darkness or whether this was something it didn't realize until afterward, after everyone else had seen it, but he knew the answer: leave me alone, I'm too old, and he remembered that Father Neumath had thrown the boy who asked the question out into the corridor, he wasn't too old back then.

After his encounter with Father Neumath, Dieter bought a roll of gray paper and covered two walls of his room, the two walls without a door or window. He meticulously covered them from floor to ceiling, securing the gray paper with glue along all the edges and giving it five centimeters' overlap: that should do it. On the ceiling above each wall he fastened a string with a pencil attached, and in the middle of the ceiling he fastened a string with a pencil sharpener attached, within reach of both pencils; nothing would be left to chance.

At the top of the first wall he wrote WRONG in big letters, at the top of the other one he wrote CORRECT. Directly under WRONG he wrote *this is what I believed before*, directly under CORRECT he wrote *this is what I believe now*; then he took two steps back and surveyed his work. There was a mistake, he stood there for a long time thinking before he went back to the one wall, crossed out the word WRONG and wrote FALSE, the American word for *wrong*; a hundred kilometers farther east he would have replaced the word in his own language with a word in Russian. Later he would change the word CORRECT, after he had been to the library to look it up; he wasn't quite sure what it was in American, he seemed to remember that it was RIGHT, but wasn't quite sure; that also meant *on the right*, and *right* and *on the right* couldn't be the same thing, could they?

The rest of the night he paced restlessly around and around his room as he rolled back time and discovered falsehoods; they grew like a carpet, dense, luxuriant, all he had to do was bend down and pluck them up, hold them up before his eyes, and hang them on the wall, sometimes with a sad smile. By the time his aunt pounded on the door and told him that was enough, and the renter down below thumped on the floor and shouted fuck you, he had covered half the wall with falsehoods, with only a few muttered circuits of the room between each.

He realized quickly that he was going to have to arrange the falsehoods in groups, not just write them down haphazardly, and he decided to start at each corner and move diagonally toward the center; economic and political misconceptions moving down from the upper right and left corners, social and personal misconceptions moving up from the lower right and left corners.

The first economic misconception he wrote was that a country has the right to take drastic countermeasures when the economy, as a result of foreign measures, is so destroyed that it threatens the very existence of the population. False, false, false, a country does not have that right, no matter how arrogant and inconsiderate the behavior of the rest of the world.

He bent down and wrote the first social truth: There is something called a national soul, with its adherent characteristics, and people can be ranked according to these characteristics. False, false, false, all people are equal, it's nonsense to talk about differences, and madness to rank them.

Dieter sat down on the bed and rolled time further back and listened to the shot from the study where his father was sitting alone, and heard him say at dinner the day before that another devaluation had been announced, this time the decimal point would be moved two places; which meant both that his savings were gone and that he could no longer afford to run the store.

Dieter stood up and started walking, he couldn't bear to sit still on the bed and listen to his mother crying the day after they sold the store and a new devaluation occurred, he couldn't bear to sit still and listen to her silent screams when the same thing happened two weeks after they sold the house.

He went over to the wall and wrote down the only critical remark he had ever heard his mother speak: 'Remember who bought both the store and the house, Dieter.' He stood there a long time and studied the remark, it was the only time he had ever heard her say anything about the chosen people; then he crossed it out. False, Mother, false, false, false; there are no groups of people, only individuals, so you can't say things like that. If people with common traits are annihilated, it's coincidence, it has nothing to do with their historical role, because only groups of people can have historical roles, not individuals. It was coincidence that the Russians annihilated the Kulaks, coincidence that the Turks annihilated the Armenians, coincidence that the Belgians annihilated the Congolese, coincidence that the French annihilated the Vietnamese, coincidence that the Americans annihilated the Koreans, coincidence that the British annihilated every single devil they came upon in their colonies. The only thing that isn't coincidence is that the

178

chosen people are now annihilating the Palestinians, because the one who has been annihilated himself has the right to annihilate, that's something everyone understands.

Dieter slammed the door so hard when he stormed out that his aunt dropped her teacup and the renter below shouted fuck you, man. Tears in his eyes, his pulse hammering, down one block, up the next; there was snow in the air. Dieter pulled his jacket tight around him, down another block, across an intersection, the cars stopped for him, people moved aside, it grew dark, the moon came up, it got colder, quieter, Dieter kept on walking until early in the morning when he sneaked up the stairs and into his room and went over to the wall and wrote that the Germans' annihilation of Slavic and Semitic peoples is an exception in the history of Western civilization due to a flaw in the German national character; he stood for a long time and looked at that sentence before he crossed it out and sank onto his bed and fell asleep fully clothed, with a smile on his lips. False, false, false.

Slowly Dieter began to fill the void from the years he had been away, slowly and deliberately. He found his way to a government office for war history with a friendly but anxious archivist, he trolled the catalogs at the library, took out books and got them to order the ones they didn't have that interested him, went to the newspaper archives and read the editorials.

Slowly the void was filled. In between funerals he sat in a little café he had discovered and filled up the void; a quiet little café with a quiet little waitress, so quiet that the only sound for long periods of time was the scratching of Dieter's fountain pen on the notebook he had started taking with him everywhere.

'Are you a writer?'

The waitress had been wanting to ask for a long time, but hadn't dared; he was a grown-up, she wasn't. Almost every morning for three weeks he had come in and sat down with a cup of coffee and his notebook; sometimes he had a piece of cake along with it, other times he drank a glass of beer, but always with his head bent over his notebook and the scratching fountain pen in his left hand. The waitress was rather surprised, left-handers didn't usually use fountain pens, it was so easy to smear the ink, until she noticed that the man with the hollowed cheeks and the rather dangerous eyes was holding the pen at a special angle to the notebook, as if he were chiseling.

'No.'

He kept on writing in his notebook without looking up. She felt a surge of something like anger, disappointment. He never looked at her, even when he ordered, he didn't look at her now, when she was talking to him. The only time he ever looked up was when he took breaks from his writing, long breaks which he spent staring out of the window.

Suddenly he turned to her.

'How old are you?'

She blushed.

'Nineteen.'

A lie. She was only eighteen and a half.

'Where were you during the war?'

She grew uneasy, flustered, didn't know what she should say.

'Where were you during the war?'

His eyes were now nailing her fast. She squirmed a bit and looked down.

'Here.'

She started wiping off the shelves with a damp cloth. This wasn't how she had imagined it, and she had been sternly warned by the proprietor not to talk to the customers about the war; from time to time elderly men would want to talk, tell her something, remember something, then she would always steer the conversation to a different topic or disappear into the back room; the war is over, the proprietor had said, the war is over.

It was the same thing at school, the war was over there too, but occasionally, when it wasn't possible to avoid it, the teachers would talk about the war as the others' war, the ones who had seduced the people and led them into disaster.

'Here where? Here in town?'
She could feel him like a shadow behind her. She nodded.
'What do you remember most?'
She wiped harder, concentrated harder.
'What do you remember most?'
She turned to face him.
'Nothing. It's so long ago. Excuse me.'
She went into the back room with brisk steps.

He was waiting for her outside the café when it closed for the night, leaning up against the wall across the street with a cigarette between his fingers. It was drizzling and dark, with only a few stalwart streetlights. He tossed his cigarette away and crossed the street as soon as he caught sight of her, and something strange swelled inside her, something that was proud and fearful at the same time.

'What do you want?'
She grabbed hold of the café door behind her, holding onto safety with one hand.
'To take a walk with you.'
'Where?'
'Wherever you're going.'
'Mother's waiting for me.'
He smiled and took her arm, led her away from the door.
'Which way?'
She pointed, he guided her with light fingers on her elbow and started walking in the direction she had pointed; reluctantly she let herself be steered, felt that she was giving in to him, that she both wanted and didn't want to give in. She looked around and relaxed more, the streets were not deserted and a few cars passed, and there was something intriguing about him.

'What's your name?'
'Hildegunn.'
A blonde name with lots of light, her mother used to say, from the time when Nordic names were in fashion.

'What about you?'

'Dieter.'

There was a bridge between them now, an opening; they were no longer café hostess and customer, but Hildegunn and Dieter.

They continued on; down the street, across the square, along a side street and out to the main avenue while he cautiously asked her questions about herself, saying her name several times before his questions, capturing her with her name.

She had the feeling of being part of a film, the feeling of sitting in a movie theater and looking at herself from the back, up on the screen as she disappeared down a night-dark street next to a grown-up man, looking at herself and the man getting smaller and smaller and walking closer and closer together and slower and slower as they approached the building in the center of town where she and her mother lived.

Hildegunn stopped and turned to face Dieter, he stopped and turned to face her.

'Here it is. Thanks for the company.'

He smiled and bowed playfully.

'Good night, Hildegunn.'

Hildegunn fumbled nervously with her key, he stood quite still and watched her trying to unlock the door, this is embarrassing, so embarrassing, damn key. She finally did it, opened the door, gave him a swift glance, uncertain. He smiled calmly.

'Tomorrow?'

Something somersaulted inside her, something that tickled, something that dropped. She nodded and closed the door, much too hard, damn door, and raced up the stairs as she looked at the images of herself as a teenager alone with her mother and just enough money to make it through high school before she had to go looking for a job; all the images she had gradually described to Dieter as he asked her questions and listened and asked more, interested, and she hadn't asked a single question about him, not one, hadn't even thought of it, damn.

The next evening a light late-summer breeze was blowing, and with it came the scent of soap when Dieter took her arm, and Hildegunn smiled with pleasure and saw that he had also brushed his hair. He held her arm as they walked down the street, a little tighter than the night before, a little closer, and she said what she had practiced saying:

'Won't you tell me a little about yourself?'

'Why?'

She was dumbstruck. That was not the answer she had expected.

They walked for a long time in silence.

'What do you want to know?'

'Whatever you feel like telling me.'

Dieter looked up at the dark sky and thought for an eternity before he said that once upon a time there was a young boy, younger than you, who went to war to seek his fortune, and on the way he met two good helpers that he took along with him; they rode into the war from one side and were there all winter and spring, and when they came back out on the other side, no one recognized them anymore.

'Why not?'

'Because they had changed.'

Dieter let go of Hildegunn's arm, pressed his fingertips against the base of his nose and breathed in, almost like a gasp, and Hildegunn stretched out her hand to touch his arm but refrained, didn't quite dare, and for a long moment they stood like that and knew that something had happened between them.

'Then what happened?'

'One flew south and one flew north.'

Hildegunn smiled at the nursery rhyme and took his arm, tucked her hand snugly under his, and leaned toward him, owning him a little. They walked on and on and on while Dieter talked about his boyhood days and his father who took his own life after the bankruptcy and his mother who shrank until she was barely visible in the one small room they had left; he talked about the club evenings at the pioneer troop and the day he was admitted to the youth movement, the only time in his life when he had ever had a whole room applaud him; he talked about the pride when he tried on the uniform for the first time and the joy when he marched through the streets the first time: There is a way, and we are that way. The teachers in school said that, the priests in church said that, the steady customers at Händel's said that; there is a way, and history has given us the right to choose that way.

'Why is that?'

'People were starving and freezing and standing in soup lines, and we marched past them and showed the way, there is a way. But all that is history now.'

Dieter fell silent. Night after night they had talked about this in the prison camp, year after year, it was our right, our historic right; gradually the voices grew fainter, it was our right, but our right to what?

They had arrived. He took her hands and held them close against his chest.

'What I remember most was the shame. We were no longer anything, none of us was. On top of everything the military leaders came and said that we had never been defeated militarily, that it was the Communist rebellion and the chosen people who had stolen the cover at their backs and made it impossible to continue the war.'

Hildegunn didn't reply. She didn't know what she should say and was afraid of saying something wrong, she didn't understand everything he said but noticed that he was growing more and more intense, as if something was flaring up that had been smothering inside him.

He let go of her hands and kissed her lightly on the cheek.

'See you tomorrow.'

She looked at him as she unlocked the door, and smiled at him as she closed it.

He brought her flowers the next evening, and what she had been wondering about was suddenly certain. She stuck her arm in his at once and looked at him, threaded the string on the flowers around her arm, and let the bouquet hang between them, tilted back, as a kind of adornment.

Without saying anything, they took a completely different route, headed in a completely different direction from the building where she lived. Outside a café he stopped and nodded.

'Something to drink?'

She smiled.

They went in, faces lifted to look at them, dense smoke, laughter, music, brown wainscoting. They found a table in the corner, he got a stein and a glass, and they had to sit with their faces close together to hear what the other person was saying. Dieter grew in his chair, told jokes, teased her; she laughed, tossed her hair back, grew toward him. They started talking about the future, cautiously opened up a tiny corner of their dreams and hopes for the other one to see.

At the next table sat two American soldiers, drunk. One of them was interested in Hildegunn, he stared at her, stared. Hildegunn noticed it, cast a glance in his direction, looked away. The soldier kept on staring, Hildegunn grew annoyed, annoyed and scared; she looked at him several more times, each time she met that bleary gaze of his. Dieter followed her eyes to the next table and gave her a questioning look. She drummed her fingers on the table.

'They think they own everything. They're everywhere.'

Dieter turned to face the next table with the two Americans, tried to catch the eye of the soldier who was staring, couldn't do it. He turned back to Hildegunn.

'Shall we go?'

She didn't reply. Dieter didn't know what kind of answer that was and he couldn't read her; she seemed annoyed and flattered at the same time, annoyed and flattered, and suddenly he felt a pang, something sharp stabbing him. He excused himself and went over to the next table.

'Would you please stop staring like that at my companion?'

The soldier who was staring like that didn't seem to hear him, his buddy looked up in disbelief. Dieter raised his voice.

'Would you please stop staring like that at my companion?'

Now the other one looked up too.

'What the hell did you say?'

'You know very well what I said.'

'I'll look at whoever I damn well please.'

Something snapped inside Dieter, a cord; he thought, I'm sure you will, I'm sure you think you have the right; he put his hands on the back of the necks of the two Americans and slammed their faces together with a bang, turned back to Hildegunn and grabbed her hand and pulled her along and heard the instructor saying: you have four seconds, two to strike and two to get a head start, and he noticed that Hildegunn gasped as they ran past the table with the bloody, shrieking faces. Someone tried to block their way, but Dieter barged into them, bent down and ran over them, and out on the street he pulled Hildegunn after him into an entrance and up the stairs until the last pursuer had run past; then they climbed over into a back courtyard and came out on the other side of the block, they heard sirens and walked quickly with their heads lowered until Dieter said here it is, and Hildegunn merely nodded, she knew that.

While she was running she had wondered how it would be. A short time later, as she lay with him panting into her throat, she thought: Is this what it's like? She turned her face to the wall with the gray paper covered with writing and the wall with the blank gray paper and tried to think about something but couldn't. When he fell asleep, she cautiously got up and found her underwear on the floor, the white cotton underwear she had washed extra carefully the night before; she picked up the rest of her clothes and got dressed and left. One of the steps creaked, she gave a start and stumbled down the next one and a voice shouted fuck you and she smiled and thought that's right. Out on the street she bent down and removed the link of braided cotton around her right ankle and imagined her girlfriends when they noticed it. Up in his room Dieter lay in a fetal position and stared at the wall with the blank gray paper.

In 1955, 6,000 of the 110,000 German soldiers who surrendered at Stalingrad came back to Germany, after twelve and a half years as prisoners of war.

DAY SEVEN

'How did you end up here?'
The priest gave Markus an intent look. They were
sitting at the big table in the living room, eating breakfast; the
priest had wanted to delay the question until they were alone
and had time. Outside the war was building, the cannons had
advanced closer and multiplied, there were rumors that Russian
forces had been introduced on the Armenian side; if this was
true, the war would soon be over. Even with the massive use of
Afghan mercenaries, the Azeris would not be able to handle the
superior force of the Russians. The cannons had kept them
awake all night long, now the radio had announced a twenty-
four-hour curfew.

'The Russians contacted me in Baku and made me an offer.
I could stay and marry Sese if I would give them a report
every six months on what was happening in the Armenian
colony; they needed, as they said, not an informant but a
listening post.'

Markus closed his eyes and let out a long breath.

Now he had said it, now the betrayal had been put into
words.

The priest stared at his plate.

'Officially they gave me an inspector job and assigned me to
the collectivization of agriculture; I traveled around for years
and tried to calm down angry farmers, tried to make the
collective system work.'

'Is that what you call building churches, making amends?'

The priest's voice had an edge to it. Markus closed his eyes again, accepted it.

'There were lots of us who believed in collectivization, we believed that large-scale operations run by the state would increase productivity, which in turn would benefit everyone.'

'And what's your explanation for why things went wrong?'

Still a tinge of sarcasm in his voice, with emphasis on the word 'your.' Markus cringed.

'We didn't take into account the Russian mentality. It's tragic to think that the Russians have been allowed to bring a word like *socialism* into disrepute for all time. It wasn't socialism they instituted, they were simply continuing Tsarist rule, but with a Party elite on top; the Russian workers and peasants still had no value. The Russian system of serfdom is sometimes compared to the European system of tenant farmers, but that's a mistake; European tenant farmers had certain rights that were tied to their status as human beings, the very cornerstone of European human rights thinking. Russian serfs did not have the status of human beings; it's more correct to compare them to American slaves; they were things, not people; things that could be sold and pawned and loaned out; things have no rights. This attitude lived on after the overthrow of power in 1917; it has been estimated that close to twenty-four million people – or things – lost their lives under Stalin's purges and forced collectivization, either as a result of direct assaults or indirectly as the result of the starvation that followed the forced collectivization. That's what happens when people are reduced to elements in a plan, a vast plan.'

'But what led you here, to Nagorno-Karabakh?'

A wistful look came into Markus's eyes.

'I lived with Sese for many years, many good years, I learned to like her silence.'

He fell silent the way people do when there's something they don't want to say.

'When I realized that I was alone, I had to move, it was too confining in Baku. I chose Nagorno-Karabakh. There were opportunities here, I built up a business as an importer; as you know, the system did have some holes. So much has been said about human beings and free will; I believe that at the important crossroads, we choose what we have to. Dieter chose to go home because that's what he had to do, it was necessary for him; I chose to stay because that's what I had to do. Manfred was the only one who made a different choice, completely different.'

Dieter had been furious.

'Manfred, come to your senses!'

Manfred didn't reply. He sat huddled up on his mattress with a burlap sack on his knees and an odd smile on his lips. Outside the wind was tearing at the walls and coming in through the gaps in the planks, but it didn't look as if Manfred noticed; he had a faraway look in his eyes.

Markus tried to calm Dieter down.

'Leave him alone. He has to make his own choice.'

'Exile? Choose exile?'

After peace came the time of dust, dust from hundreds of thousands of people migrating eastward toward the great Asian oblivion as the dictator in the union's capital decided they would be exiled for their role in the war. Tartars, Turks, Ossetians, group after group; fifty thousand, eighty thousand, a hundred thousand, the number made no difference; roots were torn up, family ties severed, the dictator in the capital didn't care. He sat at his big desk with a map of the union and a stack of papers with the names of ethnic groups, one name on each page, he studied the eastern sections of the union and wrote place names on the pages; you fifty thousand can go there, you eighty thousand down there can take the boat across the sea to that place, you four hundred thousand over there can travel by train to that place, don't waste time thinking about coming back, you're not coming back.

As soon as the dictator had written the place names on the sheets of paper, a secretary came to get them, stamped them with the union seal and put them back on the dictator's desk, unscrewed the top of the fountain pen and held it out. The dictator took the pen, squinted a bit at the nib, at the sheet of paper, wrote his name in big, angular letters and then looked at the secretary; the exile had become fact, an entire ethnic group had been banished.

'What's her name?'

'Irkuss Utsk.'

Markus and Dieter exchanged glances and then turned away so Manfred wouldn't see them smile. Considering Manfred's trouble with names, Irkuss Utsk was probably stretching the limit of what he could handle.

All summer long Manfred had been hired out to a Tatar farmer outside of town, each day he left at sunup and came back at sundown, each day he gave his day's wages to the guards: a bag of cucumbers, a head of cabbage, a smoked fish. The first few weeks he seemed annoyed at having to give the food away, but gradually it didn't even seem to register, he had acquired a dreamy look in his eyes and was quieter than he used to be. Markus, Dieter, and Manfred had made carved chess pieces and had a tournament going with three other men in the barracks; as the summer progressed, those who played against Manfred began to complain: it had become too easy to beat him.

'How do you plan to join them?'

'I've volunteered.'

'Manfred, the call for volunteers was for prisoners with technical skills. They're not lacking for people over there, enough of them are being sent over; it's people with technical skills they need, people who can help with the building.'

'I have technical skills.'

192

Manfred held up an ID card. Markus and Dieter moved closer to read it: *Wolfgang Kölz, engineer.*

As the years passed and the prisoners were given greater freedom, those who could began practicing their former professions: dentists, doctors, teachers, photographers, type-setters. A phony ID card was no longer any problem, but there was little demand; nothing could be achieved with a phony ID. With a phony passport, escape was a possibility, but passports were too difficult to replicate; for one thing, they required special paper.

'Are you crazy?'

Dieter acted as if he didn't believe what he saw.

'Don't you realize you'll get caught?'

Manfred didn't reply, just looked at him with a glimmer of a smile in his eyes.

'Leave him alone, Dieter.'

Dieter looked at Markus and started to answer but restrained himself.

Later, after Dieter had left for kitchen duty, Markus sat down next to Manfred.

'Is she pretty?'

'Like Rachel.'

They sat in silence for a while until Manfred began to talk, in a low voice, slowly, searching, without waiting for Markus to respond. With cautious words he shaped a dream and held it out, the dream of a new start, the dream of a new life, a new place, with new voices, new spaces. But there was more than a yearning for light in Manfred's dream, there was also another kind of yearning, a yearning to leave, to let go, to be done with things.

They returned to the silence, sitting next to each other with a dream between them and knew that something was coming to an end. Manfred cautiously turned his head.

'Will you bring her my greetings?'

Markus couldn't make himself speak, but he nodded, even though an avalanche was taking place in him.

They were sitting like that when Dieter came back from kitchen duty with one last admonition:

'Manfred, when they show you to the drawing board and ask you what you can design, say something that will involve the least possible risk. Not houses, they can collapse; not machines, they can explode; not boats, they can sink; not cars, they can crash; and for God's sake not planes, Manfred, promise us you won't start designing airplanes.'

Manfred nodded, and a few days later he saluted them with three fingers to his forehead: Be prepared, scouts. Then he walked backward to the lined-up column of volunteers while he looked at Markus and Dieter; he kept on looking at them as the column marched out the gate and down toward the harbor and the Tatar camp, and he couldn't see Markus's eyes or hear Dieter's sobs any longer.

Manfred took the few strides up the gangplank to the ship. It was an old ship, heavy, somber, with patches of rust and armed soldiers everywhere. The column of volunteers snaked up the gangplank and onto the deck where the Tatars, since early that morning, had been forced together, shoved together, led in weeping groups from the camp at the harbor and driven like cattle up the gangplank; women, children, old people, goats, chickens, a biblical confusion that slowly filled the brownish-black deck of the ship until not a single plank was visible and the Tatars sat close together, packed close together, and listened to the engines warming up.

The guards at the head of the gangplank checked Manfred's name off a list and nodded curtly toward the deck, he could sit wherever he liked; along the railings stood soldiers at intervals of several meters, making sure that neither he nor the Tatars had any sudden ideas. Manfred searched, shaded his eyes with one hand, and searched; it was summer and the sun stood high, strong light and deep shadows, the same as inside him; in the shadows lurked something he was afraid of, in the light flooded relief.

Irkuss Utsk was sitting with her mother and father and little sister over by the railing, they had quickly realized that this position would give them something to lean against, something other than frightened people crammed together. Manfred saw her before she saw him, he had time to study her in profile, enjoy the sight of her before she felt his gaze and turned around. Her dark, slanted eyes squinted a little in the sharp sunlight before she saw who it was, and a kettledrum thudded inside Manfred, a pounding, thundering kettledrum when the face of Irkuss Utsk dissolved completely and released a sparkling joy and a gush of tears and a shout and a scream and a laugh.

Most of what people say to each other takes place without words, with no problem; it's when words come in that the problems arise. Manfred stood still and looked at Irkuss Utsk for a long time and let her speak her fill, with her eyes and smile and tears and her whole body; if there was anyone she wanted to see on board that ship, it was him, and now he was there, and now it's the two of us and come over and sit down here and let me hold you and you must hold me too. Manfred knew with a numb feeling in his body exactly what she was telling him; he felt the shadows inside him vanish and felt that he was speaking to her in return, in the way he stood and looked at her and held his head and smiled; Kussir Tusk, he said, here you have me, I surrender.

Carefully he balanced his way among the Tatar families crowded onto the deck, and all those who looked up saw what story he was telling; people smiled, hands reached out to support him as he stepped over shoulders and legs, supported him and caressed him cautiously, as if as an afterthought. The parents of Irkuss Utsk looked at their daughter and at Manfred and at each other, looked at each other for a long time, then they smiled; the mother moved almost imperceptibly to make room for Manfred between herself and Irkuss Utsk, the father straightened his back and glanced around with a small, proud nod of his head.

Manfred sat down as close to Irkuss Utsk as he dared. They

had looked at each other all summer, in the field, in the stable, inside at the dinner table; they had talked to each other, at first only a few simple sentences, as far as Manfred's halting Russian could go, then a few longer sentences as Manfred eventually got Markus to help him with the language.

Manfred could feel it when she looked at him; every so often that summer, it felt as if someone were tending to him, watching over him; then he would glance up and always look right into her dark eyes, at the dinner table, in the stable, or in the field. One time she had come out to the stable to call him for dinner, she stood in the narrow doorway waiting for him; as he walked past her she put her hands lightly around his waist and said: You must eat more, much more, and his hands were reaching out to grab her around the waist, but his courage failed him, because there was still a part of Manfred that was back in high school and had never been to war, an undamaged part that blushed and was shy and didn't dare.

Now Irkuss Utsk put her arm in his and smiled at him, and the deck of the ship around Manfred vanished and everything behind him vanished and whatever awaited him, he didn't care.

A nervousness spread over the deck when the gangplank was removed and the ropes loosened; women and children ran to the railing to see, and behind them came the old people, tottering; soon Irkuss Utsk and Manfred sat cut off and wedged in behind the legs of the people leaning on the railing, and Manfred thought: now or never, one, two, three, then he leaned forward and kissed Irkuss Utsk on the mouth and fearfully pulled his head back to look. She had closed her eyes and was sitting quite still. Manfred leaned forward and kissed her again, a little longer and a little more boldly this time, but not much, just a little, and she still didn't move, she kept on sitting there with her eyes closed.

Suddenly the ship started moving; the deck shook and water gushed from the propellers toward the edge of the dock. From land shouted plaintive, mournful voices, and the Tatars on board ship replied; some wept, some prayed, some shouted, and some screamed as they stared at the land that the dictator in the union's capital had decided they should never see again.

Manfred grew uneasy because of all the voices and wanted to stand up to look when he felt two hands holding him down; Irkuss Utsk put her hands at his temples and leaned over him and kissed him; Manfred felt a blush burning his face, and Irkuss Utsk kissed him more and the ship blared twice, deafening, and Manfred lost consciousness; if Irkuss Utsk hadn't been holding him tight with her hands and lips, he would have evaporated, shimmered a bit in the sea breeze, and disappeared.

The ship slowly turned its bow out to sea and the stern to the dock; the Tatars along the railing ran back to watch, as if trying to hold on with their eyes to the land from which they were banished. Only Manfred and Irkuss Utsk remained seated, not kissing now because the screen of legs was gone, but close to each other and with the secretive smile of the little sister like a shout that something had happened.

The guards drove the Tatars back along the foredeck and shoved them together again; the Tatars let themselves be driven, passive, silent, but waiting to sit down; they stood with their faces turned toward land and their backs to the horizon and looked at the land they came from getting smaller and smaller.

The parents of Irkuss Utsk came back and stood at the railing. Manfred got up and went to stand next to the father; they had stood next to each other all summer, working, now they stood next to each other and were exiled. The father turned to face him and said:

'Why did you come?'

'To be near your daughter.'

'She's only sixteen summers old.'

'I'm only eighteen. That's as old as I ever managed to get.'

The father turned around and looked out across the deck, trying to find a young man, a Tatar, to see if he had any choice; he found none, and besides, he liked Manfred.

The land, far behind them, had become a gray stripe now, featureless, monotonous; Manfred tried to find his eighteen years there but couldn't, only his years as a prisoner, but they were now smaller.

'A Tatar pays for his bride. What do you have as payment?'

The father was speaking at the land, without looking at him.

'Nothing. Do Tatars give credit?'

The father's mouth twitched. He stood there for a long time without saying a word, then he turned around and Manfred could see that he had tears in his eyes.

'If she agrees, I will give my consent. But you must uphold your honor as a man; you must teach her to read and write, and when the time is right, you must give her mother and me a motorcycle.'

Manfred looked toward the land that was now becoming an empty shadow and thought: With or without a sidecar? He turned around and looked the other way, toward the open sea and the unbroken horizon; then he sat down next to Irkuss Utsk, who had been listening to the conversation between him and her father and now rested her head on his shoulder. The father sat down next to the mother as he gave her an inquiring look; she nodded, and the little sister, who had been sitting there looking anxiously at her mother, started beaming.

The mother took out a little bread and some tomatoes, the father brought hot water from one of the three shared hotplates that were set up on deck and made tea, Manfred and Irkuss Utsk sat next to each other without saying a word, and the little sister sat arm in arm with Irkuss Utsk, her head resting against her.

It grew dark, for a moment the land behind them was a slightly blacker shadow with a few lights, then it disappeared completely, and the only lights were the stars in the sky and the ship reflected in the water. It grew calmer on deck, more subdued; children were put to bed, woolen blankets spread out. Someone had brought along a big portable radio; it was turned on and sputtered and crackled for a while until it found the dictator's voice and several people on deck yelled harshly. In the silence that followed, Irkuss Utsk whispered something in Manfred's ear, he felt her lips and her breath, and she looked at him with an inquiring smile. He shook his head, embarrassed. The mother took out two blankets and spread them out; they all pulled them up to their chins and tucked their knees under them and sat with their backs against the side of the ship and the life behind them, the starry sky overhead; the father and mother under one blanket, then Manfred where the two blankets overlapped, and then Irkuss Utsk and her little sister under the second. Manfred took out his phony ID card and borrowed a pencil, printed Sirkus Stuk in big letters on the back and showed it to Irkuss Utsk, pointing at her, at the letters, said her name, read the letters aloud, one by one. She followed along, earnestly, with a tiny worried furrow between her eyes. He put down the card and moved a little closer to her, her hand found his under the blanket, put it in her lap. He could feel something soft and pulled his little finger free to explore cautiously.

To break camp, voluntarily or not, is always a new start. When the ship, in the gray light of dawn the next morning, approached land, the Tatars broke camp on deck and prepared to start anew. They had seen the sun go down over what had been, now they saw it come up over what was to come. Some of them craned their necks in an attempt to see, others got water and cooked food with greater confidence and ease than the night before, as if they felt more at home.

Manfred had stayed awake most of the night; he was too wound up to sleep, didn't want to lose anything, miss anything. Irkuss Utsk sat with her head on his shoulder, he didn't know if she slept, now and then she turned her head and took a firmer grip on his arm. The little sister had lain down with her head in her sister's lap under the blanket, Manfred could feel her breath whenever he cautiously placed his hand on Irkuss Utsk's thigh and grabbed hold. Irkuss Utsk never took his hand away, but he only dared to squeeze it for a moment each time, afraid that she would be angry.

Next to him the mother and father slept; the mother was leaning against the side of the ship, the father with his head on her left hip, both were breathing calmly.

Gradually silence had descended over the ship, only the monotonous drone of the engines and the water surging against the bow broke the silence. Manfred tilted his head back against the side of the ship; it vibrated, as if alive, he breathed in the spicy smell of Irkuss Utsk and her little sister, let his eyes glide over the dark, slumbering bundles on the deck, and knew that he was on his way with someone toward something else. He didn't need any other words for it: he was heading away from something, something sad; and that was good. For every hour the ship sailed eastward the distance back grew longer and longer; the image of Markus and Dieter and the camp with all the others grew hazy, indistinct. A melody took shape inside him, accompanying the piston strokes of the engine, rising and falling, but this melody told no story, it described only a movement, a ballet. Manfred closed his eyes and saw a flood of yellow light; he saw three men threshing grain in a barn, three men silhouetted against the yellow sunlight that was flooding through the open door and glittering on the golden grain. They were working in time to the melody; the threshing strokes and the piston strokes in unison with a heavy, inexorable rhythm, and Manfred looked at the grain and thought: life, crops, hope.

The little sister stirred in Irkuss Utsk's lap and murmured something; cautiously he reached out his hand and gently stroked her cheek. The little sister took his hand and placed it on her mouth and nose, breathed softly on it and kissed it. Manfred waited a moment before he withdrew his hand, a smile was lit inside him; he turned toward Irkuss Utsk and saw that she was sitting with her eyes open, looking at him, secretively, and he understood that now he was on his way toward something else, something very, very different.

Manfred stood at the railing and looked toward land. Dry, yellowish-brown land slowly undulating toward the horizon. At the bow of the ship lay the harbor in Krasnovodsk, an inferno of noise and colors. Five other ships with deportees had docked during that morning alone; in a harbor shed, Russian officers were waiting with armed guards behind rickety desks; name, place of birth, name of parents. The officers meticulously wrote down everything in oblong record books with blue paper, the deportees waited patiently in the line, which stretched from the harbor shed to the gangplank. One ship after another was emptied, now and then the officers would send one of the guards for tea, smoke a cigarette and drink a glass of tea, without paying any attention to the line of people standing a meter away from them.

Manfred breathed in the smoke from the cigarettes and the smell of sweat from those standing around him, hour after hour he breathed in the smoke from the cigarettes and the smell of sweat from those standing around him, and he knew that here only one thing was important. Don't draw attention to yourself. Everyone in line knew this, even the smallest children seemed to have understood; they didn't cry, didn't play, didn't fuss; a Russian officer is capricious by nature, an irritated Russian officer is unpredictable.

Irkuss Utsk stood next to him, with one hand on his shoulder for support. Her parents stood in front of them, her little sister next to them. Occasionally Manfred would put his arm around her shoulders, then she would press closer and stand very still. Manfred inhaled her scent, closed his eyes and savored the fragrance of innocence, he could feel the pulse in Irkuss Utsk's hand on his shoulder, could feel her breath close to his ear.

The ship voyage had changed something, they seemed to

consider him one of them now, someone it might be good to have along in what lay ahead; the father talked to him as to a son-in-law, the mother said the two of you when she spoke to her daughter, the two of you she said and looked at both of them, sometimes at the little sister as well; when the mother took out a water bottle, she let the father drink first, but when he was done, she handed the bottle to Manfred, and once she moistened a cloth and wiped his forehead in the suffocating heat in the harbor shed.

'Ramp two five four,' said the officer and stamped their papers without looking up.

Manfred took the lead as they came out of the harbor shed, he was the only one of them who could read such a difficult number; the mother and father and two daughters followed him, obediently; behind them came a stream of other Tatars.

The buildings at the harbor had tall windows with bars, the walls were painted in dark colors, green, brown, blue, with carved dragon heads on the ridgepoles. Between the harbor and the town, barbed wire had been unrolled in tight coils the height of a man; at intervals of several meters stood armed soldiers, stationed there by the Almighty, thought Manfred, to guard the gate, the holy gate to the Siberian tundra and the Mongolian desert and the Asian plain, no admittance to intruders, trespassers will be fined, kindly stay off this continent, new grass. Manfred smiled; when we reach the other side of the barbed wire, we'll leave this world behind, he thought, then we'll no longer exist, and the soldiers are there to make sure we don't disappear at the wrong place, because no one had that much ill will toward his fellow human beings; it's all well and good to deport people to eternal oblivion, but it's a human right to be forgotten in the right place, not the wrong place, a fundamental human right, and suddenly Manfred noticed that he missed Markus and his wordplay, but God, he thought quietly, if this means that I'll be able to sleep at night, not all the time, but a few nights or so, if from time to time I'll have some respite from the nightmares, then I'm ready to pay the price. He felt something stirring inside him at the thought, turned to face Irkuss Utsk and her little sister and was about to warm himself on a different thought when a piercing shriek suddenly woke him.

'Traitor! Filthy, miserable traitor! May you rot in a pool of sulfur with those two stinking garlic whores of yours!'

Manfred turned around. A group of people had taken up position outside the barbed wire, ten or fifteen of them, women and men. They were not the only ones; small clusters of spectators stood here and there behind the guards and followed the registration and unloading of the deportees with silent eyes. But the group the scream came from was different, the men and women were lighter-skinned and older, many of them were completely gray, and their clothes were different; the women wore long black dresses with lace collars, the men wore dark suits with ties and stiff collars; Manfred had the feeling he was opening an old photo album.

'Wretches! The likes of you should be exterminated!'

It was the same voice shouting, a thin, slightly cracking woman's voice, on the verge of tears.

'A curse upon those Mongolian whores of yours!'

Manfred glanced swiftly at Irkuss Utsk and her sister, embarrassed; they stared back, uncomprehending. He looked at the old woman, she had collapsed into the arms of another woman and was weeping in long drawn-out, painful sobs. It wasn't until then that Manfred realized she had shouted at him in German. Two guards walked toward the group, a tall, elderly man came to meet them, stopped in front of them, argued, pointed at Manfred, at the group. The guards turned around and looked at Manfred, said a few words to each other and nodded. The elderly man thanked them and stepped toward the barbed wire with his eyes boring into Manfred, walked stiff-legged, his back erect, his gaze penetrating. Manfred put down the suitcases he was carrying and went

203

to meet him, a guard shouted something after him but he paid no attention, there was something in the eyes of the elderly man that drew him forward.

They met in the middle of the square in front of the railroad platform, a dusty square divided by barbed wire stretched between the wall of the harbor shed and a post. The barbed wire was head high and threw shadows onto the face of the elderly man; it looked as if he were divided up into several layers. Between the layers glowed a pair of bloodshot eyes.

'German.'

It wasn't a question, the man was making a statement. Manfred paused for a moment before he replied:

'You too?'

The man didn't answer, merely leaned toward the barbed wire and whispered:

'I'm terribly sorry for my wife's shouting but she's out of her head, terribly sorry.'

He glanced over his shoulder to see if the woman was watching him, listening to what he said.

'Are you German?'

'We're not German, we're Volga German,' said the man proudly, a bit offended.

'Our forefathers came to the Volga in 1764, invited by the Tsar, eight thousand families in two years; they settled along the eastern shore, down by the riverbed, possibly the best and most fertile agricultural area around. They were granted rights, they were granted privileges and quickly became very, very prosperous, they were German and knew how to work hard.'

The man clicked his heels together lightly and imperceptibly bowed with his whole body, a salute to his Calvinistic forefathers, a German never works less than ten hours a day.

'We survived the previous war as a society, the Russians around us managed to keep us separate from you. We survived 1917 as a society, the new rulers were more interested in having us with them than against them. They gave us the status of an independent municipality in 1919, five years later we became an independent republic. But this war we did not survive; during the first year of the war the republic was dissolved and we were deported, every one of us, women and children, young and old. It's understandable that feelings can take the upper hand at the sight of a German soldier.'

'I'm sorry.'

'Thank you.'

'How many were you?'

'Four hundred thousand. Four hundred thousand; an entire society with schools and churches and a university, Volga German; an entire culture with poets and composers and painters, Volga German; an entire economy with agriculture, tradesmen, and industry, Volga German; now we're spread to the winds, the Volga German is no more, it's a memory, an episode in history.'

The man bowed again, stiffly, obliquely.

'It's understandable that feelings can take the upper hand at the sight of a German soldier.'

Then he turned around and went back to the others. His black suit had a rip in the seam under his left arm, the heels of his shiny, polished shoes were worn all the way down. Manfred shouted after him:

'According to what we heard, all the Volga Germans were sent as far east as it was possible to go; why were you allowed to stay here, only two days away by boat?'

The man stopped, turned around, and came back.

'The Russians have put us in charge of the unloading and onward transportation of the deportees. The Kazakhs and Uzbeks who live here aren't especially good at such matters, it's not in their nature to administrate.'

'How do they keep you here?'

A long pause.

'For each mistake we make, our children are moved a hundred *verst* farther east.'

The man turned around and left. Manfred called after him:

'How much is a *verst*?'

'A little over a thousand meters.'

The man looked ashamed, as if he had been caught in a slip of the tongue.

On the train ramp more soldiers were waiting, but with high cheekbones and slanted eyes now, they nodded expressionlessly at the rows of freight cars.

Manfred turned around and looked toward the harbor before he stepped into the car, looked toward the ship and the sea beyond, and the land on the other side of the sea and the land that lay even farther away; he felt a strange sense of relief, as if something difficult had been taken from him, a choice.

They traveled inland the way people travel inland into their own future after a sudden break, with a growing feeling of unreality; everything they encountered was foreign and yet theirs. They stood for hours looking out the window as the train snaked toward the horizon, they tried to grab the horizon with their eyes and pull it closer so they could get to know it, but it always held them at a distance. They studied the houses and the people and the clothing and the landscape and thought: Here we will stay for the rest of our lives, and something opened inside them, something fluid.

They came to new towns and new stations, their papers were stamped and the soldiers loaded them onto new trains, in new freight cars. They learned that in this part of the world distance is not measured in *verst* or kilometers or miles, but in days, days and weeks, and they knew that in this part of the world time is also measured in a different way: not in weeks or months or years, but in generations, and they understood without words that this put their lives and their fate in a different perspective.

No one told them when they had arrived, but they understood it when an officer said: You can settle in this valley here. They looked around, looked at the high mountains and the green valley and the glittering river, and for the first time on the journey they smiled; the dictator in the capital had wanted to deport them to the ends of the earth, it must be a bitter thought for him to know that it happened to be one of the most beautiful places in the union.

Irkuss Utsk and her sister and her mother looked at the father, he was the one who should decide, and he looked at Manfred:

'You build for yourselves over there, and I'll build for ourselves here.'

Manfred nodded and smiled and the little sister gave the father an inquiring look and he nodded and a shout raced across the sky.

Manfred looked around and saw in a flash all the possibilities, all the choices; he saw them bartering for seeds and livestock and slowly building up a farm, he saw himself in an office in the town they had traveled through, and he heard the shrieks of the newborn baby, not far off.

Manfred studied the bridge he had designed, sat on a rock with the warm evening sun on his back and studied the bridge he had designed, his first bridge. A fly tried to annoy him but had to give up and fly off, a man does not voluntarily let go of his first bridge.

The bridge spanned a quiet river in the middle of a quiet plain, there were no houses nearby, no trees, only the winding road that grew out of the horizon, crossed the bridge, and disappeared over the plain. Not a car in sight, not a tractor, not a horse, not an ox, not a soul. Manfred had sometimes asked himself who would actually use the bridge and what the purpose of it was, but it didn't worry him; history had chosen him to design this bridge and that was enough for him; others would have to take responsibility for its use. 'A bridge,' he said and straightened his back the way his history teacher had always done whenever he wanted to say something important, as he always did: 'A bridge is a goal unto itself, not a means to something else; a bridge binds together what was previously separate, opens up what was previously closed; a bridge is equally valuable, whether it is used or not, because it stands for the possible.'

Manfred got up from the rock and took a good grip on his right lapel with his right hand, rocked back and forth on his feet, and raised his voice into a nasal falsetto, the way the history teacher always did when he was especially eager, as he always was.

'Yes, life itself, dear friends, is a bridge, a bridge that carries us from non-existence to birth, from birth to childhood, from childhood to youth, from youth to old age, from old age to death; we must all cross the bridge of life.'

Something sparkled inside Manfred, something light and warm; he had loved the surging speeches of his history teacher, they were completely without basis in reality. He turned around and climbed up onto the rock, cleared his throat, and continued.

'What is a life without bridges, dear friends? It's a life without connections. And what is a life without connections? It's a life without continuity. And what is a life without continuity? It's a life without meaning. And what is a life without meaning? That, dear friends, is a meaningless life.'

Manfred stopped and stared. Far away, on the other side of the bridge, a figure came into view, a dot on the horizon. Manfred held his breath, the figure shimmered a bit in the afternoon sun, quivered a bit, came closer. It was a man. Slowly he grew bigger along the road, wearing a big peaked cap and worn clothing, approaching the bridge wearing a tattered, thick sweater and high boots, a streak of tobacco spittle at the corner of his mouth, unshaven.

The man stopped at the bridge and examined it. He studied it for a long time, section by section; first the ramp, then the arch, then the railing; then he scraped one boot on the ramp, spat, and said:

'Shitty bridge.'

Manfred shook his head, couldn't believe his ears at first, then he ran down to the bridge and stopped on his side of it, stared at the man on the opposite side, and said in a low, menacing voice:

'What was that you said?'

The man didn't reply, just stubbornly stared back. He had deep furrows in his face and steel in his eyes. Manfred raised his voice:

'Say it again, you damned Kirgisian wimp.'

Manfred tore off his jacket and began rolling up his sleeves, the man on the other side did the same. Manfred shadowboxed at the air, the man on the other side did the same. Like two gamecocks they stood on opposite sides of the bridge, ready to fly at each other, when the road behind Manfred suddenly erupted in song and laughter and music, an inferno of sound in the silence. Manfred turned around, a convoy of trucks full of people was on its way toward the bridge and the dedication ceremony. He put his jacket back on and sent a reluctant glance across to the other side, the man did the same.

A military band was in the first truck, they were playing a grand march as the vehicle veered in front of the bridge and stopped. On the truck behind stood a men's choir, also from the military; the singers were already warming up, they sang along with the march played by the military band as they jumped down from the truck bed, smiling. The next truck carried the inevitable Cossack dancers, then came a truck with Party dignitaries and their wives: Chairman and Mrs. Petrov, First Party Secretary and Mrs. Sevodanin, Second Party Secretary and Mrs. Dosvidankus; the men in dark suits and hats that were too small, the women in long, light dresses, holding parasols. On the next five trucks, festively dressed spectators stood crowded together, with flags and noisemakers and hip-hip-hurrah.

The spectators and dignitaries and the dignitaries' wives and the singers and corps musicians streamed toward the bridge as they shattered the silence. It was a beautiful day with dazzling sunshine and clear sky and chilled white wine in slender glasses, and in the middle of the bridge a white ribbon waited patiently to be cut. Manfred stood there with a warm feeling inside and watched his first bridge fill up with people, and the feeling grew warmer as the bridge continued to fill up with people, and something cool began tugging at him inside as the bridge continued to fill up with people and he thought: Good Lord, how many of them are there, anyway?

It was a picture unlike any other, a picture that would be handed down to future generations, but right then and there no one was aware of that; a bridge four meters wide and twenty meters long with an arch made of natural stone and cement and a meter-high steel railing on either side, split across the middle by a white silk ribbon; crammed with festively clad people on one half and a man in a big peaked cap and tattered sweater on the other.

The men's choir took up their position and began to sing, a lovely, gliding antiphony between a solitary soprano and a full complement of bass voices; the soprano rose, fragile and timid, toward the sky and was brought back down again by the bass voices, confident, strong; they hoisted themselves up and perched on the railing with the tenors in front of them and the solitary soprano off to the left, and the spectators had dreamy looks in their eyes, vulnerable looks, as if the song touched something they had tried to forget.

The band took over; a low, gentle melody with a great deal of euphonium and French horn, splendid round tones and a cautious crescendo that smiled and nodded to the flags and the spectators and the bridge and the day; hip-hip-hurrah, at last.

Someone stepped forward to the microphone that had been set up and said one two three, one two three, ladies and gentlemen, our honored and dearly beloved chairman, Genadir Petrov, and Petrov walked to the microphone, smiling, with several sheets of paper in his hand as the spectators applauded and

Mrs. Petrov gazed at him proudly from the wicker chairs that had been brought for her and the other two dignitaries' wives.

'Comrades,' said Chairman Petrov as the bridge began to tilt.

'Comrades, on this great day,' and the bridge dipped on the side where the men's choir stood, with the bass singers sitting on the railing, and a woman screamed among the spectators.

'Comrades, on this great day in the history of the revolution,' and the bridge tilted more and the band leader and the choir leader waved their hands to keep their balance, and the band and the choir misunderstood and thought this was a signal to begin, and the band launched into the national anthem while the choir started humming a beautiful hymn.

'Comrades, on this great day in the history of the revolution it is the collective team spirit that we celebrate,' and the bridge tilted even more, almost standing on its side now, and Mrs. Petrov screamed as the chairs holding her and the two other dignitaries' wives slid across toward the men's choir, and the brass band slid, and the spectators slid, and the Cossack dancers slid, squatting down with their right legs thrust out in front of them and their arms crossed on their chests; Chairman Petrov held onto the microphone, which was fastened to the upper railing, while First Party Secretary Sevodanin and Second Party Secretary Dosvidankus slid along with their wives.

The bridge tilted a little more and stood on its side, proud, beautiful; the bass singers on the lower railing lost their balance and fell, singing, the tenors kept on singing too, but uncertainly, as if the bottom of the song was missing, and besides, they were a little disconcerted when the bass singers landed in the water with a splash. The military band was better disciplined, they all continued to play until they landed in the water, and not one of them let go of his instrument; a musician goes down with his horn. Now the Cossack dancers and spectators and dignitaries with their wives lay in a festively clad heap against the lower railing, and someone stuck out a flag and shouted hip, hip, but was hushed by several others, and suddenly Mrs. Dosvidankus wriggled free of the heap and fell and ended up hanging by her left foot caught between the bars of the railing, with her dress over her head, and a gasp went through the spectators. Second Party Secretary Dosvidankus bellowed and reached down and with a firm grip, pulled up Mrs. Dosvidankus.

Manfred stood with a look of disbelief and saw the end of his career as an engineer come crawling toward him; first the Party dignitaries with their wives and parasols, then the leaders of the band and choir with their batons between their teeth, then the Cossack dancers, who clicked their heels together for every step forward they crawled, then the tenors and altos and sopranos in the choir, and finally the spectators; all of them laboriously crawling along the twisted railing toward land and the man who had designed the bridge. Manfred's eyes got bigger and bigger in their eyes for every meter they approached. There's something about people crawling on all fours, especially when there are lots of them, it's not always easy to take them seriously, and suddenly laughter spurted out of Manfred. He threw back his head and laughed, surrendered to it completely, and a deep snarl rose up from the crawling crowd, low, dangerous, and from the river bubbled up scraps of the national anthem and men's bass voices, and the crowd reached land and kept on crawling on all fours toward Manfred.

Manfred fell over with laughter, he lay with his hands covering his face and howled, and that would have been the last thing he did if the wives of the Party dignitaries hadn't crawled up onto the hems of their long dresses and toppled over, falling flat on their faces and hurling curses at their husbands because they didn't come to their aid quickly enough. Behind them the crawling crowd came to an uncertain halt; it has never been wise for rank-and-file soldiers or civilians to crawl past Party dignitaries who are down on all fours, wiping the mud from the faces of their weeping wives; and it gave Manfred the time he needed to get to his feet and take off from the bridge and the river, toward town, shaking with laughter.

On the other side of the bridge stood the man with the big peaked cap and the tattered sweater, regarding the scene on the opposite side. He shoved back his cap, looked at the bridge, and spat again:

'Shitty bridge.'

Then he turned on his heel and disappeared in the direction he had come.

Manfred folded up the letter he had written and put it in the envelope they had given him; he placed it on the table, leaning it against the candle, and sat there looking at it. It was like an icon, an image that told a story, just as the candle behind it did. In the beginning they had refused to give him any light; he woke up with the sunlight that came through his cell window and went to bed with the darkness. Then one day a guard had slipped him a candle and matches and merely nodded, without saying a word, and later another guard brought him paper and a pencil and said: 'Can you design a bridge from here to eternity that the Russians can cross to leave here?' and a smile glinted in his slanted eyes.

In the daytime they put him to work digging ditches, which he then had to fill back up, but they let him take longer and longer breaks and spent more and more time keeping him company; in the evening came the sound of drums and the scent of Irkuss Utsk through his cell window. He sensed her as a movement, something that filled the room, and he knew that as long as the shaman's drums sounded, she would be with him; he breathed in the fragrance of her hair, her skin, her secret, and one night she brought with her someone else, someone who was also stripped naked, and with cautious fingers Manfred stroked them both at once, looked into deep, dark eyes, and saw, far down, far ahead, a long table in the courtyard of a farm with food and wine and the first colors of fall on the courtyard tree; he saw himself standing with a glass in his hand, holding

213

a speech, he heard laughter from children crowding around the table, and from the road came the sound of a motor, first from one motorcycle, then from two.

Thea felt someone's gaze on the back of her neck. She lifted her face from her clasped hands and looked up. On the altar burned two white tapers with steady flames; behind them the cross cast long shadows on the whitewashed convent wall.

The prioress was standing in the doorway to the chapel. There was something in her expression, something out of the ordinary, as if someone had touched her and confused her. Thea gave her an inquiring look, the prioress met her glance and held it. In the next room they could hear the other nuns singing, a low, mournful hymn; the women of the convent had renounced all speech for good – the only words we need are already written down, in the great book, all other words are the work of the evil one – but they had given themselves permission to sing, to utter praises in music.

The prioress stuck her hand inside her black robe and took out something, handing it to Thea with a slightly reproachful glance.

She gasped for breath and looked at the letter the prioress was holding, looked at the letter and met the eyes, which said: We do not encourage contact with those outside, it takes our thoughts away from Him, but Thea had seen the name on the envelope and heard a roar start up, far away, deafening, paralyzing.

Back in her cell she knelt down and said a prayer for her brother before she dared open his letter, didn't know exactly what to pray: that he was alive – he was – that he wasn't wounded, crippled, but she didn't think this thought to the end, they had gradually heard enough about the campaign in the east to understand that they would be wounded, every one of them, by what they had taken part in, and she ended up praying that he would be allowed to keep his music; please, let him keep his music, and she opened the letter, cautiously, hesitantly.

Dear sister,

The same handwriting, the same rather clumsy letters, as if he wasn't used to writing and was surprised at every letter he managed to shape.

Dear sister, I hope you are well and that Father and Mother are both well . . .

Let us hope so, Manfred, for they are no longer here.

. . . it has been a long time since we last saw each other, and much has happened, more than one letter can contain, and the censor will not let us write more than ten lines, if only I could play for you, I could tell you the story; I have moved to a country called . . .

Blacked out by the censor . . .

. . . it is so beautiful here, with tall mountains and swift rivers and air that is so clean and fresh that you can drink it; I have a sweetheart named . . .

Blacked out by the censor . . .

. . . when I have saved up enough money for a motorcycle I will marry her, and when I have saved up enough money for another motorcycle I will marry her little sister too; in the meantime . . .

Blacked out by the censor, Blacked out by the censor, Blacked out by the censor.

. . . they are very free in that way. I am happy living with them, there is a low, calm song coming from them that I like. What about you, Thea?

Thea lowered the letter, her eyes brimmed over, inside she was singing and screaming at the same time. She lay down on the pallet, jumped up, knelt down and said a prayer of thanks, back to the pallet, one arm over her eyes, and then she let the tears come, in shuddering, painful gasps; that's how she lay

215

when the prioress came in and took the letter away from her, read it, and looked at her with ominous silence: Is it Christ or your brother you have wed? Then she took the letter with her and left.

Thea didn't move when the cell door shut behind the prioress, she lay there with her arm over her eyes, the tears running down both cheeks and into her ears; it reminded her of her childhood. She smiled, took her arm away from her eyes, sat up on the pallet and looked around the cell. A window with bars high up on the wall, too high to see out, a table and a chair, a washstand with a washbasin. On the table lay a Bible, she went to get it and then sat back down on the pallet, paging back and forth through the book and thinking: Where, in all these words, these words that are all the words we need, where in these words does it say in which country men have to have motorcycles in order to marry? She set the Bible down and thought: If I just travel long enough, sooner or later I'll find it, I can just follow the sound, the land of thousands of motorcycles, and if there's something about those motorcycles, if they do it on motorcycles, then I can just close my eyes and settle for the sound, the sounds.

God forgive me, forgive me.

But Thea's shouts for forgiveness came from far away, faintly, and her nipples had turned hard and she whispered: Manfred, how do you plan to do it with two at once? I mean motorcycles. And a sudden crash thundered in the convent walls and from the keyhole the prioress screamed.

DAY EIGHT

'Have you heard about the fire worshippers of Baku?'
The priest didn't have time to answer before a shout came from the stairwell:

'Wait! I've got to hear this one.'

It was the nurse, she had come to check on them.

There was a cease-fire now, thirty-five thousand killed and a million refugees had forced the sides to the negotiating table; neither of them could afford a lengthy war anyway. With the cease-fire the nationalistic cries had also been silenced, at least for a while, and in the silence the true sound of the war could be heard. Markus and the priest listened to the news on the radio every hour, waiting and waiting, and in the meantime they exchanged stories.

'A short distance outside Baku there's a temple made of yellow sandstone; walls four meters high surround a temple courtyard, as big as a handball court, with an altar tower in the middle. On the altar burns a fire, in a hollow in the ground a little farther away burns another one. On each corner of the tower roof burn smaller flames, visible for miles around. The temple courtyard is hexagonal with Oriental arched doorways in the thick wall, twenty-six in all. The doors lead to small cells; the wall is at least five meters thick, more than thick enough. Above the gate stands a tower with a tower room, which has three windows facing east and three facing west, two facing north and two facing south.'

Markus spoke in a low voice, for a religious calm hovered

over the temple courtyard, an intimidating silence over the flame flaring up from the altar.

'This place is just as sacred for the Zoroastrians as Mecca is for the Muslims and Jerusalem is for the Jews and Christians. For over two thousand years they made pilgrimages here to see the eternal fire, in many cases to die beside it.

'The place was first mentioned by the Byzantine historians, they think it was discovered about three hundred years before the beginning of the Christian era. It's likely they were mistaken, historians frequently are, it's likely that Zarathustra lived and worked here at least six hundred years before Christ; but it's possible that this too is wrong, no one knows with certainty when or where Zarathustra lived.

'The fire comes from natural gas issuing freely from a crack in the ground, it has probably been burning for thousands of years. German aviators used the fire as a navigational marker in the campaign I took part in, it turned out to be impossible for the people who lived there to extinguish it and black out the area.

'A thousand years ago the trade caravans between east and west used the fire as a sign: when the caravans from the east saw it, they knew they had reached their destination; when the caravans from the west lost sight of it, they knew they were on their own.

'The temple itself was built in the thirteenth century, first as an inn by merchants from India, practical men who saw the value of a heated place to stay after weeks and months on camelback.

'Gradually, however, as news of the eternal fire seeped southward and into the Indian subcontinent, pilgrims began to arrive, ordinary fire worshippers like you and me, with no other goal in their lives than to be united with the eternal fire, that which comes out of the sacred eye.

'The most ordinary of them all was Patel Patel, a failed Indian fakir. He had tried to sit on a pole in the desert but couldn't keep his balance and fell off; he had tried to crawl into a jar like a contortionist with his thighs pressed to his torso and his calves folded behind his head and his arms under his groin and his hands stuck into his rectum, but he couldn't do that either; the jar tipped over and tumbled down the incline of the village marketplace and into a Buddhist convent, where the nuns had just sat down in the convent garden to meditate together, and the brown jar with Patel Patel inside came rolling in and struck the statue of Buddha which the nuns were sitting around, meditating. Patel Patel fell out and the nuns screamed in terror and broke their vow of silence; twenty-two years without a word, half a year away from having their names carved into the convent wall, if it hadn't been for Patel Patel.

'Patel Patel's life was never the same; whenever he showed himself in the village he seemed to hear whispering from inside the gates, and sometimes when he walked past children playing, he thought he heard a whistling sound. Being a fakir is difficult enough, being a failed fakir is almost impossible; that's why Patel Patel was happy when someone suggested that he should join a caravan making a pilgrimage to the eternal fire in the land far, far away to the north.'

Markus looked at the caravan riding into the temple courtyard; there were at least fifty camels, fully loaded with woven saddlebags and plaited baskets with lids. The camel drivers walked alongside the camels; twenty-five lean, sinewy men wearing black desert garb, with steel in their eyes. Behind the camels trotted the camel boys with close-shaven heads and big dark eyes. At the very end came Patel Patel wearing a white loincloth, his torso bare, and with a white 'Y' painted from his nose and out to the side of each eyebrow. He had a peculiar, halting gait, as if he couldn't make up his mind whether to walk or run, stand still or sit down, and his long gray hair fluttered up and down with every hop he took into the temple courtyard.

'The camel drivers muttered at the camels, they stopped; the camel drivers poked them in the sides, they knelt. After that the camel drivers walked through one of the cell doors in the wall and left the unloading, watering, and foddering to the camel boys.

'Evening darkness had long ago descended on the temple courtyard, a velvety soft, gentle evening darkness, full of stars and sounds and smells. Around the altar with the eternal fire knelt twenty or so men with their faces turned toward the fire; now and then they bowed down and pressed their foreheads to the ground, but for the most part they stared at the flame as if hypnotized. All of them wore only loincloths, tattered, filthy loincloths; all of them were gaunt, with long gray beards and matted gray hair. One of them had heavy chains hanging around his neck, they jangled every time he bowed to the ground. Another one had slashed himself all over his body; blood trickled from the striped wounds.

'At the gateway to the temple courtyard stood two men, each of them striking a mallet against a gong, two meters in diameter. In the fire pit a short distance from the altar two corpses had been placed for cremation, wrapped in reed mats; the sweetish smell of scorched human flesh blended with the smell of spices and food and tea and sweaty, unwashed bodies.

'Patel Patel now stood in the middle of the temple courtyard; he stood as if in a trance, with his eyes fixed on the eternal fire. Slowly he began to unwind his loincloth until he stood there naked; the two men began striking the gong more vigorously, and the two corpses in the fire pit began to burn more briskly.

'Something spread over the temple courtyard, something that flapped against the wall and cast a shadow over the flames; the camel drivers, holding tea glasses in their hands, came out of the doorway through which they had disappeared, the camel boys turned their big dark eyes toward Patel Patel, the fire worshippers turned to face him, from a concealed door came two female temple dancers with big naked bellies; they straightened their hair and looked at the Indian fakir with heavy, moist eyes.

220

'Patel Patel may have registered all the attention, he may have registered that the scene was his and that history lay at his feet, but if he did, he didn't let on; slowly, almost regally, he walked up the steps to the altar and fell to his knees before the fire; he kissed the stones for a long time and then stood up like a man with a calling. All eyes in the temple courtyard were now turned toward the naked fakir, a gasp raced like a ripple over the spectators when he took two steps forward and sat down astride the altar with the eternal fire.

'The fire went out where Patel Patel was sitting; there was a crackling from scorched flesh and the reek of black smoke, but Patel Patel stayed where he was; in front of him and behind him the eternal fire kept burning, from below the natural gas streamed into him. He pressed his nostrils closed with one hand and clamped the other around the tip of his penis; two fire worshippers understood what he was up to and came running forward, one of them stopped up his ears with his fingers, the other sealed up his mouth with his hand.

'Patel Patel grew and grew; like a balloon he let himself be inflated by the natural gas, laboriously, slowly, until the skin of his gaunt body was stretched to the breaking point, and his head was transformed to a peg on top of a mighty barrel. The men at the gong put down their mallets and took out their drums, they began drumming a low, insistent beat; the temple dancers ran out to the middle of the square, tore off their clothes, and began dancing; with big naked bellies and even bigger naked rumps they danced toward the audience, shaking in time to the drums. The fire worshippers covered their faces and wept, the camel drivers stomped their feet, the camel boys fell to their knees shrieking, with both hands at their groins.

'Patel Patel turned around with a smile, as if to thank them, then turned away again; a modest man. He looked down at his hand clamped around the tip of his penis and loosened his grip a little, a thin jet of natural gas streamed out, he loosened it more, the jet grew bigger and stronger. Patel Patel aimed the jet at the fire in front of him, calmly, with dignity, like a king with his scepter. The jet ignited and shot like a pillar of fire out into the temple courtyard, ten meters long; Patel Patel let it sweep over the spectators, they threw themselves in terror to the ground, he aimed it at the two temple dancers and lit them on fire from behind, they screamed; the camel drivers came running to put it out, the temple dancers screamed again. Patel Patel aimed the jet at the dark evening sky and lit a new star, then he tore himself away from the two fire worshippers who were still holding him by the mouth and ears and did a cartwheel over the eternal fire on the altar; a clumsy, jolting Patel Patel cartwheel, but a cartwheel all the same, and very effective; jets of fire shot out of his ears and nose and mouth, and from his backside, stronger than the others, strong enough to send Patel Patel like a sputtering rocket around the temple courtyard among the howling spectators.

'Patel Patel spun back and forth between the temple walls for a while before he whirled up the steps to the altar and stopped in front of the eternal fire.'

Markus paused and smiled.

'He must have been quite a sight: A skeletal old man with gray hair and beard and fire spurting out of every orifice of his body, and a temple courtyard full of terrified spectators who devoutly took each other by the hand and watched Patel Patel perform the masterpiece above all other masterpieces in the history of Indian fakirs; slowly and solemnly he bent forward with his mouth open wide until he had swallowed the flame from his own penis and then the penis itself and then his testicles, and the spectators gasped when Patel Patel began rotating and more and more of him disappeared into his mouth; his backside vanished, and his knees and his feet waved goodbye, and his diaphragm and his chest and his neck; Patel Patel even managed to turn and wink at the spectators before his head disappeared inside his own mouth and dissolved in a puff of air, and the blazing drops rained down over the eternal fire and someone pointed toward the altar and shouted: Look! and they saw one of Patel Patel's eyes in flames, smiling, and someone pointed toward the cremation pit and shouted: Look! and they saw Patel Patel's other eye in flames there, angry, and from that moment on Patel Patel became renowned in history as the fire son: half fire and half human, who had come down to earth to bring the passions of human life – love and hatred – back home to the eternal fire, where they shall burn forever.'

The nurse stood up in the silence that followed and left the room. They could hear her running water in the next room. She came back with a full zinc bucket, which she dumped over Markus's head; then she turned on her heel and left.

Markus sat there for a moment, listening to the water running onto the floor from his head and shoulders and arms and lap before he took off the bucket and continued:

'I began to take an interest in the Zoroastrians, I was curious about their ancient *haoma* cult. An old Armenian had connections, he got hold of some *haoma* juice.'

Markus drank from the cup held out to him. It tasted bitter. He swallowed, gave the old man an inquiring glance.

'Wait.'

Markus waited. He listened to the bird song outside the window, looked at the sunlight flooding in, smelled the odor of age and death in the room.

'Wait.'

Markus waited. He didn't know what he was supposed to be waiting for, he didn't know whether he would notice when it came, he didn't know whether he would notice if it didn't come.

He had almost no experience with intoxication. Sometimes he and Erich Maria would stop in at Händel's on their way home from training on Fridays, but just to stop by; Rachel didn't like him to go there:

'There's no reason to go there, Markus.'

Markus listened to her voice and smiled. For Rachel, life was like that; either there was a reason to do something, and so it had to be done, or there was no reason to do something, and so you refrained.

No reason to go to Händel's? His friends were there, with a piano, songs and laughter, faces shining with joy behind their steins. Once when he was there Dieter came over and wanted to talk about Rachel; Dieter had stuck the thumbs of both hands under the bandolier of his uniform and talked about Rachel while a flock of white birds slowly rose up and flew soundlessly toward the sky, higher and higher, and Markus didn't realize that he was flying with them until he saw Dieter far below, angrily calling after him; he had taken his hands out of his bandolier and was shaking his fist at him, and out of his clenched fingers grew orchids.

Markus climbed higher, it grew brighter, warmer. The warmth filled him, spreading from his groin, upward; the light fell on him, reaching through his outer layer, downward, until he smiled and hugged himself, warm, open; launched himself forward in a long, lazy dive, rolled over, and flew back toward the flock up there with his hair flowing, and the other birds said:

'You can leave now.'

Markus looked at the old Armenian.

'Leave now?'

The Armenian nodded and gave him another cup. Markus gave it a puzzled look, the old man nodded again.

'*Haoma* has three stages. The first is the rejuvenation stage, in which life supplants death, joy supplants sorrow. It was this effect that originally prompted the Aryans to start drinking *haoma* nectar six thousand years ago. Life must have been frustrating back then, cold and dark and lonely.'

224

Markus accepted the cup and drank. It tasted just as acrid and bitter, but this time he was prepared. He put down the empty cup and closed his eyes.

'Markus, come here.'

Rachel was tugging on his arm.

'And you, Erich Maria, you stay here.'

Markus smiled behind his closed eyes; when Rachel made up her mind about something, she made up her mind. One day at school she made up her mind to kiss Markus, the first time for both of them, and arranged it with a firm hand; Erich Maria stood guard, Markus came over to an empty bay window, soft lips pressed tentatively to his, stayed there, her body closer and closer until what was surging inside Markus touched the inside of his skin and he shouted to let it out, and Erich Maria shouted that someone was coming, and someone shouted behind a locked door, and he stormed across the marble floor with four horses galloping on each side, up the stairs with suits of armor on every landing and toward the locked door where the shouts were coming from, Rachel's shouts. Uniform pants were hanging on the door, olive green; in front of the door sat a wild boar, staring at Markus with evil eyes; evil, piercing eyes, deep-set. Markus grabbed the head of the wild boar and forced open its mouth, ripped the upper and lower sections of the jaw apart with a jerk so the entire head split and gleaming black snakes poured out. Markus stomped on the snakes and for every one he killed, Rachel screamed; Markus gathered himself for a leap, a wind gusted up, blowing behind him, with him; Markus leaned sideways, backward, and attacked; bashed in the wall with the locked door and bellowing swept into the room with the soldiers and Rachel, thundering toward them like an avalanche; the soldiers held up their arms, tried to protect themselves; Markus rolled over them and crushed them and lifted up Rachel all in one movement; feather-light, naked Rachel with skin that grew warmer and warmer for each light-year he flew out into the universe, naked Rachel who put her arms around his shoulders and kissed him and whispered: Markus, you must go on.

Markus opened his eyes. The old Armenian had fallen asleep. Markus lightly touched his cheek, the Armenian opened his eyes and smiled.

'The vitality stage, in which a victorious wind blows and everything swells; not until this stage is the cult formed, not until this stage does worship come in. The first stage is enjoyed, the second stage is worshipped. Are you ready for the last one?'

Markus nodded and accepted the cup offered to him. He raised it to his lips and looked at the stars in the drink, small, flickering stars that rocked back and forth when he shook the cup; he tilted it over to the right, the stars floated up to the left; he tilted it over to the left, the stars floated up to the right. One of them waved to him:

'Don't do that, Markus. We're getting dizzy.'

Markus smiled and drank, smiled and drank the stars. They floated down into him, deep inside him, like a silver ribbon across a dark landscape, a river that mirrors the moon.

He took a deep breath, the stars came along, started to grow, fill him. They shimmered, melted together, took shape, melted, took new shapes. A figure glided forward, quivered, whispered:

'Welcome, Markus. Good to have you here.'

The figure melted together with the rest of the light, another came forward.

'We've been waiting for you, Markus.'

Markus turned around.

'Why?'

The figure didn't reply, just smiled, smiled and melted. The light had now completely filled Markus, it was so strong that it blinded him; everything inside him was white light, blinding white light. Far away he could see something dark, something coming closer. The light reluctantly released it, let it come closer, take shape, grow darker. A bright figure came around it, dancing.

'Step in, Markus, step in.'

Markus stepped in. He added his light to the sum of the light, let himself melt together with the light, undulating back and forth as he drank *haoma*. The light drank with him, cups were raised, he heard laughter.

He turned toward the dark, glided toward it, a sacrificial stone with a boy on top, wearing a red tunic, his eyes wide. A light figure whispered to him:

'Take it easy, Markus, we will soon win.'

A blaze was lit under the sacrificial stone, it grew rapidly until it covered both the stone and the boy, two blazing mirages in a blinding white light.

Suddenly someone was calling him, he heard running footsteps, pounding, a voice calling his name, trying to reach him. He walked toward the sacrificial stone and the fire, the gods stepped aside to allow him through; let Markus through, the king. He parted the fire with his hands, leaned over the boy who lay there, and studied his face; it was Rachel's face and someone else's, a face he knew he had seen before, but something had made him forget it.

He turned toward the gods, they applauded him without a sound, and a kettledrum resounded blue; he sank to his knees with one hand stretched out in front of him and looked at the worn shoes and arms of the old Armenian who was holding him.

Markus sensed the village getting closer with a sinking feeling in his stomach, a numb feeling in his groin. It grew quieter around him, the colors were duller. He leaned forward over the steering wheel and stared at the snow-covered mountains at the head of the valley, wondering what it looked like on the other side, where he had once come from.

The road climbed laboriously upward along a roiling river between steep cliffs, the white water cutting like a streak of light through the green landscape. Here and there a single house appeared with gardens full of grapevines; beyond them waited the village. Markus felt nausea rising inside him, but it was too late to turn back; the village had seen him, it stood and pointed at him with its dark rooftops and precipitous alleyways.

Markus parked at the marketplace, which sloped down toward the river; he placed a rock under the left front tire. Then he bought a home-brewed beer and a sausage at one of the little stalls and sat down at a sunny wall. People came and went without taking notice of him; that was their way, and he was grateful for it. After a while he stood up and started walking; by this time he figured that the news of the stranger had spread over the whole village; if anyone had recognized him, they would be ready for him now.

He crossed the bridge over the river and followed a steep road up to the right, first through low, dense trees, then in between stone walls on either side. At intervals of several meters there were doors in the walls; outside one of them two women stood studying him, outside another were three children, squatting down. He tried to say hello, they looked away.

The road meandered onward, the cobblestones rose up before him, merging with the walls. He waited for a blow to the back of his neck, an arm on his shoulder, the whistling sound of a rock; nothing came. The road divided into three, he walked straight ahead, certain of which way to go. In a window he could see a silhouette moving. The day was waning, and the sunlight was low, making the stone walls cast deep shadows.

The wall on the right side of the street stopped abruptly and changed into a low stone fence. Markus found the gate, opened it, and walked through. A green grove met him, received him, with tall grass and thick bushes and a tree; beyond the tree stood an old stone church, quite small and dilapidated; an ancient Christian monument in a Muslim land.

Markus sat down under the tree, leaned his back against the trunk, and studied the church, looked at the windows in the low dome, the ruined entrance, the destroyed roof. He heard the gate in the fence open and closed his eyes. He heard footsteps approaching, something approaching, something else. The footsteps stopped beside him, he could feel eyes on him and thought: Is it now, is this it?

Markus opened his eyes, a middle-aged man was standing and looking at him, his clothes worn, his face worn, thin, gray hair, gaunt. The man pointed inquiringly at the ground beside him, Markus nodded. The man sat down and said something in Azeri, Markus answered in Russian. The man studied him a while from the side, switched over to Russian.

'Do you know the story of this church?'

Markus had the urge to scream: Yes, I know it, and couldn't you ask instead what I'm doing here? But he saw that the man wanted to tell him, and he shook his head.

'No.'

'It's six hundred years old, but underneath it are the remains of a church from the year 70 in the Christian era; it was the Apostle Tadeus who had it built, he lived and worked in this area. In the past this was a holy place for Christians; the Armenians used to come here, the Russians used to come here. Now nobody comes here anymore, only you.'

Something moved behind Markus's back, something between him and the tree trunk he was leaning against, something soft.

'Tadeus was one of the seventy apostles who gathered in Jerusalem after Jesus had risen from the dead and asked them to wait until they were enlightened by the Holy Spirit before they went out to make all peoples his disciples.'

The man turned to face Markus to see whether he was listening. Something moved behind Markus's back again, tried to escape.

'Tadeus journeyed on foot the entire length of the Caspian Sea to come here; that's a long way. Just imagine, where we're now sitting sat a man who saw the Son of God, a man who heard the Savior speak. For that very reason, the Armenian church still preserves the head of Tadeus, to this day. Wouldn't you think that a place where such a person had a church built would be so sacred, so filled with light that nothing evil could befall it, no shadow could descend over it?'

Markus stretched out his hands behind him and held on tight to the trunk; the thing that was moving was now kicking him, a voice shouted something he either couldn't or wouldn't understand, he sensed the smell of blood, that sweet, intense smell of blood. He turned to face the man:

'Are you a Christian?'

'I was once. But one day Christian soldiers came down from the mountains up there and into our village. One of them took away my daughter and tied her to this tree and raped her, raped her and killed her.'

The man started to cry. Markus put a hand on his shoulder and thought: I know, it was me.

Markus drunk now, his head between his knees, muttering, incoherent, resigned, angry. He was sitting on the bed of the truck with a wool rug wrapped around him and an empty bottle of home-brew beside him; the taste of raw liquor was so strong that he had already thrown up twice.

After leaving the weeping man at the church he had driven on up the valley toward the mountains, stopped at a stand and bought two bottles of home-brew, started drinking in the truck. After a while he started talking to himself, first in Russian, and then, as he got drunk, in German. He worked himself up, grazed something, there was a thud, he didn't turn around to see what it was, kept on going until he found the place where they had rested on their advance down toward the village; a green sloping plain with a view of the whole valley, the white silver ribbon in the middle, the mountains above, and the village below.

Markus backed the truck onto the plain so that he could sit on the bed of the truck and look out, found his wool rug, wrapped it around him, and continued drinking into the twilight. The green valley grew darker, the white silver ribbon grew lighter, a carpet was pulled over the sky, in the village lamps were lit. Markus drank straight from the bottle, without eating anything, threw up again, and again. He stood up to take a piss, tottered backward on the truck bed, stumbled over the tailgate, and fell, fell with all his weight, his fly open, down onto the soft grass and remained lying there, face down, with one hand inside his fly; he smiled, thought about the cabbalist who was found dead behind the synagogue and thought: If I die now, they'll say that he died the way he lived.

It started raining. Markus rolled over on his back, closed his eyes, felt the raindrops on his face, stuck out his tongue and tasted them. He opened his eyes again and looked at the sky and shouted with all his might:

'God!'

A bolt of lightning struck the dark sky carpet, thunder rolled down toward him. Markus screamed:

'Why didn't you stop me? Have you ever managed to stop anything at all?'

The sky exploded, the ridges shook, Markus was about to scream again when he suddenly heard a voice in the woods, a voice that called his name, stopped him. It was Rachel, and Markus rolled over, weeping in the rain and got to his knees and shouted toward the woods: Rachel, Rachel; and for the first time as an adult he clasped his hands and raised them toward the sky and said *dear God*, and the vomit spurted like a jet out of him, he fell on his side and whispered *dear God I can't bear this alone, can you help me*, and the sky rumbled.

Markus got to his knees again and once more clasped his hands toward the sky and shouted: Dear God, you helped Jefta and accepted what he had promised you, will you help me if I make you the same promise? and the sky was split by furious lightning from a god who refused to be bargained with, and Markus shouted: Forgive me, I make the same promise as Jefta, and Rachel called Markus, Markus, but Markus didn't hear and didn't understand, he was more concerned with the Apostle Tadeus who came walking toward him without a head and asked: Do you know where my head is? and blood bubbled up from the stump of his neck when he spoke, and Markus replied that the Armenian church has it preserved in Vagharsapat, and Tadeus said: How am I going to find the way there without a head? and Markus replied that we all have our problems, and as he toppled over and passed out on the ground, he remembered how good it had felt to kill her, master of life and death.

Dear Rachel, wrote Jochen. He had never called her Mother, and his stepfather he had never called anything at all.

Greetings from the Crimea. Hope you're feeling better, you'll see, soon everything will be like it was before. It's nice here at the pioneer camp, there are participants from twelve countries here, boys and girls, mostly boys but also some girls. I've gotten to know a Russian boy, he can drink a liter of milk in eight seconds, and then he can pee two and a half meters. I've also gotten to know a Bulgarian girl, she smells strange and is kind of sticky, but she can hold a pickled pepper in her mouth for eight minutes and twenty seconds, I can only do it for seven minutes and twelve seconds. In the morning we have political history, it's hard to stay awake, in the middle of the day we work in brigades, in the afternoon we have political history again, and it's even harder to stay awake. In the evening we have a campfire and international folk dancing, I think that Bulgarian girl has tits. Take care, hug from Jochen.

She had tried to hide the card, but the administrator found it; I want a little respect here in this house, a little respect; he had screamed so his tight black hat leaped in the air and the locks of hair at his temples danced; if you showed me a little more respect, it might rub off on him; respect, Rachel, respect, not just obedience, but respect; and deep inside her brain a light switched on, for the first time since the sanitarium, it followed

232

the track of the surgeon's scalpel and filled the void between the severed threads and sliced tissue, so that when the next card arrived, the way lay open, the light flooded into her like an explosion, and she had to hold onto the wall with one hand as she read it again:

Dear Rachel, on Saturday I'm going to meet Markus, he's alive, on Saturday I'm going to meet my father, now I have a father, and he's alive, and on Saturday I'm going to meet him. I was called in to the camp leaders today, there were lots of men I didn't know there, somber men, they had arranged everything, the train ticket and everything, they knew that Markus is in Baku, alive, they were going to send him word that I'm coming, I just had to memorize some numbers to tell him, he'll understand what it means, they said, oh mamma, mamma, on Saturday. Hope you are well, hug from Jochen. P.S. She does.

Markus read the handwritten note and gave Sese a puzzled look, but she merely pointed at the piece of paper and looked at him. Markus read the words again: *Jochen is arriving on train 624 from the Crimea to Baku on Thursday the 24th of this month,* and asked who in heaven's name is Jochen? but Sese just kept on looking at him.

Notes with messages on them tend to disappear; this one didn't disappear, it stayed on the table until the 24th. Sometimes Markus would wake up at night and look at it, a few times he thought some sort of light was coming from it.

He found out what time train 624 was due to arrive; on the 24th he left the house in plenty of time and started walking toward the railway station. On a side street two blocks away from the house the cavalrymen were waiting for him, dusty, grimy, exhausted; some of them with their clothes in rags, many of them gone. He nodded to them, they nodded back, set their gaunt horses in motion, followed behind him, Markus first, then the cavalrymen. Some of them had pulled their

233

scarves up over their mouths and noses, others had closed the visors of their helmets and rode with their lances straight out, proud.

The cavalrymen followed Markus from street to street, from building to building; along the beach promenade, toward the center of town, past the palace monument built by the prisoners of war, up toward the town. The clatter of hooves echoed off the building façades, completely filling the streets; like a wave the sound rolled toward the railway station with Markus in front. He turned around and looked; the cavalrymen had the sun at their backs, they bobbed up and down like shadows in the backlight. Markus smiled sadly, he felt himself merging with the group of cavalrymen, felt himself whole in their presence; this was not the way he thought it would be.

The parade grounds in front of the railway station opened, Markus and the cavalrymen crossed the space slowly and majestically, with their heads held high. From the little stalls selling fruit and vegetables and salted sausages and bread and beer, frightened eyes stared at them. Markus led the cavalrymen up the first stairs, across another square; there he stopped in front of another stairway, turned around, and raised his hand:

'You can wait here.'

The cavalrymen nodded, some swung a leg over the saddle, others bent forward and lightly rested on one elbow. In the vendors' stalls fear gave way to amazement; the people stared at the light-haired man who was talking in front of the stairs. Markus turned around and walked up to the entrance and into the dark railway terminal. He asked which platform train 624 would arrive at and went over there to wait, sat down on a crate next to the track and looked out over the town, which streamed from all directions down toward the harbor, a mish-mash of apartment blocks and low houses and tin sheds and trees, everything on its way toward the harbor and the gray horizon far off in the distance; it was as if the sea made the town real.

Markus was offered a little bread and cucumber by an elderly couple also waiting, and he thanked them politely, leaned against the crate he was sitting on, and studied the crowds; soldiers in new uniforms on their way home or leaving, farmers in worn clothing on their way to or from the illegal vegetable markets in town. Markus saw that a railway station mirrors the soul of the place where it's located, and he tried to put into words the soul of this place where he had spent the last years when train 624 rolled in, first as a smell of stoked coal, then as a shadow of black steel in gray smoke.

Markus moved away from the platform to get a better view, he watched train 624 empty out farmers and seasonal workers and mothers with children and soldiers and officers and Rachel, God, no, Rachel; Rachel climbed down the two steps from the car, agile, eager, wearing shorts and a pioneer neckerchief and a red cap and blue eyes and looked around eagerly, and everything stood still for Markus when he saw himself in the boy's open face, not a sound from outside, not a sound from inside, quiet, quiet, only a voice whispering: *Welcome home, Jefta.*

The boy started walking along the platform toward the station terminal as he looked around, craning his neck. Markus stepped back into the shadow of a vendor's stall and stood quite still, stood quite still in the shadow of a stall and watched his son searching for him.

The boy stood right in front of the stall now, Markus could have reached out his hand and touched him, and he recognized again Rachel's slightly crooked, thin knees.

The boy moved on toward the terminal, he went from stall to stall, as if he hoped that Markus might be among the customers, that he would be standing there buying something for them. Markus grabbed the front of his shirt, started tugging and tearing at it, the boy went out onto the steps in front of the station, the shirt split with a ripping sound, the boy came back, looked around the terminal one more time, walked toward the platform and sat down on a low fence. He took off his pioneer cap and put it down next to him, Markus saw that his lower lip began to quiver.

The sun sank behind a ridge and a cold shadow fell over the railway station, the boy pressed his bare knees together and shivered. Markus was still standing half hidden behind the stall and watching him; then a brisk woman in a railway uniform came and talked to the boy, took him by the arm, led him to a ticket window, back to the train. Markus leaned forward as the boy climbed up the two steps, leaned forward and saw Rachel and Markus climbing up, leaned forward and saw the train with Rachel and Markus slowly set in motion and pull away.

Markus stayed there until the last car had vanished around the bend and he suddenly noticed how cold it was; he walked toward the terminal, tried to hold his shirt together where it had ripped.

A Zen master gathered the wind from the universe that had collapsed because of the choice made by men. Markus gazed after him, then he went over to one of the stalls and bought a bottle of home-brewed beer and a roll, no, *pivo* and *bulka hleba*, *pivo* and *bulka hleba*, continued on toward the exit, and people looked at the light-haired man with the ripped clothing who was eating and drinking as he walked down the steps from the entrance and out onto the square.

The cavalrymen were gone.

THE LAST DAY

'Did anyone win?'
The priest looked up.

'In Nuremberg the Allies introduced a whole new principle of justice for war and used it to judge us. A soldier must at all times evaluate the orders he is given; if he thinks that they constitute a crime against humanity, he must refuse.'

'And be shot?'

'Yes.'

Outside the cannon thunder had ceased. The sound of war was gone: the engines of the tanks were shut off, the machine guns secured, and the helicopters landed. The sound of peace was back: cars honking, trains rolling, and a song came on the wind, low, plaintive, it came from both sides of the front, sometimes as sobs, sometimes as shouts, now and then as a gasp, a single gasp.

Markus listened to the song as he looked at the priest.

'Has it occurred to you that the sound of a war just ended hasn't changed in fifty years, probably not in a thousand, and that it's identical on both sides of the front, regardless who has won and who has lost? It's only when the speeches and trials begin that we can differentiate between the victors and those who were defeated; on the first day after the war, everyone has won and everyone has lost, won peace and lost themselves.'

Markus put his hands behind his back and paced back and forth over the floor as he talked; the priest followed him with his eyes.

'I'm not trying to explain away anything, I'm not trying to excuse anything, I know that the Germans were the ones who started the war, I know that we caused an entire continent inhuman suffering, I know that we must atone for that, forever afterward, both as a nation and as individuals. I'm just asking whether anyone won this war, whether the light conquered the darkness, or whether the opposite was true.'

The priest didn't reply.

'Up until the early summer of 1940 the Allies only bombed German military targets. But on May 10th Churchill tightened the noose; that's when he decided that the whole German war effort would be bombed, from then on neither the residential areas nor the civilian population would be spared. Would the Nuremberg court have approved such a directive?'

Markus went over to the window and looked out; he was in the habit of doing this when he talked with the priest.

'In February of 1942 Field Marshal Arthur Harris took over command of the British bomber fleet with the following orders: "From now on the main target of attack will be the morale of the enemy population." And with that the carpet bombing of German cities began, a systematic attempt to break the endurance and working ability of the German civilian population. Would the Nuremberg court have approved such an order?

'The planes came in waves by the thousands, and they came at night; in the daytime the Allies' own losses would have been too great. Over Essen alone, in one night five thousand tons of bombs were dropped; I've done the calculations, Father: if each bomb weighs a hundred kilos, that's fifty thousand bombs. Let's say that the nighttime darkness lasts nine hours, then one and a half bombs fell each second, for nine hours. Nine hours.'

'You don't have to call me Father.'

'Dresden was bombed for two nights in a row, the city was overflowing with refugees, and the Allies knew that. The residential areas in the center of town were so massively bombed that a firestorm broke out; do you know what that is? It's when the area on fire inside a city is so great that the air becomes overheated and rises up and cold air is sucked in from the surrounding streets, sucked in at a furious rate. That's a firestorm. In Dresden the storm was so powerful that people were lifted up and carried on the cold air several blocks into the fire. The Allies say that between sixty and ninety thousand were killed, but they've never shown any particular interest in finding out exactly; German historians say between sixty and two hundred and forty-five thousand. Would the Nuremberg court have called that kind of bombing attack a crime against humanity?'

Someone was pounding on the door. Markus went over to open it; he had started locking the door after the house had been evacuated. It was the second-lieutenant and the nurse. They looked exhausted, the nurse's uniform was filthy and covered with blood, the second-lieutenant's face was grimy with soot. They didn't come in.

'We thought you'd want to know, they're executing the collaborators now.'

'On both sides?'

'On both sides.'

They said goodbye, got into the ambulance, and drove off. Markus went back to the priest.

'Bad news?'

'Now it's the collaborators' turn.'

'My God.'

They sat for a while, each on his side of the table, one of them fingering a pencil, the other a crucifix; each reading his own thoughts and the thoughts of the other man. It struck them how alike they had become, so alike that when they stood up, it was as one: one thought, one decision, one movement.

It's after a war that the true hatred is created, thought Markus as they walked up the stairs; it's in the revenge that hatred is allowed to grow, when the slightest trace of suspicion is proof enough.

And the law is an eye for an eye and a tooth for a tooth, thought the priest, do not turn the other cheek, old bitterness can find an outlet and old enmity can be brought out, because now is the time for scores to be settled.

They went to their sleeping places in the closet and hall in front of the bathroom; neither of them had felt like moving back into the bedrooms after the house was evacuated; the smell of blood and despair was still too thick. They started going through their belongings, each of them knew exactly what he would take along.

They met at the top of the stairs, one wearing the ankle-length black priest's robe, the other in a dark suit. Markus stood still as the priest put a chasuble over his head and handed him the two silver orbs, one containing holy water, the other incense. Markus tried swinging them in a circle on the meter-long silver chains, sprinkling the priest with holy water, leaving a trail of incense in the air as they walked down the stairs and out the door.

At the front door they turned and headed left; both of them knew where they were going. Markus hesitantly took the priest's hand, holding one of his fingers with two of his own as he spoke:

'On the one hand we have the Spinozan view of life, the world seen from the perspective of eternity: God is a power that permeates everything and everyone, also what we call evil. Evil is merely an illusion, resulting from the fact that we fail to see through things, don't see the large view of life. The illusion that something is evil will vanish when we look at it from the perspective of eternity; then everything balances out, then those things that seem to be discordant notes will become harmonies that meld naturally into a symphony.

'That's how I sometimes manage to see the war, both this one and the previous one, from a distance; I imagine myself flying, higher and higher; first I see all of Armenia, Nagorno-Karabakh, Azerbaijan; I fly higher, now I see all of the Caucasus; still higher, down there is the Ukraine, there is Europe, over there Siberia, and there Central Asia. I see great movements, great masses of people on the move; two million Russian colonists are at this moment on the move after the collapse of the empire, on their way back to a Russia that neither can nor will receive them; a million people are at this moment on the move west from Siberia and Central Asia, where they were deported a generation ago; Turks, Tatars, Ossetians, the whole kit and caboodle, determined to return to what they call their homelands. This is what we call ethnic migrations, more or less voluntary. Along with it comes flight: three hundred thousand Armenians are at this moment fleeing from Azeri pogroms, and I mean real pogroms; two hundred and thirty thousand Azeris are fleeing from Armenian pogroms, here only the names are reversed; three hundred and fifty thousand people are at this moment fleeing from Georgian ethnic cleansing, and a million people are in permanent flight from this war; believe me, it will be that many.

'I roll back time and see the same thing: ethnic migration after ethnic migration, Mongols and Turks from the east, Germans from the west; for three hundred years, Europe had the biggest population growth in the world, the number of people doubled in only three hundred years, that's enormous, and we were the most populated country. Were we just following the same law of nature as the Mongolians and the Turks: expand or perish? In the century preceding the Great Patriotic War, or the Second World War, as it's now called, sixty million Europeans emigrated, no doubt many of them by choice, but most of them because they had to; emigrate or starve. Under that kind of starry sky everything falls into place and everything grows calm; what we call evil is merely a link in a natural process, part of human destiny.'

They were getting close now, they could see it, hear it, smell it. The priest withdrew his hand, took his friend by the arm, and replied:

'On the other side, we have the individualistic view of life, the world seen from the perspective of time. In this view, ethnic migrations consist of individuals, of people with an "I." The Book of Job can be read as a criticism of God, criticism of a god who had become too abstract and who sent a son in order to become more concrete. It's true that we feel more comfortable if we take away the word "I" from both God and evil, but then we also take away the divine nature of human beings, and we're not about to do that, are we? We're not about to become Darwinists, are we, Markus?'

'And do absolutes exist for a divine nature? Everything is not relative for a divine nature?'

'Is that a true German Catholic asking? For Christians it's a question of the presence of God or the absence of God. It's either-or, you can't get anything more absolute than that.'

'What about when man falls?'

'Then you Germans have set up a safety net: Kant's categorical imperative. You just have to act according to such norms as you might want to make into a universal law – dear God what a language – not much different from the golden rule you find in all Mosaic religions, but German, thorough and binding.'

They had arrived. An armored car was parked in the middle of the street, blocking the way; next to it sat six soldiers around a small table, drinking tea. Four soldiers stood guard, two on either side of the street.

Markus and the priest walked past the blockade without looking to the right or the left; they managed to count twelve steps before someone shouted at them:

'Halt!'

An officer got up from the table and came toward them, followed by a private with his rifle ready. The officer was an older man, in his mid-fifties; he had two gold wreaths on his epaulettes: a captain.

'Where are you going?'

His gold teeth gleamed.

'We're going to stop something.'

'What?'

'You know. Why don't you stop it?'

'What?'

The officer was surly, he felt on edge.

Markus turned to face him.

'Civilian law distinguishes among three groups of people in connection with acts of violence: those who commit the violent act, those who contribute to it or incite it, and those who witness it. Which group do you think you belong to?'

The officer grew angry.

'Turn around. That's an order. Go back where you came from.'

The priest turned his back on him and continued walking down the street. Markus did the same. They walked next to each other, their backs straight, their shoulders high.

'Do you want to get shot?'

'Would you like that on your conscience too? A priest and a choirboy, in the back?'

Markus smiled.

'Quite a choirboy.'

They heard the officer give an order, they heard running footsteps, two soldiers came up behind them, moved past them, in front of them, stopped with their guns held out, trying to stop them.

Markus and the priest slowed their pace but kept on walking, the soldiers took a step back. They were young, pimply, with hesitant eyes, they had been taught to respect their elders, show reverence for the church.

The priest stretched out his arm and separated them.

'Move aside, children.'

243

They looked from one gray-haired man to the other and encountered only calm expressions, firm, calm expressions. They glanced uncertainly at each other and stopped, let the two pass, stood and stared after them. Over by the armored car stood the officer; he was about to shout something but refrained, looked at his soldiers, looked down.

The priest touched Markus's sleeve.

'There is a third possibility, in addition to viewing evil from the perspective of eternity or time. Do you remember Epicurus, three hundred years before Christ?'

Markus smiled and quoted:

'Either God wishes to prevent evil, but cannot do so: then He is not almighty; or He can but does not wish to do so: then He is not good; or He neither wishes to nor can prevent evil: then He is neither good nor almighty; or He both wishes to and can prevent evil: and then there is no solution to the problem of evil.'

The priest nodded.

'Hard for a priest to swallow, but difficult to refute. It hasn't given us a solution, Markus; viewed from the perspective of eternity, everything falls into place and everything has its explanation and nothing is good or evil, merely natural; but viewed from the perspective of time, much is chaotic and much cannot be explained and much is evil; much good, but much evil, and in spite of everything, it is time we live in, not eternity. So each one of us has to take responsibility for his own actions, and we must atone for the injustices we may have committed, and after we have atoned, we must forgive ourselves, otherwise others won't be able to forgive us, and if we have offered up a sacrifice, we must forgive ourselves for the sacrifice, do you hear me, Markus, we must forgive ourselves for the sacrifice.'

They continued on down the street and onto a side street. They walked toward the sound, stopped in front of an open gate, and crossed themselves before they stepped into the back courtyard. It was filled with people, men in rough clothing and heavy work boots, some of them with bottles in their hands. They stood facing two open doorways in the building that formed the back wall of the courtyard, crowding close together as they craned their necks to see. The muttering and shouting and laughing rose and fell in waves, sometimes faint enough to let sounds from the two doorways slip through; from one of them came the sound of blows and screams, hard blows against something soft and long drawn-out screams; from the other doorway came the sound of agitated men's voices and women sobbing.

Markus and the priest tried to force their way through the crowd, they advanced a few meters but were held back, blocked in. The priest shouted angrily, held up the cross; the people who stood nearest tried to move aside but couldn't; the spectators were packed too close together.

Markus stayed close to the priest, lifted the silver orbs with the holy water and the incense over his head so as not to lose them in the crush.

A woman was shoved into one of the doorways, she was naked and weeping, her head had been shorn, almost shaved. The mob in the back courtyard roared, tried to press toward her, she screamed in terror, struggled against the hands that were holding her from behind.

Markus and the priest tried to shout, to scream: *Leave her alone, in God's name*, but no one paid any attention to them; the men in the courtyard stamped and bellowed and moved toward the woman in the doorway until they covered her completely.

From the other doorway suddenly emerged two men wearing olive-green military sweaters and hooded masks: their eyes and lips were the only things visible; brown eyes and lips that smiled. They were each holding a rope, the mob moved aside to let them through, the two masked men walked out into the courtyard until the ropes grew taut behind them, then they yanked on them and two men tumbled out of the doorway with the ropes around their necks and their hands bound behind them. One of them was an older man of stocky build, the other was a young boy; blood was running from the ears and mouth of both of them. The two masked men dragged them out to the courtyard, toward a children's swing set, the prisoners tried to resist but were struck on the back and sides by the spectators. The two masked men threw the ropes over the bar of the swing set and grabbed hold of the ends, ready to pull. The older man looked at them in silence, the young boy wept.

One of the masked men turned to face the spectators and raised his hand:

'This is what happens to collaborators!'

The spectators roared.

The priest raised the cross:

'*In God's name!*'

The crowd roared.

The priest tried again:

'*In God's name!*'

The crowd roared again.

The masked man raised his hand and shouted: *Look, even the church blesses our revenge.*

The priest shouted:

'*In God's name!*' but fainter, as if he were about to give up, and put his hand to his chest.

Markus held up the silver orbs with the holy water and incense, someone took them away from him and passed them forward so the executioners could be blessed.

The two masked men drew the ropes tight and leaned back and tugged, the prisoners kept on struggling against them, the executioners pulled harder, and the spectators bellowed yes, yes, yes, keeping time, in unison, and broke into wild applause when the feet of the two prisoners lifted off the ground and they desperately kicked to find a foothold and tried to twist their bound hands up toward the ropes that were tightening around their necks.

Markus and the priest threw themselves at the backs of people standing in front of them, once, twice, three times, four times; the wall of backs gave way and let them through, they tumbled and fell against the two hanged men.

The spectators laughed and clapped, someone shouted *God is with us*, the two masked men fastened the ends of the ropes with a half hitch, over by the gate facing the street someone shouted a name, we're going there next, and suddenly it was over; the spectators streamed excitedly through the gate. Markus and the priest sat down; one of the masked men came over to them:

'Thank you.'

He walked toward the gate. Markus shouted after him:

'When you have to explain this to your God, what will you say?'

The masked man didn't answer. Markus and the priest watched him go, then they sat in silence for a long time before they slowly got to their feet, unsteady and gray-haired. Above them swayed two bodies from a swing set; from a doorway came scraps of a lullaby, in a window crackled a poorly tuned radio.

A NOTE ON THE AUTHOR

Gunnar Kopperud was born in 1945 and studied theatre in Strasbourg and at RADA in London. He also took a master's degree in philosophy at the University of Oslo. He has worked as a journalist for, among others, Associated Press and the leading Norwegian daily paper, *Dagbladet*. He has spent the last few years mainly in Africa, winning acclaim and respect for his journalism. He lives in Norway.

Tiina Nunnally is the prize-winning translator of *Smilla's Sense of Snow* by Peter Høeg and many other Scandinavian novels.

A NOTE ON THE TYPE

The text of this book is set in Bembo; the original types for which were cut by Francesco Griffo for the Venetian printer Aldus Manutius, and were first used in 1495 for Cardinal Bembo's *De Aetna*. Claude Garamond (1480–1561) used Bembo as a model and so it became the forerunner of standard European type for the following two centuries. Its modern form was designed, following the original, for Monotype in 1929 and is widely in use today.